"You we ~~everyone stares at you as~~ if they've seen a ghost?" Jean-Paul asked.

He knew she did. What he failed to understand was the terror those unknown answers held. She hesitated a moment, then nodded. "Yes, I want to know."

Jean-Paul wrapped his arm around her waist and pointed to the wall above the librarian's desk. "Look, Angeline."

Taking a deep breath, she obeyed his command. There, in an ornate gilt frame, was a portrait of a woman who looked identical to her.

Angie gasped. And in that instant, she knew: *her entire life had been a lie.* "What's going on here, Jean-Paul?" she asked, her voice trembling. "Who am I?"

Dear Reader,

Talk about starting the new year off with a bang! Look at the Intimate Moments lineup we have for you this month.

First up is Rachel Lee's newest entry in her top-selling Conard County miniseries, *A Question of Justice*. This tale of two hearts that seem too badly broken ever to mend (but of course are about to heal each other) will stay in your mind—and your heart—long after you've turned the last page.

Follow it up with Beverly Barton's *The Outcast*, a Romantic Traditions title featuring a bad-boy hero— and who doesn't love a hero who's so bad, he's just got to be good? This one comes personally recommended by #1-selling author Linda Howard, so don't miss it! In *Sam's World*, Ann Williams takes us forward into a future where love is unknown—until the heroine makes her appearance. Kathleen Creighton is a multiple winner of the Romance Writers of America's RITA Award. If you've never read her work before, start this month with *Eyewitness* and you'll know right away why she's so highly regarded by her peers—and by readers around the world. Many of you have been reading Maura Seger's Belle Haven Saga in Harlequin Historicals. Now read *The Surrender of Nora* to see what Belle Haven—and the lovers who live there—is like today. Finally there's Leann Harris's *Angel at Risk*, a story about small-town secrets and the lengths to which people will go to protect them. It's a fittingly emotional—and suspenseful—close to a month of nonstop fabulous reading.

Enjoy!

Leslie Wainger
Senior Editor and Editorial Coordinator

Please address questions and book requests to:
Silhouette Reader Service
U.S.: 3010 Walden Ave., P.O. Box 1325, Buffalo, NY 14269
Canadian: P.O. Box 609, Fort Erie, Ont. L2A 5X3

ANGEL AT RISK

LEANN HARRIS

INTIMATE MOMENTS

Published by Silhouette Books

America's Publisher of Contemporary Romance

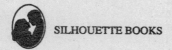 SILHOUETTE BOOKS

ISBN 0-373-07618-5

ANGEL AT RISK

Books by Leann Harris

Silhouette Intimate Moments

Bride on the Run #516
Angel at Risk #618

LEANN HARRIS

When Leann Harris first met her husband in college, she never dreamed she would marry him. After all, he was getting a Ph.D. in the one science she'd managed to avoid—physics! So much for first impressions. They have been happily married for twenty-one years! After graduating from the University of Texas at Austin, Leann taught math and science to deaf high school students until the birth of her first child. It wasn't until her youngest child started school that Leann decided to fulfill a lifelong dream and began writing. She presently lives in Plano, Texas, with her husband and two children.

ACKNOWLEDGMENTS

I would like to thank the following people for their
generous help:

My agent, Evan Fogelman,
for his input and knowledge of Louisiana law
and customs.

Debbie Hancock and Donna Caubarreaux,
for telling me how to cook crawfish.

Becky Edwards,
deputy clerk of the court for the parish of Lafourche,
who helped with parish records.

Judy, Karen M., Anne, Karen L. and Dora,
who constantly keep me on track.

Chapter 1

Angie Fitzgerald glared at the closed hood of her white rental car. The steam escaping from it told the grim story. She wasn't going to drive another mile in that torturous vehicle. The compact had been nothing but trouble since she'd picked it up from the small rental company at the airport in New Orleans.

On this deserted stretch of state road, she doubted help would appear any time soon. So that left only one option—she'd have to walk the rest of the way to Mirabeau. From the sign she had passed on the road a while back, she guessed that the town was another five miles ahead.

Angie retrieved her purse from the front seat and began walking. Within minutes, the stifling heat of the Louisiana day plastered her cotton blouse to her body.

Lush plants crowded the edge of the pavement, giving her the impression that they were trying to obliterate the road and reclaim what man had taken. The intense green of the leaves was so dark it gave the landscape a sinister air. A chill

ran up her spine. This place was untamed and uncon-
quered, ready to eat novices like her.

The sun beat down, making her light-headed. Rivulets of
sweat ran down her neck, further dampening her blouse. No
wonder her aunt always insisted on coming to Vermont on
her vacation. Louisiana in July was a miserable place. How
could anyone breathe, let alone function, in this sauna bath?

Angie swatted at the gigantic mosquito that landed on her
bare forearm. Of course, what wasn't beneficial for hu-
mans certainly seemed to be favored by the vegetation and
bugs.

Her knees were turning to mush and the edge of her vision beginning to blur, when she thought she heard the
strains of a waltz played on an accordion. Angie stopped
and cocked her head. Sure enough, the upbeat rhythm filled
the air. If there was music, then there had to be people
nearby. Relief flooded her. Since rescue seemed imminent,
Angie tried to repair the damage to her appearance. She
tucked her blouse back into her skirt and stuffed stray ten-
drils of hair hanging down her neck and face into the braid
at the back of her head.

She resumed walking, and just as she suspected around
the sharp bend in the road was a collection of buildings
strung out on either side of the blacktop.

Angie stopped before the first building. This was the
source of the music she'd heard. The old wooden structure
was a combination gas station, garage and grocery. The
clapboard was gray with age and a few chips of what was
once white paint clung to the wood. A faded, round metal
sign hanging by the torn screen door proclaimed something
about a cola.

"You old cheat. Put those pieces back." The rich masculine voice came from inside.

A laugh punctuated the air. "You are just a poor loser, Jean-Paul. That move, it was legal. Now crown me."

Angie pulled open the door and stepped inside. The building wasn't air-conditioned, but an overhead fan moved the thick air. It took a moment for her eyes to adjust to the dimness. To her left, a high counter ran the length of the room. Behind it were shelves filled with dozens of cans and cartons. On the countertop was an odd collection of items. At one end was a forty-cup electric coffeepot, a big crock-pot, foam bowls, plastic spoons in a cup, and a handwritten sign proclaiming gumbo a dollar a bowl. At the other end was an ancient cash register and a beat-up radio, the source of the music she'd heard. On the back wall, auto supplies, belts and tools hung from hooks. Cans of oil and transmission fluid and car batteries were stacked in front of the wall display.

In the center of the room three men were gathered around a lopsided card table, a checkerboard in front of them. Two of the men were seated, the third standing, observing the game.

They glanced up and all conversation in the room died, leaving only the scratchy sound of the radio filling the air with exotic music.

Angie was tempted to look down and make sure she was properly dressed, that no buttons were undone and her blouse hadn't ridden up. "Uh." She swallowed her nervousness. "My car overheated a few miles back. I was wondering if I could get someone to go back with me and fix it."

No one moved. They stared at her as if she were some alien from another world. Or an apparition.

"Is there someone here who can help me?"

The men looked gravely at each other, then back at her. They were quite a collection of characters. The man standing was in his late teens and dressed in a faded T-shirt and jeans. One of the men at the table was easily in his sixties, with a full head of white hair and a bushy beard.

It was the other man who drew Angie's attention. Though he was seated, she could tell he was tall, his shoulders massive, straining against the seams of his workshirt. A lock of black hair fell over his broad forehead. High cheekbones, aquiline nose and full lips added to his incredible good looks. His green eyes locked with hers, and she felt a charge of pure sexual awareness race along her nerves. Oddly enough, she thought she saw a flicker of recognition in his penetrating gaze. But that couldn't be. She'd never seen the man until this moment.

"Well, I'll be damned," the older man mumbled.

"Of that we have no doubt," the handsome one replied.

The older man chuckled. "And you will keep me company, yes?"

A wicked grin that made Angie's heart skip a beat flashed across Green Eyes' face. "But of course."

The old one looked back at Angie. He shook his head. "Who would've believed such a thing?"

"I beg your pardon?" Angie cut in, becoming frustrated with their aimless dialogue.

Rising, the old man came toward Angie. "Forgive our lack of manners, *mamselle*. I'm Pierre McKay." He offered his hand.

Reluctantly, Angie shook it, but before she could pull back, Pierre brought her hand up to his mouth and placed a kiss on the back. Angie wanted to jerk free, but the good manners her mother had so painstakingly taught her kicked in and she smiled stiffly and endured his gesture.

He pulled her toward the table. "The cheat playing checkers with me is Jean-Paul Delahaye."

She watched Jean-Paul carefully place the checker he'd been holding on the board. He had beautiful hands, large palms and long, slender fingers. The picture of those hands on her body popped into her head. Stunned, she shook off the thought.

He stood and came toward her. Her own five-foot-four frame only came up to his shoulders, and she had to look up to meet his bold appraisal. He followed Pierre's example, took her hand and kissed it. The deep heat curling in her stomach set off more shock waves.

"A pleasure," Jean-Paul murmured.

His soft, sensual reply rumbled through her. He released her hand and the odd tension gripping her body eased.

"And this—" Pierre pulled the youth forward "—boy with his mouth hangin' open is Martin Andrew."

Angie offered the youth only a smile, keeping her hands wrapped around her purse.

Martin nodded, then whispered something in Pierre's ear. The older man shook his head. *"Non."*

"Pierre, your lack of upbringing is showing again, *mon ami*," Jean-Paul said, a thoughtful look on his face as he studied her. "The lady looks like she is about to collapse. Offer her a seat and something to refresh her."

Pierre slapped his forehead. "Of course, how stupid of me." Giving a wide, graceful gesture, he offered her his place at the table.

With a sigh of relief, Angie sank down.

Jean-Paul resumed his seat. He leaned back in the chair, assuming an indolent pose, much like a panther watching its prey.

"Would you like some coffee?" Pierre asked.

Angie's head jerked around and she stared at the older man. Surely he was teasing her. No one in his right mind would want *hot* coffee on a day like this. Her horror must've shown on her face, because a deep laugh vibrated through Jean-Paul's chest.

"I think your guest would prefer somethin' cold, *non?*" The end of his question was directed at her.

"Something cool would be heavenly," she replied, her lips dry. And indeed, the thought was so appealing that she closed her eyes and gave herself over to the feeling of cold liquid sliding down her parched throat. When she opened her eyes, she found Jean-Paul staring at her, his green gaze like a laser cutting deep into her soul.

"Such abandon, *chère,*" Jean-Paul whispered, the musical syllables washing over her. "I would like to know the name of the woman who knows how to appreciate the simple things of life."

Before she could answer, Pierre boomed, "Martin, get one of those expensive French waters from the ice chest."

The youth went to an old-time refrigerated chest that was meant to hold soft drinks, opened the lid and brought Angie the water. Without waiting, she unscrewed the cap and took a deep swallow. She knew Jean-Paul was watching her, but thirst overrode manners. Placing the bottle on the table, she smiled shyly at the men. "Thank you."

"*Bien sûr,*" Pierre replied. He pulled up another chair to the table and sat down. He did not say anything, but after glancing at the three men, Angie knew they were waiting for her to introduce herself.

"I'm Angeline Fitzgerald."

"And what is such a lovely lady doin' in this outta-the-way place?" Pierre asked.

The men seemed to lean in, eagerly awaiting her answer. "My aunt lives in Mirabeau. When I called a couple of days ago to wish her a happy birthday, I got a recording that the number had been disconnected. I called the operator, but she couldn't tell me anything more. So I came down here to see what happened to her.''

The men looked at one another again.

"What is your *tante*'s name?" Jean-Paul asked.

This time the men avoided looking at one another, but Angie picked up the strange tension in Jean-Paul's voice. "Marianna Courville. Do you know her? Do you know what has happened to her?"

Silence.

The song on the radio ended and another began. Still, no one spoke.

"Are you sure of your *tante*'s name and where she lived?" Pierre asked.

"Of course I am. What's going on here?"

"Marianna died in March."

Angie stared at Pierre. "That can't be true," she murmured, trying to convince herself that the men had made a dreadful mistake. "If my aunt died, someone would've notified me, since I'm her next of kin. Perhaps you're thinking of someone else."

"Non," Pierre answered slowly, shaking his head. "There is no mistake. Marianna is dead."

"Then why didn't her lawyer notify me?"

"No one knew she had any living relatives."

Angie stood so quickly her chair tumbled backward to the floor. "How can that be? I've called her. Written her. She visited my family every summer. Are you telling me she never told a soul in this town that she had a married sister and a niece?"

Jean-Paul leaned back and pinned her with his gaze. "Marianna was an only child."

Outrage raced through her. "That's a lie. Aunt Marianna and my mother were sisters."

Jean-Paul didn't waver. "Ask anyone in the parish and they'll tell you Marianna was the only child born to the Courvilles."

Reaching in her purse, Angie pulled out her wallet and flipped it open to the picture of her mother, Marianna, and herself. "Here's a snapshot of the three of us taken two years ago." She threw it on the table.

Looking away, Angie fought the tears and confusion while the men studied the photo.

"I don' know what to say, *chère*," Pierre said as he ran his fingers through his hair. "We thought Marianna was the last Courville. That's why the court is holding a hearing on Monday to decide what to do with Marianna's house and land. It's a good thing you showed up when you did."

"Maybe it's too good," Jean-Paul said, rising to his feet.

Even though she was standing, she still had to look up into Jean-Paul's eyes. "What is that supposed to mean?"

"It means, sugar, that I don't believe in coincidences. And you showing up the Saturday before the hearing on Marianna's estate, claiming to be her *niece*, makes me wonder what you're up to." He ran his finger along her chin, then shrugged. "Personally, I don't give a damn what your motives are, because your appearance will tie a knot in Roger Boudreaux's tail. Me, I'm going to be in that courtroom to watch." He turned and walked to the side door. "I hope you have a good lawyer," he called over his shoulder. "You'll need one."

She heard the roar of an engine, then a horn sounded. What was going on here? Nothing seemed to make sense. The horn blared again.

Pierre stood and took her hand, leading her outside. "Your car is sick, *non?*"

"Yes."

"Jean-Paul is my mechanic. You go with him. He will fix the car."

The last thing on earth she wanted to do was accompany Jean-Paul Obnoxious Delahaye anywhere, but fate had given her no choice. Pierre pulled open the truck door for her and she slipped in without saying a word to Jean-Paul or glancing his way. As they pulled away from the gas station, the grief she'd held at bay caught up with her. Silent tears coursed down her cheeks.

He didn't need this. He didn't need this exquisite impostor tugging at his heartstrings. Picture or not, anyone who showed up claiming to be Marianna's *niece* was as dishonest as that old rascal Roger Boudreaux. He wanted to laugh out loud. Roger was legendary in Louisiana. No one could name a more corrupt, slimier or smarter man than Roger. What irony. Roger's grand scheme for getting legal control of Marianna's estate would be blown to hell by a lady who looked exactly like Roger's sister, Jacqueline.

And once word of Angeline's appearance got around, it would rock Mirabeau to its foundation. Why, when he'd first seen her standing in the doorway of Pierre's store, he'd thought her a ghost.

Angeline. The name was French. Cajun, maybe? She had pronounced her name in such a cold, clipped manner that it in no way resembled the sweet sensuality with which her name was meant to be murmured.

He stole another look at her and caught her wiping away the moisture from her cheeks. The afternoon light poured through the side window, outlining her in gold. She had the serene beauty reserved for angels; milky white skin, sky blue eyes, pale rose lips and hair the color of sunset.

"How did my aunt die?"

Her question startled him out of his thoughts. "Her car was found in the bayou. She was inside."

The little color she had in her cheeks fled, making him feel like a first-class heel for giving her the news so harshly. He kept his eyes on the road, but he heard her choking back her tears. Damn. He would *not* feel pity for her. And yet her reaction to Marianna's death seemed to be genuine, touching the raw spot in his own heart.

Despite the overwhelming evidence against him, Marianna Courville was the only person in all of the parish who had believed him innocent of the charges brought against him, and she had spoken out for him. When he'd been caged in that hellhole they called a prison, Marianna had written and visited him. Over the past few years she had never wavered in her support, and they had become close friends.

"H-how did the accident happen?"

He wanted to ask Angeline why she thought it was an accident, but refrained from voicing his personal suspicions. "Can't say. No one saw. When she didn't show up for work at the library, the sheriff started looking for her."

"But—"

He didn't want to dwell on the ugly memories of pulling Marianna's car from the bayou. "That yours?" He pointed to the white two-door sitting on the side of the road.

"Yes."

He stopped beside the compact and jumped out. It didn't take long for him to spot the hole in the radiator.

He was aware of her pacing behind him. "Can you fix it?" she asked, stopping to peer over his shoulder.

He pulled a rag from his back pocket and wiped off his hands, then turned to her. She looked so regal standing in front of him, arms crossed, looking down her aristocratic nose at him. She thought him some backwater Cajun, who could neither read nor write. Probably thought he couldn't fix her damn car, either. He'd run into that attitude often enough in the past, first from his public-school teachers, then from the well-bred teachers at the East Coast boarding school he'd attended. Well, why not give her the peasant she expected?

He leaned one hip on the car. *"Mais sho',* I can fix it, but not here, *chère.* The car, she will have to be towed back to the garage. I'll drive you to Pierre's, then come back with the tow truck."

She frowned and he read skepticism in her eyes.

"You doubt me, *hein?"* He motioned to her. "Come, I show you."

She hesitated, her body vibrating with tension, like an animal cornered by a hunter. Suddenly the air seemed heavy and expectant, reminding him of the moments before a violent thunderstorm.

He waited, watching, anticipating. She gnawed her bottom lip, then her tongue darted out to soothe the self-inflicted hurt. His physical reaction to her movement was like a gut punch. He nearly moaned with the hot desire gripping him.

Steady, Jean-Paul, he sternly told himself. *Remember who this woman claims to be.*

He thought she was going to turn tail and run. Instead, she stepped closer. The lady had courage, he'd give her that. Resting his elbows on the car, he pointed to the small hole near the bottom of the radiator.

"See that hole?"

She squinted. "No."

He sighed. She wouldn't see a thing that far back from the engine. Slipping his arm around her shoulders, he pulled her down so she could see where he was pointing. She stiffened.

Her reaction fired his already simmering temper. She was acting as if he was going to throw her down on the ground and ravish her. Well, tough—let her think what she wanted. He wasn't out to seduce her, only to show her the problem.

Liar, a voice in his head whispered.

"Do you see where the water is running out?" With his index finger he touched the spot.

She leaned closer. "Yes."

Jean-Paul swallowed hard as he felt every inch of her pressing against him. "Because the hole is there, any water I put into the radiator would leak out and the engine, she would be ruined. You want to do that, *hein?*"

She turned her head, and her lips were mere inches from his. Immediately, she straightened and backed away. "The rental company wouldn't appreciate that. I guess you'll have to tow it."

He bowed his head in gracious acceptance of her surrender to his diagnosis. *"Bien."* He slammed down the hood and strode to his pickup.

"My suitcases," she called out, stopping him. When he turned to her, she gave him an apologetic smile. "I think it would be wise if I took them. I don't know how long it will take you to fix the car and I might need something in them."

He shrugged and followed her to the trunk. She opened it and reached for the two cases. He brushed aside her hands and grabbed the luggage.

"I can do that," she protested.

"Non. My *maman* raised me with manners."

She grumbled something under her breath that sounded suspiciously like *Could've fooled me.*

He stopped and looked over his shoulder. "Did you say somethin', sugar?"

"No," she replied innocently. She didn't wait on him but hurried to the truck and slipped inside.

He hid his grin. The lady was sassy and smart. A deadly combination.

Chapter 2

"So, you think I'm a liar."

Jean-Paul threw her a startled glance but said nothing.

The first wave of shock and grief had passed and she was beginning to think coherently again. The bombshell Mr. Delahaye had dropped before they left the gas station, that Marianna was an only child, came to mind. How could that be?

"Why would I want to masquerade as Marianna's niece?"

He lifted his shoulder in a careless shrug.

"What would I have to gain from such a charade?"

"You tell me that, *chère.*"

The man was determined to be difficult. All she wanted was to find out what had happened to her aunt. What purpose would it serve to lie about Marianna? "How do I know you're not the one telling the lies?"

His head jerked around and the deadly look in his eyes made her recoil. "Ask anyone in the parish. Better yet, I'll take you to visit Eleanor Flanders. She's been clerk of the court for the last thirty years. You can ask her yourself if Ben and Julia Courville had any other children besides Marianna.''

''My grandparents' names weren't...'' A light went off in her brain. Of course, in the chaos of her initial meeting with Jean-Paul, Pierre and Martin, she had forgotten to explain about her grandparents' divorce. ''There's a simple explanation for this confusion.''

Jean-Paul raised his eyebrows in disbelief.

''Mother told me that when she and Marianna were very young, their parents divorced. My grandfather, Edward, took Mother and stayed in Vermont. Grandmother took Marianna and moved back to Louisiana to be with her family. Later, both remarried.''

He shook his head. ''*Non.* Marianna's parents can trace their families back to when they came to Louisiana from Nova Scotia. No one ever left. No one ever divorced.''

His words were clear, distinct, his diction perfect. ''My, what has happened to your accent?''

The muscles of his jaw flexed and Angeline knew her jibe had hit home. She'd been floored when he put on that thick accent to explain that he'd have to tow her car. He was getting back at her, but why?

''I'm calling your bluff, Angeline.''

Liquid heat raced along her nerves. Her name on his lips was a delicate caress, invoking images of scented breezes, moonlit nights and lovers sharing secrets.

''You want to see which one of us is lying, *hein?*''

The soft glow shattered.

''Yes, Mr. Delahaye, I want to know which one of us is the liar.''

''Jean-Paul, *chère.* You must call me Jean-Paul. M'sieu Delahaye is much too formal. Such respect is not due a liar.''

She wanted to hit him with the crowbar lying on the floorboard. If he thought he could intimidate her, he was in for a big surprise. She'd let one man push her around, but she vowed it would never happen again. "John-Paul."

He shook his head. "*Non, non.* It is *Jean,* not John. You must place your tongue in the bottom of your mouth to make the proper sound. J—Jean."

They rounded the bend in the road and Pierre's place came into view. Jean-Paul pulled onto the shoulder of the road. He rested his wrists on the steering wheel and looked at her.

"What will it be, Angeline, Pierre's or Eleanor's? Which is it?"

Nothing had made sense since she'd landed in Louisiana, but at least she could clear up one thing in the next few minutes. "Eleanor's, John-Paul." She deliberately said his name with the English pronunciation, wanting to see his reaction.

He sighed, then shrugged. "Maybe it's for the best. I think hearing you say my name as my *maman* meant it to be said would bring us both trouble, *non?*"

Relief swept over her in waves. He wasn't a bully. Unfortunately, what he was—a virile man who made her want to whisper his name with sweet abandon—was worse for her mental health than any bully.

He gripped the wheel and guided the truck back onto the road. "We must stop at Pierre's and call M'dame Eleanor. It would be impolite to visit without telling her we are comin'."

Angeline watched in amazement as he parked the truck and jumped out. Why would a man with the sensitivity of a goat think of a woman's feelings . . . unless he was up to something? She shoved open the truck door and followed him inside.

* * *

"Ah, hell," Jean-Paul muttered, coming to a halt just inside the door of Pierre's.

Sheriff Dennis Mathers placed his beer on the table and pushed back his hat. "Is that any way to greet an old friend, *mon ami?*" The bloated features, red eyes and spare tire around Dennis's middle were testimony to his years of heavy drinking and hard living. Yet, in spite of that, there were traces of the handsome youth he'd once been.

"*Non,* but then you and me were never really friends, were we? You were more like a snake to my breast."

"Tut, tut, Jean-Paul. Do you hear that, Pierre? He calls me a snake. Do you think that's right?" The sheriff's gaze never wavered from Jean-Paul.

Jean-Paul glanced at his employer, whose fear shone bright in his eyes. "This is between you and me, Dennis. Don't involve anyone else."

With a calculated move, the sheriff stood and turned to Pierre hovering by the cash register and studied him. As if considering the old man not worth his effort, Dennis shrugged. "He doesn't matter, anyway."

"That's right. He is only a peon, *hein?* No one with money or power."

"You got that right, Jean-Paul. The real reason I'm here is because Martin called his brother and told him he saw a ghost. I came to investigate."

Before Jean-Paul could respond, he heard the screen door slam and a small body barreled into his back. He whirled and snagged Angeline's wrist so she wouldn't fall.

"I'll be damned," Dennis said, staring at her.

"Why do I get that reaction from everyone in this town?" she asked, brushing back a lock of hair from her face.

"If I didn't see it myself, I wouldn't have believed it." Dennis shook his head. "Kinda spooky, ain't it, Martin?"

Martin stepped out from behind the counter. "You got that right, sheriff." His Adam's apple bobbed as he nodded his head.

Jean-Paul wanted to strangle the youth. Martin wasn't a bad kid, but he was the biggest tale-teller in south Louisiana. Usually, Martin's penchant for gossip didn't bother him. Today, it did.

Dennis Mathers possessed the meanness of a rabid hound and the deadliness of a cottonmouth snake. Jean-Paul knew from bitter experience that Dennis had no morals and was in Roger Boudreaux's back pocket. Dennis had set up Jean-Paul. The idea of letting this slime anywhere near Angeline made him sick.

Dennis sauntered across the floor and stopped in front of her. He gave Angeline what Jean-Paul considered an oily smile, then swept his hat from his head. "I'm Dennis Mathers, the sheriff of this parish."

"Angeline Fitzgerald." She held out her hand.

"A pleasure, *mamselle*." Dennis grasped her hand and brought it to his lips.

"What brings such a lovely lady like you to Mirabeau?"

Jean-Paul could just imagine Dennis pumping Angeline for information, then running straight to Roger with the entire story. And of course Roger wouldn't like the idea of Angeline turning up, spoiling his plans. She didn't have a snowball's chance in hell of surviving against the evil duo.

Yet, what could Jean-Paul do? If he tried to prevent her from talking to Dennis, it would only cause more suspicion among the different parties. And for all he knew, Angeline was lying, her purpose yet to be exposed.

"I've come to check on my aunt, Marianna Courville, sheriff. These gentlemen have told me that she's dead. Is that true? Is my aunt dead?"

Dennis scratched his chin. "It's true that Marianna is dead. But..."

Angeline's expression turned grim. "But you don't know how she could've had a niece, isn't that right, sheriff?" Anger laced her words.

"That's right. Marianna dinna have any brothers or sisters."

"I can see how you would arrive at that assumption, but as I told Mr. Delahaye, my grandparents divorced when the girls were quite young and each took one of the daughters. The both grandparents remarried."

Dennis shook his head. "Hah. You are wrong. Marianna's parents were Catholic, and Catholics don't divorce, at least not in this part of Louisiana. Besides, Marianna was born, lived and died in this parish."

She threw her hands up in disgust. "Is this entire town involved in a conspiracy? I feel like I've landed in the twilight zone. Next you'll be telling me that up is down."

Jean-Paul leaned down and whispered in her ear, "Have you considered that maybe you're the one who's wrong?"

Her gaze locked with his and he read her confusion, doubt and fear. "That can't be," she whispered back, her voice shaky.

Illogically, he wanted to reach out and soothe the worry from her brow and tell her everything was fine. But it wasn't. No matter how they sliced it, Marianna didn't have any siblings.

"There's no conspiracy, here, sugar," Dennis replied. "But there might be another explanation. Marianna's daddy was gone a lot of the time, working on offshore rigs and other things. Mebbe he had himself a bastard and didn't tell no one."

She shook with rage. "How dare you!"

Dennis's eyes narrowed, taking on that ruthless look that signaled trouble for all.

"How dare you imply my mother was illegitimate. Why—"

Jean-Paul couldn't leave her to her fate. He grabbed her hand and pulled her toward the door. She reminded him of an enraged hummingbird, sputtering and waving her free hand.

"Martin, take the tow truck and get Miz Fitzgerald's car. I'll be back later to fix it." He nodded to the sheriff. "Excuse us. I need to take the lady to see a friend."

Before anyone could respond, Jean-Paul pushed open the screen and thrust Angeline out.

"What are you doing?" she demanded as he hauled her to his truck.

"Keep your voice down." He jerked open the driver's door, scooped her up and deposited her on the bench seat. He hopped in beside her. "Scoot over."

He shoved her with his hip. The old engine roared to life and Jean-Paul floored the accelerator.

"Have you lost your mind?" she yelled over the noise.

What was he doing trying to protect a woman who was spouting an impossible story? "I might have, *chère*. I just might have."

"What was all that back there with the sheriff? I wanted to ask him some questions about my aunt's death."

"Let me clue you in, Angel. Sheriff Dennis Mathers is as crooked and dishonest as they come. He is the paid bully of this town's wealthiest resident, Roger Boudreaux. You showing up spells only trouble for them. Beware. Under no circumstances should you trust either one."

"Why should I trust you over them? You called me a liar and believe me a cheat. What proof do I have you're one of the good guys?"

"I can't give you any. I left my white hat at home. You'll just have to take my word for it."

"That's a weak reason, at best."

Didn't he know that?

The sheriff's ugly suggestion caught hold in her mind and she couldn't banish it. Not with all these people telling her the same thing.

A dozen different feelings slashed her. Sorrow, pain, doubt, fear. And on top of it all, remorse that Marianna was dead.

What was going on here?

Little, niggling doubts that had cropped up during her childhood came roaring back. Questions like why she didn't have pictures of her mother and aunt when they were growing up. And why her mother's accent was so different from her aunt's. The explanation of her grandparents' divorce seemed reasonable, but there was always something not quite right about the story. Every time she had asked her aunt about growing up in Louisiana, she would always manage to steer the conversation off her personal history.

And there was the little question of where she had been born. Her mother could never identify the state she'd been born in since her birth had occurred on a flight from their home in Vermont to Florida where her dad had been transferred. The odd story had satisfied her when she was sixteen. Now, it fell short.

But the incident that stuck in her mind was the Christmas they had spent with her maternal grandparents. She'd been close to ten. After Christmas dinner, she had asked her grandfather if he didn't miss his first wife and other daughter. Her mother had yanked her from the room and told her never, never to ask that question again. She was told that Grandma Newberry had been extremely hurt at the mention of Grandpa's first wife. Angie had been forced to apologize to her grandparents, then sent to bed. Thinking about it now, she remembered hearing her mother and grandparents arguing.

The child needs to know the truth. Suddenly, that phrase took on new and ominous meaning.

"*Chère,* pay no attention to that snake," Jean-Paul said, snapping her back to the present. "He likes to think he's important. He is nothin'. Less than the dirt under your feet."

Angeline looked at Jean-Paul in disbelief. "He only said what everyone else did."

"True, but he delighted in saying what he did. It pleases him to hurt others."

The distinction wasn't lost on her. She looked out the window at the passing scenery and tried to ignore the handsome man next to her. His effort to comfort her disturbed her. She would rather he remained hostile. It was better for her if he kept his distance.

When she'd stumbled into Pierre's earlier today, she'd immediately been drawn to Jean-Paul. What woman wouldn't be, unless she was six feet under?

"Where are you taking me?" she asked, trying to focus on something else besides him.

A mischievous glint flashed in his eyes. "To M'dame Eleanor's, of course. Where else would you like me to take you?"

"You didn't call her."

"I couldn't, not with you runnin' off at the mouth like you were."

"Running off at the mouth?" she squealed, offended he would say such a thing.

"*Mais, yeah.*" He shook his head. "There's gonna be trouble, no matter what."

"What do you mean?"

When he didn't answer, she laid her hand on his forearm. The muscles were like iron. He glanced down at her hand, then up into her eyes.

"I'm afraid you'll find out soon enough. Too soon, I'm thinking."

He turned onto a quiet side street. Old-style Acadian houses, constructed in timber frame and set up on cypress blocks, lined both sides of the street. The last home was painted a pale yellow with an extensive flower garden running along the side of the house. Jean-Paul parked the truck and jumped out.

"M'dame Eleanor," he called in a loud voice. "You here?"

Angeline followed.

"M'dame Eleanor, are you here?"

A tiny woman with white hair and sparkling black eyes came around the side of the house. "Quit your bellowing, Jean-Paul. You will scare my darlings to death."

He waved aside her concern. "You, m'dame, are much too crazy about your roses. Loud noise won't cause them not to bloom."

She shook a gnarled finger at him. "You are wrong. My *bébés*, they will no' show their beauty if they are shouted at. And you know that." The old woman turned to Angeline. "Oh, my," she murmured, her eyes wide. "Have you brought me a ghost, Jean-Paul?"

He smiled. "*Non,* but I have brought you a young lady who thinks Marianna Courville is her aunt."

She lovingly slapped Jean-Paul on the arm. "Quit teasing this old woman."

"I'm not teasing. I have brought Angeline to you so you can tell her about Marianna."

The old woman's gaze rested on Angeline. "Is this true? Jean-Paul is not pullin' this old woman's leg?"

Angeline stepped closer. "It's true. Please help." Her voice quavered, and a single tear slipped from the corner of her eye.

Eleanor slipped her arm around Angeline's waist and gave her a motherly hug. "Come, *ma petite*. Let us go inside and you tell me this story."

Eleanor crossed her arms and leaned back in her chair. "I am sorry, *chère*, but what Jean-Paul has told you is truth. Me, I have lived in this parish for all my sixty years. I knew Marianna's *maman* and *papa*. We grew up together. Julia and Ben wanted more children besides Marianna but were never blessed with any."

Angeline's brows crinkled into a frown. "But—"

"You still don't believe us?" Jean-Paul asked.

"How can I?" Desperation sounded clearly in her voice. "If I believe you, then everything my parents and Marianna told me is a lie. Why would they do that?"

"Is it easier to believe an entire town is lying?" he softly inquired.

Her shoulders slumped, her head bowed, she whispered, "I don't know. I don't know."

The confusion he read in her face and heard in her voice touched him deeply. She seemed desperately in need of reassurance, but how could he give her any? She claimed to be one thing, yet her face was proof of another. Somehow, some way, Angeline was connected to Roger Boudreaux. Could she be in league with Roger, trying to gain access to Marianna's property to turn it over to him? The explanation seemed logical, but his heart wasn't buying that line of reasoning.

"Would a copy of Marianna's birth certificate help convince you, Angeline, that she was an only child?" Eleanor asked.

"There's a copy of it here in the parish?" The revelation surprised Jean-Paul.

"Oui."

"But I thought all birth and death records were kept in New Orleans," he shot back.

With a smile that told him the old woman was enjoying herself, she began, "What you say is true, Jean-Paul. But what you don't know, and should, a man your age still single—"

"M'dame," Jean-Paul interrupted. "You are drifting from the point."

Giving him a reprimanding look, she continued, "When a man and woman apply for a wedding license in this parish, they must produce a copy of their birth certificates. After that, they are kept on file at the courthouse."

M'dame Eleanor was enjoying this too much, but because he had neglected to visit her as often as he should, Jean-Paul played along. "But Marianna never married."

She acknowledged that point with a regal nod. "True, but that doesn't mean she did not apply for a wedding license."

Too many surprises were turning up today for Jean-Paul's taste. "When did she do this?"

"I don't remember exactly." She waved her hand, dismissing the exact time as unimportant. "Sometime in the early seventies."

He still couldn't believe his ears. "Who did she plan to marry?"

"Charlie Tate."

"Charlie Tate," Jean-Paul parroted in a strangled voice. "I can't believe Marianna would ever consider marrying him."

Miss Eleanor shook her finger at him. "What do you know of the ways of the heart, *hein?* You do your best to avoid such things."

The old woman's black eyes locked with his and she silently challenged him to contradict her. Several replies came to mind, but he held his tongue. If nothing else, Miss Eleanor deserved his respect.

"Why didn't she marry this man?" Angeline asked, breaking the tense quiet.

"Who can say?" A Gallic shrug accompanied her answer. "All I know for sure is Marianna was the one who called off the wedding. But, I will tell you this. Marianna acted like a woman who had loved intensely, passionately and lost her love. She mourned him the rest of her life."

"I don't remember any of this," Jean-Paul complained.

Eleanor waved off his objection. "You were in short pants and only interested in what wiggled in the mud of the bayou."

"If Jean-Paul didn't know about the wedding, then maybe he's wrong about Marianna having a sister?" Angeline questioned, her voice filled with hope.

"Non, chère." Miss Eleanor's voice held no doubt. "He is not. Come, I will take you to the courthouse and show you."

Chapter 3

Angeline's heart pounded as she read over the birth certificate.

July 20, 1944...Marianna Courville...Father—Benjamin Courville, age 22,...Mother's Maiden Name—Julia Mouton, age 17...Father's occupation—oil-field worker.

She frowned. This didn't make sense. Her grandfather's name was Edward, and he was a shipbuilder. She continued to read.

Birthplace of parents—Mirabeau.

That was wrong. Grandfather Edward was born in Burlington, Vermont.

Her eyes focused on the most damning piece of information the document held.

Number of live births to mother—one...

If what she'd been told by her mother was true, then that line should have read two. Sarah, her mother, was the older of the sisters by a year. Marianna should have been the second live baby born to Julia.

But there it was, bold as brass, staring back at her, shouting that she'd been lied to.

She heard footsteps behind her, then felt Jean-Paul's warmth.

"Do you need any other proof?" The richness of Jean-Paul's voice washed over her in the dark dankness of the tiny ground-floor room of the court building. "The Catholic church has baptismal records."

The ache inside her seemed overwhelming. Carefully, Angie laid down the paper. Any sudden move might shatter her. "No," she murmured.

Jean-Paul squatted by her chair. She tried to hide her pain and confusion by turning away, but he would have none of it. With a gentle hand he forced her to meet his gaze.

"I'm sorry, *chère*." His fingers stroked over her cheek.

"I guess I'm the liar." A tear slipped from the corner of her eye and slid onto his fingers. She swallowed hard, trying to stem the flow of emotion. Gazing into Jean-Paul's deep green eyes, she asked, "What is going on? My entire life, I've been told one lie after another. My mother, father, Aunt Marianna. Even my grandparents, for heaven's sake. But why? Why would they all tell the same lie?"

He soothed the wisps of hair away from her face. "Who can say why? You will have to ask your *maman* why."

"I can't. My parents are both dead."

"Your grandparents, then, they can answer your questions, yes?"

She shook her head. "They died years ago. There was no one left but Marianna. Now...There is no one to answer the question why."

An awkward silence settled on the room.

"Jean-Paul," Miss Eleanor said, capturing everyone's attention, "take Angeline to the library. She needs to see the picture. Maybe it will answer some questions."

"What picture?" Angeline asked, glancing from Eleanor to Jean-Paul.

He hesitated, then shrugged. "You're right, M'dame Eleanor. The lady needs to see the picture."

Angeline wanted to protest and ask him what he was talking about, but he pulled her to her feet and out of the room into the dim hall.

"What are you doing?" Angeline demanded as he led her out of the building. It was a question she'd been constantly asking the man since she'd met him. "And what was Miss Eleanor talking about, Jean-Paul?"

He stopped so suddenly that she ran into him. "I wish you'd quit doing that. I'm beginning to feel like a Ping-Pong ball."

The charming grin he flashed her caused butterflies to assault her stomach. "So, my little northern wren knows how to say my name. *Merci, Angeline.*"

She couldn't stop the flush of red racing to her cheeks. Funny, how such an inappropriate feeling could pop up now, in the midst of this crisis. And yet, in a way, Angie welcomed the diversion.

He tugged on her hand. "Come. There is something you must see."

He guided her across the grassy knoll in the center of the town square to a lone building surrounded by a black wrought-iron fence. A garden filled with dozens of different flowers and plants occupied the space between the fence and building. Carved into the stones above the entrance was the word Library.

"Isn't this where Au—Marianna worked?" she asked.

"*Oui,* but that's not why I brought you here." He opened the door and motioned her inside. The cool interior air flowed around her. She closed her eyes, enjoying the respite from the heat. A sigh of relief escaped her lips. A choked sound made her eyes fly open. Jean-Paul towered over her, the dark hunger in his gaze making her knees weak.

He leaned close, his warm breath fanning her lips. "You, Angel, have a gift, one that makes others want to share your little sips of life." Tenderly, he ran his thumb over her lips as if he were a blind man wanting to learn the texture of her mouth. But he was sighted, and she feared Jean-Paul saw much more in her than any other person ever had. She stepped back.

"You were going to show me something in here," she prompted.

After a moment's study, he gave her a sad smile that spoke of regret and cowardice. Hers. "Come." He held out his hand, challenging her.

She placed her hand in his. His strong fingers curled around hers and she wondered if he could feel how her pulse rate shot up. He led her through a second set of double doors into the main floor of the library.

Angeline glanced around the quiet room, unease tightening the muscles across her shoulders. She slowed. The certainty that there was something here, in this building, that was going to shake the foundations of her world gripped her heart. She wanted to pull her hand out of Jean-Paul's and run pell-mell out of the library and not stop until she was safely aboard a jet on her way back to Vermont.

Jean-Paul must have felt her reluctance. He glanced over his shoulder, his brow raised in question.

One of the teenage girls working at a table near the door glanced up and froze. At a neighboring table, a man reading the latest copy of the local newspaper peeked over the top of the paper and went still.

Angie's unease multiplied a hundredfold. "Maybe this isn't a good idea." The explanation sounded weak at best.

Jean-Paul stopped, but didn't release her hand. "You want answers to your questions, *non?*"

She glanced at the staring duo. "Yes."

"And you want to know why everyone stares at you as if they've seen a ghost?"

He knew she did. What he failed to understand was the terror those unknown answers held. "Yes, I want to know."

"Then we must do this."

She hesitated a moment, then nodded.

He gave her hand a reassuring squeeze, then started toward the circulation desk.

Angie kept her eyes focused on his back and counted the steps. There were six before he stopped. When she didn't move or glance around, Jean-Paul wrapped his arm around her waist and pointed to the wall above the librarian's desk.

"Look, Angeline."

Taking a deep breath, she obeyed his command. There, in an ornate gilt frame, was a portrait of a woman so identical to her that if she didn't know better, she would have thought someone had done an extremely flattering painting of her.

Angeline gasped, bringing the librarian's attention to her. The woman's mouth flew open and she dropped the book in her hand. The thud echoed through the room like a gunshot.

"Mattie," Jean-Paul said, his voice casual and reassuring, "I would like you to meet Angeline Fitzgerald. I brought her here to see Jacqueline's picture. She wondered why everyone in Mirabeau stared at her as if she were a ghost."

Mattie nodded her head, her eyes still wide with shock. "I understand. Why, she—she could be Jacqueline, herself."

Jean-Paul stepped back, then looked from Angeline to the painting. "You got that right. Look, they have the same red-gold hair—'' he fingered a strand of Angie's hair ''—blue eyes and fair skin. Why, the smile is even the same. Smile for Mattie, Angel.''

In some part of her brain, Angie heard the conversation between Jean-Paul and the librarian, but shock of seeing the picture kept her motionless. ''Who is she?'' Odd, her voice sounded flat and lifeless.

''There's a plaque on the bottom of the frame.''

She located it and read aloud the name engraved in the metal. ''Jacqueline Boudreaux. 1910-1970. Who was she?''

''Jackie was the sister of the richest man in this town, Roger Boudreaux. She gave the money to build this library. She and Marianna were close, and not just because Marianna worked here.'' He paused and tapped his mouth with his forefinger. ''Come to think of it, Jackie and Marianna were a lot alike. Neither married nor had children. And yet, here you are, claiming to be the niece of one woman and the very image of the other. How very odd.''

His words sliced through the numbness of her soul, and circumstances rushed in on Angie. Nothing was as it should have been. Tremors began deep inside her and quickly enveloped her body. She tried to hide the shaking by wrapping her arms around her waist.

Jean-Paul grasped her upper arms. ''Are you all right, *chère?*''

She wanted to answer him, but nothing came out of her mouth. Her eyes sought out his, silently asking him to take her out of this place.

''Come, let us go.'' He laced his fingers through hers and tugged her forward.

Once outside in the hot Louisiana sun, Angie tipped her face up to welcome the warmth, hoping it would banish the deep chill that had settled around her heart.

"Ah, don't cry, Angel," Jean-Paul commanded, wiping away her tears.

Stunned by his comment, she touched her cheek to discover tears streaming down her face. She hadn't made a sound, would have never been conscious that she was crying if he hadn't said something.

He slipped his arms around her and gently pushed her head onto his shoulder.

The more she tried to stem the tide of tears, the harder they came. The emotions she'd been fighting all day—grief, fright, bewilderment and rage—crashed upon her like breakers on the beach during a violent storm. Once one emotion hit, shaking her, another would come, just as strong as the previous one, giving her no time to recover her equilibrium.

It seemed as if she cried on Jean-Paul's shoulder for hours. It probably was only minutes, but finally she gained control of herself and pulled out of his embrace. The first thing she noticed was the large wet spot on the front of his shirt.

"I'm sorry," she said, wiping dry her face.

He gave her a tender smile, one that eased her embarrassment. "Think nothing of it."

"I'm not usually an emotional person."

"You've had reason."

Now that the violent storm of weeping had passed, Angie was left with one terrible question. "What's going on here, Jean-Paul? Who am I?"

His expression thoughtful, he brushed her chin with his fingers. "I wish I knew, *chère*. I wish I knew."

Staring down into Angeline's puffy, ravaged face, Jean-Paul knew how it felt to rip the wings off a butterfly. Lousy.

The three years he'd spent in prison had taught him any number of harsh lessons. Among them was how to read people and the subtle signals they gave off. Of course, the pain radiating from her wasn't subtle or hidden, leaving him with only one conclusion. Angeline had told the truth as she had known it. Or she was a damn fine actress.

So where did that leave them? He didn't know.

"Jean-Paul?"

His name on her lips struck deep into his soul. The longing to hear her whisper his name in the heat of passion coursed through him. He shoved aside the dangerous thought. His little northern wren was trouble, and if he wasn't careful that trouble would blow up in his face.

"Jean-Paul?"

"*Oui,* Angel."

"Could we go somewhere where I could sit down? I feel kind of shaky."

He shook his head. "*Bien sûr.* You have had an eventful afternoon, *non?*"

A chuckle that boarded on the hysterical escaped her lips. "An understatement if I've ever heard one. I feel like an amnesia victim who knows nothing about herself or her past."

For the first time, he noticed the crowd of onlookers that had gathered around them. Several of the people were straining to see Angeline's face. He ignored them, slipped his arm through hers and headed across the town square toward his truck.

"Thank you," she whispered as they walked away.

"They don't mean to be rude. It is just they are amazed by the resemblance."

"I understand."

Nothing more was said until they were in Jean-Paul's truck, heading out of town.

"Where are you taking me?" she asked, her voice sounding like a lost child's.

"To Marianna's. Maybe there we can find some answers."

She turned to him. "Do you think so?" She looked so hopeful and expectant he couldn't tell her the truth, that the chance of their finding something was slim to none.

He shrugged. "Perhaps."

The lie didn't set well.

Chapter 4

Angie, numb from the events of the morning, stared out the window of the truck at the passing scenery.

"It's much different than your Vermont, *non?*"

Angie glanced at Jean-Paul and saw the twinkle in his green eyes. "Oh, yes. The college where I teach is nestled in a small valley. My house is perched on the side of the mountain, overlooking a babbling brook."

"So, there is such a thing as a babbling brook? I've never seen such a thing. Here, there are just slow-moving bayous."

That she didn't doubt. The contrast between the two places was startling. Her hometown was a quiet, peaceful spot. Her neighbors were no-nonsense folks and the rugged land was a perfect backdrop for their strong ideals. Here, the earth seemed to pulse with uninhibited life that spilled over into the lives of the people, coloring their actions.

But the strangest thing about this spot was that, at some

subconscious level, it called to Angie. It was as if some part of her inner self had come to life in the heat and humidity.

"So, *chère,* you are a teacher. What do you teach?"

Angie welcomed Jean-Paul's question because it drew her attention from her disturbing thoughts. "I teach English composition and literature."

Jean-Paul lifted his right hand from the steering wheel and shook it. *"I yi yee! Un prof d'Anglais."*

He was acting as if she'd just declared she was a carrier of the plague. "Do you have a problem with that?"

The grin he flashed her throbbed with wickedness. *"Non,* sugar, I have no problem with you."

Heat pooled low in her abdomen, and for a brief moment Angie surrendered to the wonder of the feeling. But sanity quickly returned, and with it the realization that Jean-Paul had not answered her question. "Don't you like English teachers?"

His body tensed and an odd darkness seemed to descend on him. *"Anglais* teachers are the scourge of all Cajun children. In the seventies, the public-school system in Louisiana decided all children would speak proper *Anglais.* No more backwater Cajun would be spoken. And to their credit, they almost wiped out the language. But that's not the worst part. They've taught the children to be ashamed of their parents."

"No, you're wrong. Teaching children to speak correctly will help them when they go out and try to find a job."

Jean-Paul's eyes turned cold. "There is a difference between teaching a child English and teaching a child shame because his parents cannot speak proper upper-crust English."

Angie winced at his harsh but correct pronunciation of the word English. When he said English using the French enunciation, the word was lyrical, soft and seductive. But the way he'd just said it told her that there was a wealth of bitterness and hurt in Jean-Paul. Had he been one of those small boys in elementary school who'd been belittled because of his heritage?

She fought the urge to reach out to him and offer some sort of comfort, shocked that she would feel anything so tender for Jean-Paul.

He turned his truck onto a single-lane crushed-shell road. The lush foliage dropped away and the flat land was covered with knee-high grass. Occasionally, Angie could see a clump of bushes dotting the landscape. But what caught her attention was the half dozen oil pumps, their spindle arms moving up and down.

"I didn't know Aunt—" Angie bit off the word, fighting the tears that filled her eyes.

Jean-Paul reached over and laid his hand on hers. "It's okay, Angel."

She gulped. "I don't know what to call Marianna now." She felt foolish admitting her confusion.

"Don't worry. Things have a way of working out."

"Do you think so?"

"Mais yeah."

They both knew his assurance rang hollow, but she grasped the thin thread of hope he held out.

"Now, you wanted to ask something about Marianna?"

"Yes. I'm surprised to see all these oil derricks. Marianna never mentioned having oil on her land."

"They are not derricks, Angeline. Derricks are the tall, steel structures they use to drill for oil. What you see are pumps, or what we call grasshoppers. They keep the oil flowing once it's been discovered."

A grin tugged at the corners of her mouth. "They do kind of look like grasshoppers."

Jean-Paul stopped the truck in front of a small, dilapidated frame house that could have been built in the last century. Angie glanced around, thinking that maybe she'd missed the lovely house that Marianna lived in. But there were no other buildings anywhere in sight.

She looked at Jean-Paul, expecting him to see his error and start the truck again. Instead, he pulled the keys out of the ignition.

"This is Marianna's house?" she asked in disbelief.

"*Oui*, this is it."

"B-but, I don't understand. With all the money from the oil, surely Marianna could afford something more modern."

"The oil wasn't Marianna's."

"What?"

"The oil wasn't Marianna's."

"How can that be?"

He turned, resting his arm along the top of the seat. "Marianna's *papa*, along with every other landholder in the parish, sold his oil-and-gas rights to Roger Boudreaux for a pittance days before oil was discovered in the parish. Only one man got rich from the oil and gas." There was a harshness in Jean-Paul's voice that made her shiver. "Come, *chère,* let's get you settled."

Angie scrambled out of the truck cab and followed Jean-Paul up the steps to the porch.

"Do you have a key?" she asked.

"*Non,* but Marianna kept one under the flowerpot on the porch." He retrieved the key and opened the door.

Angie stepped into the living room and stopped, frozen by the chaos before her. The room looked as if a whirlwind had ripped through it. The cushions from the chairs and sofa were ripped up and tossed on the floor. The desk drawers were pulled out and their contents scattered about the room. Angie could see into the room beyond—a bedroom—which looked in much the same condition.

Angie heard Jean-Paul curse in both French and English and tried to ignore the coarse language.

"I knew it. I just knew it wasn't an accident."

Angie whirled to face Jean-Paul. "What wasn't an accident? What are you talking about?"

Her question seemed to snap him out of his angry tirade. He studied her for a moment, then shook his head. "Nothing."

Before she could question him further, he moved to the bedroom, then disappeared through a door at the rear of the room. A moment later he appeared in the kitchen, which opened onto the living room.

As Jean-Paul walked through the destruction, his suspicions that Marianna had been killed grew. It made no sense for anyone to trash Marianna's house, since she didn't own anything of great value. That is, unless the culprit was looking for something specific. But what?

The day Marianna died, she had driven to New Orleans to talk to Edward Dias, an old friend of his and fellow member of the task force investigating corruption in state government. Maybe someone had discovered why Marianna wanted to talk to Edward and had killed her to keep her quiet, then searched her house to dispose of any incriminating evidence she might have had. It was a wild theory, but it was all he had.

Angie sagged down into a wooden chair by the door. "Who would do something like this?"

"Someone without a conscience." Jean-Paul could list a number of candidates in the parish, but Roger Boudreaux would be his first choice and Dennis Mathers, the sheriff, his second.

She peered up at him. "And do you know anyone like that?"

"Yeah."

"What's this about, Jean-Paul?"

He wished he trusted her enough to tell her, but at this point he didn't know spit about her. Hell, he wished *he* knew enough to be able to understand what this was all about. "I don't know."

The look in her eyes challenged him, telling him she didn't believe him. He boldly met her steady gaze, as though he had nothing to hide. She glanced away.

Standing, she walked into the bedroom. He followed. Together they surveyed the disarray. The dresser drawers were piled on the bed, Marianna's underthings tossed on the floor. Her dresses, skirts and blouses had been pulled out of the closet and thrown about. Boxes, which must have been on the closet shelves, were lying next to the clothes.

"Whoever ransacked this place did a thorough job," Jean-Paul said.

Angeline bent and reached for a flowing print dress on the floor. Jean-Paul squatted beside her and his hands covered hers. Her head came up and moisture shone bright in her eyes.

He cupped her cheek in his palm. He told himself he was simply comforting her. But his conscience called him a liar. His action sprang from a need to touch her and feel her satin-smooth skin beneath the calluses of his hand. His thumb ran along the edge of her lower lip. He felt her tremble and wanted to lean closer and cover her sweet mouth with his. He started to lower his head, but she pulled away and scrambled to her feet. *Idiot,* he silently scolded himself. She didn't need him to make a pass. He sighed.

"I'll hang these up," he told her. He motioned with his head toward the bed. "Why don't you put Marianna's things back in the bureau drawers?"

She glanced over her shoulder and nodded.

They worked quietly for several minutes. He'd replaced most of the clothes when he noticed the shoe box full of letters and pictures. Bending down to pick it up, he froze when he saw the postmark on one of the envelopes. Vermont.

The sound of a car engine penetrated his brain. Since Marianna's house was the only one on this road, he knew someone was coming to meet Angeline. He hurried to the front windows and saw the sheriff's car rumbling down the crushed-shell drive.

They were in for trouble.

He rushed back into the bedroom, spotted a suitcase under some of the dresses and pulled it out.

"What are you doing?" Angeline asked.

He didn't reply, but opened the lid and emptied the shoe box into the case. He also snatched up the photo album lying on the floor and threw it in.

"Jean-Paul, what's going on?"

He slammed the lid closed. "There's gonna be trouble, sugar. You just let me handle things. You got that?"

"No, I don't got that."

Jean-Paul grinned, liking her sass. Cupping her chin, he said, "That's a pretty temper you got there, *chère*. But now's not the time to show it to me. Later."

She opened her mouth to argue with him, but the front door flew open and the sheriff strode inside.

"Well, well, what we got here?" Dennis glanced around the room and shook his head. "Tut, tut, what have you done to this place?" He walked over to the couch and picked up a cushion. After examining the ripped fabric, he flung it back. "Well, in addition to breakin' and enterin', I could book y'all on vandalism."

"The house was in this condition when we came here, sheriff," Angie hotly replied.

He shrugged. "I have only your word on that."

Angie stepped toward Dennis. "We've been here less than five minutes, sheriff. How could we have done this much damage in that amount of time?" she demanded, hands on her hips.

"Again, I have only your word for that, Miss Fitzgerald. The last time I saw you, you were at Pierre's, and that was over an hour ago."

Jean-Paul stared at Angeline in amazement. His little northern wren looked madder than a wet hen. If challenging the sheriff wouldn't bring such dire consequences, he'd let her have at the old boy. He stepped between the two. "All you have to do is check with Mattie at the library. Angeline and I were there less than ten minutes ago."

Dennis puffed up like an ugly toad. "I will. But that doesn't change the fact that you're trespassing. And it's my job to enforce the laws of this parish. Leave."

"Oh, yes," Jean-Paul answered in a voice deadly and still. "You enforce the law as made and twisted by your patron."

Dennis took a step toward Jean-Paul. "You callin' me crooked?"

Jean-Paul didn't bat so much as an eyelash but met Dennis's stare.

Being the bully he was, Dennis backed down. He gave a nervous laugh and said, "Look who's calling me crooked."

Everything inside Jean-Paul was screaming for him to knock Dennis's crooked teeth down his lying throat, but he heard Angeline move.

"Sheriff," she said, "don't I have a right to stay at my aunt's house?" She sounded calm and in control of herself, but Jean-Paul suspected she wanted to defuse the tension between the two men.

Dennis's cold, fish-eyed stare moved from Jean-Paul to Angeline. "You got proof that you're Marianna's niece?" he asked in a tone so nasty that Jean-Paul almost gave in to the urge to punch the lout.

With her cheeks turning pink, she admitted, "No."

"Then you're outta here. Like I said before, I'm sworn to uphold the law. And you, missy, are where you don't belong."

Jean-Paul turned and saw the light of battle flare in her eyes. He knew that Dennis had backed down once, but if Angel tried to challenge him, Dennis wouldn't let the insult pass. Then he would have to step in, and from then on out Dennis would be looking for some way to even the score. It was better to avoid the confrontation in the first place.

Grasping her hand in his, Jean-Paul gave it a gentle squeeze, drawing her attention to him. Silently he pleaded with her not to answer. He breathed a sigh of relief when he saw her swallow whatever she was about to say.

Jean-Paul retrieved the suitcase he'd packed from the bed.

"What are you doing?" Dennis demanded.

"I'm getting Angeline's things. Do you have an objection?"

Scratching his face, Dennis thought a moment. "Naw."

Jean-Paul gave a prayer of thanks that Angel didn't set up a fuss about the bag and that she'd played along with him. Dennis watched them get into the truck and was still standing on the porch as they rounded the bend of the road.

"All right. Are you going to tell me why you hustled me out of that house without a word in my defense?"

Would she believe him if he told her the danger she'd been in? "Remember I told you that the sheriff is as mean as a rabid hound? Well, I didn't want you to find out firsthand how nasty he can be."

"Yes, but—"

"Besides, *chère,* you didn't have a legal leg to stand on. You have no proof you are who you say you are."

Her head dropped forward and he could feel the pain radiating from her. *You're crazy,* a voice inside his head whispered. And as much as it didn't make sense, he knew he was feeling her agony.

"What's in the suitcase that you hid from the sheriff?" Angie asked, pointing to the bag.

He glanced at her, then down at the case on the floor. "Why, I think, *chère,* that I may have found the answer to who you are."

Chapter 5

Angie stared in shock at Jean-Paul. She couldn't say what her feelings were. She should have welcomed any clue to her real identity. But for some unknown and frightening reason, she didn't want to know. Not at this moment.

"Aren't you curious, Angel?"

His question was like a whip across her soul. He laid his hand on her forearm, and she jerked away in response.

"What is it, *chère?* What's wrong?"

"Nothing," she murmured, wincing at the lie. Everything was wrong, nothing was right, and they both knew it. Her world had been turned inside out, and she didn't know if she could take another revelation without completely falling apart. She wished she could just close her eyes and lose herself in the lyrical rumbling of his deep voice and the warm strength radiating from his big body. But it would be foolish to depend on this gorgeous stranger, no matter how much she was tempted.

He turned onto the blacktop and headed the opposite direction from town. He drove for about a mile, then took another dirt road.

"Where are you taking me?"

When he didn't answer, she glanced at him. He'd been waiting for her to look at him, and he gave her a mocking grin.

"Don't you trust me?"

How could he ask for her trust? He was a virtual stranger who had openly expressed his skepticism about her. Granted, his attitude had changed; still, she knew he had doubts about her. Besides, after the revelations of the morning, Angie didn't know if she'd ever trust anyone again. "Trust's not the issue here. I simply wanted to know where we're going. Obviously, this is not the way to Mirabeau."

He shook his head. "*Non*, you are wrong. Trust is the entire issue. Do you think I'm like that snake back there at Marianna's?" he asked, his voice filled with outrage.

She didn't understand his reaction. What had she done but ask a logical question? When she remembered the solace he'd offered her at Marianna's, she realized her conscious choice not to trust him with her feelings must have angered him.

"You haven't answered my question, Angel. Do you think I'm like the sheriff?" There was a tension in him that spoke of something more than his query.

"No, I don't think you're anything like him." And heaven knew his gaze evoked a different range of emotion in her than the sheriff's insolent looks.

He nodded. "*Bien.* Now, as to where we are going, I'm taking you to my house."

She opened her mouth to protest, but he raised his hand to stop her.

"Wait—let me explain."

Angie leaned back and folded her arms.

"The safest place for you to look through the evidence in that suitcase is at my house. There might be something that will set this town on its ear, and you don't want to do that with an audience."

He had a point. She was tired of being stared at like a bug under glass. Whatever that suitcase contained, she wanted to review it in private. And Jean-Paul was offering her that very opportunity.

"Thank you for your thoughtfulness."

"You're welcome."

The truck rumbled down the pitted road, throwing Angie against the passenger-side door. Again, oil pumps dotted the field before her, but this time, because of what Jean-Paul had told her earlier, she knew oil didn't mean wealth for his family.

The road curved around a group of trees and then widened into a driveway. The house beyond was set up on blocks and at an angle to the road. The structure was slightly larger than Marianna's and lovingly cared for. The clapboards had been recently painted white and the shutters a deep green.

He stopped the truck and turned off the motor. Angie didn't wait for Jean-Paul but scrambled out of the truck. She leaned into the cab and grasped the handle of the suitcase. Jean-Paul's hand covered hers.

"I'll take that."

His warm breath fanned her neck, causing shivers to race up her spine. Angie stepped back, overwhelmed by his heat and bulk. He hefted the case and started for the house, seemingly unaware of his effect on her. After a moment of hesitation, she followed him.

The inside of the house was as well taken care of as the outside. The simple furnishings looked as if they were from another era. Suddenly, Angie realized that these pieces were a history of Jean-Paul's family. The hand-carved rocker in the corner could easily be a hundred years old, but the bright cushion on it had been made by hand in the last few years.

An overhead fan moved the air in the room and Angie noticed all the windows and doors were open. The little house had no air-conditioning.

Jean-Paul walked to the cherrywood table and set the suitcase on the surface. She stumbled over the large rag rug in the center of the airy room. Suddenly, Angie felt drained and utterly weary. Her knees turned to jelly, and she collapsed into one of the dining room chairs.

"Why don't I get us something to drink before we explore the contents of the suitcase?"

Angie peered up at Jean-Paul. Either he was the most observant man she'd ever come across or he was psychic. Either way it made her nervous that he seemed so in tune with her and her feelings.

"That would be nice."

He disappeared. "What would you like?" he called from the kitchen. "I have Cajun coffee, but I don't think that would appeal to you. I have some white wine or brandy."

"Water would be fine."

He didn't reply but reappeared a few minutes later carrying two large glasses of iced tea. "If I can't convince you to drink coffee or wine, at least I can give you some tea fixed Louisiana style."

She accepted the glass from his hand, grateful for his consideration. The cold, sweet liquid flowing down her throat felt heavenly, and for an instant she reveled in the pure pleasure of it.

"Ah, Angel."

At the sound of Jean-Paul's voice, her gaze flew to his. He studied her, his green eyes hot with a passion that she didn't want to define.

"There is inside of you a Cajun, waitin' to come out and enjoy," he whispered in a tone so intimate that Angie wanted to close her ears and rush from the room.

His assertion hit home. All her life she had seemed somehow out of step with the people around her. She loved her hometown, loved the crisp, vibrant colors of autumn, the quaintness and history of Easton. But here, in this hot, humid place, a part of her soul had sprung to life. The rhythm of life here sang to her, and little things that she wouldn't have ever considered doing in Vermont, such as chugging down the iced tea and then wallowing in the cool feel of it, she found herself doing automatically here. And it scared her.

"Do you want to open the suitcase so I can see what you found?" she asked.

He shook his head, obviously disappointed that she refused to respond to his observation. He opened the case and motioned for her to begin sifting through the items.

At least two dozen letters and a photo album were inside. She picked up several of the envelopes and studied the writing on the outside. Instantly, Angie recognized her mother's handwriting. With trembling hands, she pulled out the sheets of paper and began to read.

Jean-Paul watched carefully as Angeline went through the letters. Her eyes grew moist and the turmoil in her heart was clearly reflected in her expression. He stood and walked to the window, knowing that if he sat there a moment longer, watching her unveiled reactions, he would pull her into his arms and try to erase her hurt.

Damn, he didn't need or want this protective emotion she brought out in him. A mere three hours earlier Angeline

Fitzgerald had been a stranger who wandered into Mirabeau with the wildest story he'd heard in the past year. He knew nothing about her, except that her coming was going to cause trouble for him and for this town.

And yet he wasn't willing to throw her to the gators. The lady resurrected things in him he'd thought long dead.

He ran his fingers through his hair.

You are a fool, Jean-Paul, he told himself.

Glancing over his shoulder, he saw her wipe away a tear. Oh, yes, he was a fool. But that wasn't going to stop him from helping her.

She was connected with Roger, but how? He glanced at the suitcase. Maybe the answer was there.

He moved back to the table, retrieved the photo album and opened it. The pictures on the first page were of a baby, held in the arms of the woman Angeline had identified earlier as her mother.

"Angeline."

She looked up at him. Her eyes were bright with tears.

He held out the album to her. "I think we should look through this together."

She glanced at the photos and her brow furrowed. "Those are pictures of me as a baby."

"Oui," he gently replied.

She took the book. As they went through the snapshots, Angeline explained each one. There were numerous pictures of Marianna with the Fitzgeralds. On the last page was a duplicate of the picture Angeline carried in her wallet of herself, her mother and Marianna.

Angeline closed her eyes, and her fingers absently moved over the back inside cover of the album. "Jean-Paul, it feels like there's something hidden here."

He took the album from her and carefully examined the paper glued to the back cover. There was a slight crinkling at the top, as if it had been reglued to the cardboard. Retrieving his pocket knife, he loosened the edge and tugged it away from the backing.

"Is there anything there?" she asked, craning her neck to see.

"It appears some sort of paper has been stuffed in here." He pulled it out of its hiding place. "I think there's more than one sheet."

Unfolding the pages, they stared down at Angeline's birth certificate. Marianna Courville was listed as her mother. The place of birth: Boston. In the space for the father's name was typed *Unknown*.

Jean-Paul shook his head. That had to be a lie. He was certain the woman he knew and called friend would know the name of the man who had fathered her child. For some reason, Marianna had chosen not to list it.

He looked at Angeline. She was ghostly white. "Show me the other page, Jean-Paul," she whispered.

He took a deep breath and set the birth certificate aside to reveal a copy of Angeline's adoption by Sarah and Thomas Fitzgerald.

Angie stared at the damning document. "Adopted," she murmured.

Her voice sounded odd to his ears. "Angel."

"Yes."

The detached, faraway look in her eyes worried him. She was pulling into herself, wounded and bleeding from the emotional blows dealt to her, and he knew that if she was ever to heal, she had to give voice to her pain.

He placed the paper on the table, knelt beside her chair and grasped her hands. "Talk to me, Angel."

Angie tried to yank her hands out of Jean-Paul's, but he refused to let her go. "What do you want me to say? Do you want me to talk about all the times I asked Marianna about her childhood and how she would always turn the conversation away from herself? Or maybe you want me to tell you about the countless times I wanted to visit Marianna and how my mother always had a logical excuse why I couldn't go."

Her hands tightened on his until her knuckles were white with the tension.

"Or which of the other countless lies would you like me to tell you?"

She bent over their clasped hands, fighting the shattering pain. Her body began to tremble. "Oh, Mama, why?"

Jean-Paul could no longer stand idly by and watch her go through hell. He rose and pulled her into his arms. And held her.

She clutched his shirt in her fists and tugged. He could physically feel her battling the wrenching tears.

"Let go, *mon coeur*," he whispered in her ear. "Don't fight what is good."

With a final tremor, she surrendered to her grief.

He cupped the back of her head and drew it down to his shoulder. His sweet, little northern wren had endured too much. Her whole world had been blown apart. Nothing she knew as truth in her life when she came to town this morning remained.

The devastation she felt he could easily identify with. He remembered the day he'd been arrested at his office for drug possession and corruption, with his colleagues witnessing his humiliation. His world had come crashing down on him much as Angeline's had today. But what had been the bitterest part of the entire incident was that he'd been innocent. Someone had set him up and he'd taken the fall.

His pain mingled with hers. His hand moved from her hair to wipe away the moisture from her cheek. Her eyes met his and Jean-Paul was lost to everything but bringing comfort to this woman.

His lips softly brushed hers. Angeline moaned and her mouth followed his. Rejoicing at the invitation, he settled his mouth firmly on hers. The salty taste of her tears mingled with the sweetness of her lips. It was better than any wine he'd ever had, and more intoxicating. His tongue ran across the fullness of her lower lip, then traced the seam of her closed mouth.

"Open for me, Angel. Let me in."

She gasped and he slipped his tongue into her mouth. With light strokes he tasted the inside of her cheeks, the roof of her mouth, tangled his tongue with hers.

Shyly, she returned the caress. Her response raced through him like a flash fire.

The muscles in his arms contracted and he pressed her closer to his body. All logical thought shut down and he felt as if he'd been hurled a thousand years back in time and stripped of all outward trappings of civilization. The raw emotion he experienced shook him to his core. He knew what lust felt like. This feeling surpassed that weak emotion.

His instinct for self-preservation kicked in and he set Angeline away from him. She looked confused and vulnerable. It took a moment, but her disorientation disappeared, and her cheeks turned hot pink. Turning away from him, she walked to the window. With trembling fingers, she wiped away the remaining moisture from her face, then tried to smooth back the fallen strands of golden hair into her braid.

"I hope you'll forgive my behavior." A small hiccup interrupted her. "I'm not known to give in to my emotions. I never cry. Twice in one day..." She lifted her shoulder.

Damn, he hadn't meant to embarrass her, only to offer comfort. Well, his good intentions had been incinerated in the flames that flared between them.

"Think nothing of it. As you said, the circumstances were extenuating."

She stole a glance at him as if to assure herself that he wasn't making fun of her. His expression must have reassured her, because she faced him again.

She took a deep breath. "Those documents solve part of the mystery. I now know that Marianna was my mother. And that I was adopted by the Fitzgeralds."

He nodded. "What was in the letters?"

A tender, little smile curved her lips. "I haven't read them all. But the ones I did read were just one mother relating to another mother all the things her child had done. First word, first step, first day at school."

She moved to the table and touched the documents. "There are still too many questions left unanswered, Jean-Paul."

Questions, he knew, that were as explosive as the information they'd just uncovered. "And which questions are those?"

Angie laid the papers on the table. "My birth certificate doesn't name my father. Why do you suppose that is?"

He had his own theory, but at this point he didn't want to share it with her. Instead, he said the first thing that came into his head. "Perhaps Marianna didn't know the father's name."

"Rape?" she gasped. "Are you suggesting that I'm a product of rape?"

That possibility had never occurred to him. "*Non,* that thought never crossed my mind."

"Then are you suggesting that Marianna had a one-night stand and didn't bother to ask the man's name?" She didn't give him the opportunity to answer. "No. The woman I knew never would've done something like that." Tapping her mouth with her finger, she continued, "Maybe she had a reason for not naming the man. Maybe she didn't want him to find out. What do you think?"

What he thought was that this lady was one smart cookie. In spite of the trauma she had been through, she hadn't given herself over to pity. Instead, she was fighting back, trying to discover the mystery surrounding her birth. "I think you're right."

"But why would she do that?" She began to pace.

It was only a matter of time before she came to the same conclusion that he had. Her father was a Boudreaux. She stopped in front of the wall mirror by the front door and looked at herself. Her eyes met his in the reflection.

"Jacqueline," she whispered. "I'm a dead ringer for her. That leads to only one conclusion. My father was a Boudreaux." She whirled to face him. "That's what you think, isn't it?"

He shrugged. "It's the only logical conclusion, *chère.*"

"But you said that Roger was—"

He couldn't stand the horror dawning in her eyes. He caught her shoulders in his hands. "Roger has a son who was close to Marianna's age. He could be your father."

This time Angie refused to give in to the hysteria pounding in her head. There were questions that needed to be asked and she needed a clear head to voice them. She pulled out of Jean-Paul's grasp and walked to the table. Picking up the adoption declaration, she studied the piece of paper that had upended her world.

"You know, the arrangement Marianna had with my parents was unusual for the time. They had what in today's terms would be called an open adoption—except I didn't know I was adopted. So that means it was probably a private adoption."

He moved to her side and took the document from her hand. "I think your reasoning is sound. I don't think any states were allowing open adoptions thirty years ago."

Being reminded of her age, she couldn't help but wonder how old Jean-Paul was. The hair at his temples had turned gray, and there was a certain look of weariness in his eyes that spoke of suffering beyond his years.

She must have been staring, because he smiled. "Are you wondering how old I am, *hein?* I'm thirty-six, but sometimes I feel like a hundred."

That he answered the question that had been floating in her head made Angie nervous. She didn't want this man to be able to read her mind, because if he knew the effect he had on her, she'd be lost.

Remember the last time you gave in to your feelings, a voice in her head taunted. *You were played for a fool, and the entire town witnessed your stupidity.* She, the admired and dignified English professor, had fallen head over heels in love with a con man who had swindled her out of thousands of dollars.

Shoving away the painful memory, she tried to recall what she'd been talking about. "So, we both agree that my adoption—" The word seemed to catch in her throat. She coughed and went on. "The adoption was probably a private one."

He nodded.

"So how did Marianna get together with Sarah? I mean, if you'd ever seen the two of them together, you'd know what good friends they were and how much they enjoyed each other's company."

"A lawyer?"

Angie sank down onto the couch. There was a memory at the edge of her mind, teasing her.

"What is it, Angel?"

"I remember something. It had to do with a basketball game. My parents were watching TV and Tulane was playing. Mother said she was glad that Marianna had talked her into going to that basketball game or else she wouldn't have met my father." Excitement hummed through her. She grabbed Jean-Paul's arm. "What if they were college roommates?"

"That's a possibility. Marianna had a university degree. I remember seeing her diploma, but I can't recall where it was from." He picked up the phone on the end table and punched in a number. "M'dame Eleanor, this is Jean-Paul again. Angeline and I have come across another mystery you might be able to solve. Do you happen to remember where Marianna went to college?"

Angie watched him carefully as he talked. He nodded. "Is that so? Do you recall if Marianna ever mentioned her roommate's name?"

Angie bit her lip, wishing she could hear the old woman's answers. Finally, he bid her *adieu*. The instant Jean-Paul hung up Angie was on her feet, waiting for him to speak.

"According to M'dame Eleanor, Marianna went to Tulane. And although she couldn't recall the name of her roommate, she knew the girl came from the northeast— Vermont or New Hampshire."

"Yes. We're on the right track."

Before he could reply, her stomach growled. Angie's hand went to her middle, and she tried to smile her way out of the awkward moment.

Jean-Paul leaned back against the cushion of the sofa and studied her. "When did you last eat?"

"At home this morning."

"And what time was that?"

"Five."

He shook his head and muttered something in French. He stood and caught her hand. "Come." He didn't release her but pulled her along behind him into the kitchen.

"What are you doing?"

He stopped and grasped both her arms. "You are always so full of questions. Are you sure you aren't a lawyer?" The twinkle in his eyes eased the tension in her.

"The reason I'm always so full of questions is that you always expect me to follow you blindly, without any explanation."

He raised one hand and traced the line of her jaw. "That's trust, Angel, and so far you don't trust me." The mirth had left his expression.

With the memory of her fiancé's betrayal and her parents' and Marianna's lies fresh in her mind, she said, "At this moment, Jean-Paul, I find it hard to trust anyone."

His thumb moved over her chin to trace the line of her bottom lip. "Too much has happened, hasn't it, Angel? Don't fret. I have just the thing for you."

The picture that filled Angie's head made her gasp.

Jean-Paul chuckled, a knowing, masculine laugh. "*Non, chère,* that is not what I had in mind." He leaned down and whispered in her ear, "Gumbo."

She jerked back. "Gumbo?"

"*Mais sho'.* Crawfish gumbo. It will satisfy your hunger. But if you have other hungers in mind—"

"Gumbo...gumbo sounds fine to me."

As he turned away, she thought she heard him say, "What a shame."

Chapter 6

Angie swallowed the last spoonful of gumbo, enjoying the richness of the flavors. At first the mixture had burned her tongue. But she'd been so hungry, she'd ignored the sensation and continued to eat.

Leaning back in her chair, she said, "You were right. The gumbo certainly helped my outlook. Did you make it?"

Jean-Paul, who was standing at the counter, glanced over his shoulder. "*Non*. Maria Theresa down at the diner fixed it. When she makes crawfish gumbo, she saves a big pot for me."

"I bet that Maria Theresa isn't the only female in this town who looks out for you."

Angie was expecting some sort of laughing response. Instead, Jean-Paul's movements stopped. "There are no others."

Angie wanted to ask why, but the harsh tone of his voice discouraged any further questions. She gathered up her bowl and spoon and set them in the sink. Leaning back against the counter, Angie marveled there wasn't a legion of women banging down Jean-Paul's door. He certainly was handsome enough. And he possessed that air of untamed male that drew women like flies.

So what was the reason the women of this town stayed away from him?

"You're staring, *chère.*" His voice held a teasing note.

She was, and there was no sense in denying it. "What are you making?" she asked, nodding to the silver bowl in front of him.

"A treat. *Café brûlot.*"

Angie eyed the brandy bottle sitting beside the stove.

"Watch." He poured the brandy into the bowl, then added sugar, cinnamon sticks, allspice seeds, cloves, pieces of lemon peel and orange peel. He ignited the mixture and let it burn until the sugar had dissolved, then added the fresh dark-roast coffee he'd made.

"If I was doing this right I would put this in *brûlot* cups, but if you don't tell anyone, I'll just use regular coffee cups."

She raised her hand. "I swear your secret is safe with me."

He stopped stirring the mixture and his gaze locked with hers. An odd tension crept into the room. It occurred to Angie that she knew next to nothing about this man. And she sensed he had his share of secrets.

Jean-Paul nodded toward the side door. "Why don't you wait for me on the back porch? It's much cooler out there."

Grateful for an excuse to escape the stuffy room, Angie hurried outside. She settled on the top step, tucking her skirt around her legs. The tall grass and trees were bending with the light wind blowing through the field.

In spite of the lingering heat and humidity, the breeze felt heavenly. She closed her eyes and threw her head back to get the full impact of the wind cooling her skin.

What was it about this place that made her experience things on a deeper level? The day had been hellish with its draining heat, and yet here she was reveling in a light breeze, savoring the feel as if it were a precious commodity. She was not a sensuous person. She ate only to sustain life; she appreciated the beauty of nature, but didn't go out of her way to celebrate it. There never had been time.

Practical is what everyone agreed she was. There was nothing frivolous about Angeline Fitzgerald.

Until now.

The sight that greeted Jean-Paul as he pushed open the screen door nearly caused him to drop the cups of *café brûlot*. Angeline's head was thrown back, and the look of complete abandon on her beautiful face nearly brought him to his knees. This woman possessed a sensuality that he'd rarely seen. But the odd thing about Angeline was, he suspected that this side of her nature was something she had suppressed. Why she would fight against such a gift, he didn't know, but he vowed to find out.

"Here we are," he said, purposely announcing his presence.

Just as he expected, her eyes flew open and she sat up straight. A blush stained her cheeks, as if she were embarrassed about being caught enjoying herself.

Jean-Paul hid his smile at her telling actions. He handed her the cup, then settled next to her. Instead of commenting on her behavior, which he knew would further embarrass her, he sipped his coffee. Only he didn't hide the deep pleasure he had experienced. Maybe if he showed his little northern wren that enjoying the pleasures of life was not a sin, she would give in to her natural inclinations.

"Ah, what a joy." He glanced at her and found her studying him. "Go ahead. Try it."

She brought the cup to her lips and took a small sip. The look of surprise on her face made him smile.

"This is wonderful." She took another taste.

"You see, *chère,* I wouldn't steer you wrong."

She smiled in response.

"I'm sorry there is no air-conditioning in the house except for the window unit in the bedroom. Several times I offered to have it put in, but *maman* refused. After she died, there wasn't any need."

They drank their coffee in a comfortable silence. The night creatures began their serenades. Crickets and cicadas filled the air with a comfortable rhythm. The breeze rustled the grasses, adding to the symphony of sounds, with an occasional *ribbit* from a frog punctuating the air.

Life throbbed around them.

He drained the last of his coffee, then set the cup beside him on the step. There was a subject of immediate urgency he needed to discuss with Angeline. Resting his elbows on his knees, he clasped his hands.

"Angel, do you remember me telling you that on Monday there's going to be a hearing on Marianna's estate?"

"Yes. I also remember you thought my timing was a little too perfect to be accidental."

He shrugged. He had his reasons not to trust, but she didn't need to know about them. "The reason I mention it is, now that we have proof that you're Marianna's daughter, you are her legal heir. Monday morning the court will decide the disposition of her estate. You'll need to be there to claim what's yours, and what I'm sure Marianna wanted you to have. And for that, you'll need a lawyer."

She rubbed her hands up and down her thighs as she considered his words. Jean-Paul's eyes were drawn to her slender legs, outlined by the flowered fabric covering them.

Such lovely legs. He wondered if her skin was as silky and white as the patch revealed by the neckline of her blouse.

The sound of her voice finally penetrated through the images crowding his brain. "Forgive me, *chère*. My mind wandered. What did you say?"

"Do you know any good lawyers who would take a case on such short notice?"

"*Mais sho'*, I know plenty of lawyers." He ran his fingers through his hair. "But you said you wanted a good one. That narrows down the field. Does he have to be honest?"

"Of course."

"But there's a difference. I know many good lawyers, tops in their speciality, but honesty has nothing to do with their skill." He leaned forward and whispered conspiratorially, "As a matter of fact, I know several who are sharing cells with their bankers."

She shook her head and laughed. "I want a good, honest lawyer."

She thought he'd been teasing her. He hadn't. He'd been set up by someone, most likely a lawyer in the pay of Roger Boudreaux, and framed for a crime he hadn't committed.

Jean-Paul made a show of racking his brain for a proper candidate. "Hmm, I have a friend in New Orleans. Let me call him and see if he might represent you."

Peering down into her face, the face of innocence, Jean-Paul felt a longing for a time when he'd been untouched by the evil of this world, of this place. Maybe he'd never been innocent. But something told him that Angeline could teach him how to see the world through eyes unclouded by corruption.

"Thank you, Jean-Paul."

The brilliant smile she gave him only confirmed what he had thought. Angeline was a force that would forever change his life.

* * *

Through the screen door, Angie could hear the deep rumble of Jean-Paul's voice. Although she couldn't make out any of the words, just the sound of his voice brought her comfort.

Who was this complex man who worked as a mechanic at the local gas station? Although Jean-Paul's speech was colored with Cajun endearments and phrases, it had an educated ring to it. If she were a gambling woman, she'd bet money he'd gone to college. So why was he working in a garage in this tiny town?

And why did she get the feeling that Jean-Paul had very few friends here? What had happened to set most of the residents against him?

She heard his footsteps crossing the kitchen, then he rejoined her.

"You're in luck. My friend Ted Peters has agreed to meet with you tomorrow and discuss the case."

"That's nice of him to drive here to talk to me."

Jean-Paul shook his head. "*Non.* You weren't listening to me. I said Ted was willing to go over the case with you. I said nothing of him driving here."

"Then how—you mean he wants me to go to New Orleans?"

"I said Ted was honest. I didn't say he was a saint. He has an appointment tomorrow morning. He said he could see you at two."

"How am I supposed to get there? As you so intimately know, my car is not well." She purposely used the term Pierre had used to describe the problem.

His black brow arched and wicked laughter danced in his green eyes. Angie reviewed what she'd just said and realized her blunder. *As you so intimately know.* She'd been so intent on making the point that he knew her car wasn't in any condition to drive and tried to be cute. Her "cute" had backfired on her—big time.

"*Mais sho', chère.* I know you're without transportation. That's why I planned to drive you to New Orleans tomorrow morning."

"That's not necessary, Jean-Paul."

Her stiff reply amused him. His little northern wren was showing her independence. "Oh, how you gonna get to New Orleans?"

"Isn't there a car in town I can rent?"

He shook his head.

"Could I borrow your truck?"

"What?" He gaped at her.

"You heard me. You could lend me your truck. I'm a very safe driver and have never had a wreck."

"Ah, Angel, you don't understand men, do you?"

Her chin went up. "How does understanding men have anything to do with your truck?"

"No man worth his salt would let a woman borrow his car. I'd let you borrow my toothbrush before I'd let you have my truck."

"That's ridiculous."

He shrugged. "That may be, but it's the truth."

She fell silent, but he could see her trying to come up with an alternative.

He took her hand. "Let me do this, *chère.* I'd worry about you the entire time you were gone. You could get lost in New Orleans, have a blowout on the road, or any other number of things could happen."

"I assure you, I can change a tire."

He wasn't going to convince her unless he revealed more than he wanted to. "Angeline, it could be dangerous."

"What do you mean?"

There was a look in her eye that told him he needed to confide his fears about Marianna's death to her. Nothing else would convince her of the need to be careful. "I don't think Marianna's death was an accident. I think she was murdered."

She went deadly pale. "Why do you say that?" she asked, her voice unsteady.

He wanted to reach out and comfort her, but she needed to be aware of the danger surrounding them. "There is something not right about the events surrounding your *maman*'s death."

"Do you have any proof?"

"If I did, I would've gone to the state police. All I have is this feeling that something isn't right. I don't want to risk you, too."

She wavered for what seemed like endless seconds, then her shoulders slumped. "All right, Jean-Paul. You can drive me."

He tenderly cupped her chin. "Thank you."

Angie had the foolish urge to throw herself into his arms and let him take care of all the problems swirling around her. The notion startled her. Never had she run from her problems or fobbed them off on someone else. Why would she start now? What was it about this man that drew her so? She pulled back out of his grasp and looked out over the field.

"It's getting dark. Maybe you should drive me to the local motel so I can get settled for the night."

His gaze flew to hers. "You're here. This is where you're staying the night."

"What would lead you to believe I'd spend the night here?"

"Because there are no motels in Mirabeau, and the only boardinghouse in town is full. Now, I couldn't leave such a lovely lady out in the middle of the road, could I?"

"What about Miss Eleanor? Couldn't I stay with her?"

He waved aside the notion. "*Non.* Sheriff Mathers is not happy with you, *ma petite,* and for you to stay with M'dame Eleanor would put both of you in jeopardy. Would you want that, *hein?*"

"You're kidding me, aren't you?" But even as she spoke, Angie knew Jean-Paul was sincere.

"*Non.* I kid not. The only difference between Dennis Mathers and the inmates at the state pen is that Dennis pins a badge to his chest and has Boudreaux money behind him. The sheriff has committed as many crimes as any three prisoners in the joint."

Angie still couldn't believe her ears.

"If you need more reassurance, call Pierre. Ask him how much money he gives the sheriff each month to protect his garage from vandals. Or call Mattie, the librarian, and ask her what happened to her husband when he tried to run against Dennis in the last election. Henry ended up with broken kneecaps."

The ugly picture he painted only confirmed the feelings she had about the sheriff.

"You can sleep in the bed. I'll take the couch."

His gallant gesture made her smile. "That's not necessary. I don't mind sleeping on the couch."

The expression of mock horror that crossed his face made her laugh. "You can't do that. If I let you sleep there, my *maman* would come back from the grave and haunt me." He shook his finger at her. "Positively not. I wish to let that sainted lady rest in peace. Therefore, allow me to be the gentleman she wished me to be."

How could she refuse? "You win. You can take the couch."

He took her hand and kissed the back of it. "Thank you, for myself and my *maman.*"

He was such a handsome, charming man. What more could a woman want? But the last time she had trusted a handsome, charming man, she had suffered a broken heart and an empty bank account.

"Why are you doing this, Jean-Paul?"

"Sleeping on the couch? Because I haven't had an invitation to join you in the bed."

His teasing comeback held an appeal that shocked her. Ruthlessly, she shook off the extraordinary image it brought to mind. "No, that's not what I'm talking about. What I want to know is, why are you helping me?"

"Do you mean what purpose does it serve? What will I get out of it?" The edge in his voice let her know she'd offended him.

"I've come to learn, the hard way, that people have specific reasons for doing the things they do. If you don't ask and understand them, then you're likely to get burned."

He studied her, a speculative gleam in his eye. "You've been burned, huh, *chère?* Some man took your trust and abused it, yes?"

She looked away, ashamed her folly could be so easily deduced.

With his fingers, he turned her face to him again. "It's not your shame, Angeline. It is another's."

"There's a saying, 'Fool me once, shame on you. Fool me twice, shame on me.'"

"And you will not be shamed again, *hein?*"

"I learned my lesson, Jean-Paul."

"*Non,* you learned distrust. Not of others, but of your own heart."

His observation found its mark.

He leaned over and lightly brushed his lips across hers. "Trust your heart, Angel. Yours is a good one."

Startled at his kiss, she leapt to her feet and wrapped her arms around her waist. "You still haven't answered my question."

He sighed. The sound carried out into the night. "I have a debt to repay to Marianna. She believed in me even when I didn't. By helping you, I can return her generosity."

He spoke with such honest conviction and sincerity that there was no room for doubt.

He looked over his shoulder at her. "Does that satisfy your Yankee practicality?"

The fact that he had failed to mention why he didn't believe in himself could have been a sticking point, but she felt he was entitled to his privacy. "Honesty is honesty, whether in Vermont or Louisiana. But, yes, it satisfies me."

Laughter rumbled through his chest. "Ah, Angel, you are such an innocent. But I'll let you keep your fantasies." He stood. "Come. It's time we went to bed, if we're to drive to New Orleans in the morning."

She watched him walk into the house. The man unnerved her. He saw too much of her soul that she didn't want to reveal. If there was a place she could have stayed instead of here in his house, she would have snatched up the offer. But unless she wanted to sleep in his truck or out in the field somewhere, she had no choice.

As she followed him into the house, she wondered just how uncomfortable his truck would be.

Chapter 7

As Angie searched through her cosmetic bag, she discovered that she'd forgotten to pack toothpaste. She could search the drawers in the bathroom, but the idea of snooping through Jean-Paul's personal things seemed too intimate to her.

Tying the belt of her robe securely around her waist, she opened the door.

"Jean-Paul?"

"*Oui.*" He walked into the hall, his head cocked. He was shirtless and barefoot. At the sight her mouth went dry. A light sprinkling of hair covered his well-sculpted chest, disappearing into the waistband of his jeans. She should have looked for the tube of toothpaste herself.

"I forgot my toothpaste. I was wondering . . ."

His mouth quirked into a naughty grin. "What were you wondering?"

"If I could use some of yours?"

"*Mais sho', chère.* What I have, I'll gladly share with you."

It irritated her no end when he turned on his Cajun charm.

"The toothpaste will be enough."

The look of mock disappointment in his green eyes robbed her of her irritation. "It's in the medicine cabinet above the sink."

"Thanks." She closed the bathroom door and hurried through her nightly ritual.

With a final fortifying breath, she steeled herself for the short trip back to the bedroom. The moment she stepped out of the sheltering confines of the bathroom she spotted Jean-Paul by the front door, looking out into the night. He didn't turn to face her, but she knew he was aware of her.

"Good night," she called.

Glancing over his shoulder, he said, "Good night, *chère.*" The word was a whispered endearment that caused her heart to skip a beat. "I hope you sleep well."

Not likely, since she was sleeping in his bed. She nodded and rushed into the bedroom. The cool air from the window-unit air conditioner raised goose bumps on her arms. Or was it the image of Jean-Paul's wonderful chest that caused chills to race over her skin?

Annoyed with her thoughts, she snatched Sarah's letters to Marianna off the dresser and climbed into bed. For several moments she stared at the outside of one envelope, at her mother's handwriting. With shaking fingers, she pulled out the sheets of lavender stationery. The letter was about her first day of kindergarten.

Slowly, she worked her way through all the correspondence. Angie's throat clogged with emotion as the words from her mother to Marianna took on a whole new meaning. After returning the last letter to its envelope, she turned off the light and scooted down between the sheets.

Her head hurt. For that matter, so did her heart. So many new, disturbing feelings were hammering at her. When she'd walked into Mirabeau this afternoon, she'd been Angeline Fitzgerald, daughter of Sarah and Thomas. Now, she knew she'd been born Angeline Courville, daughter of Marianna and an unnamed man.

She'd been lied to by those she had loved. Why, oh, why couldn't they have told her the truth?

And now there was the ugly fear that Marianna had been murdered.

As the tears came, she turned her face into the pillow. Murder. Her aunt—no, *mother*—might have been murdered. What could have been worth Marianna's life? And how unfair life was, that she could never call Marianna mother.

As much as she wanted to, though, she couldn't give in to the despair filling her. For Marianna's sake, she had to be sure the truth was uncovered.

She took a deep breath and was immediately distracted by the manly scent of sandalwood clinging to the pillowcase.

Jean-Paul.

In addition to all the other traumas she'd endured today, her body had picked the oddest time to turn traitor and run amok. The man did odd things to her heart and blood pressure.

Hadn't she learned from her experience with Richard how fickle the heart could be? When the handsome actor had shown interest in her, shy, boring Angie, she'd gone against her better judgment and followed her heart.

What a disaster that had been. She'd trusted him, and he'd swindled her out of her life savings. She'd learned then not to listen to her heart. But here it was again, demanding to be heard.

She hugged the pillow to her breasts and tried to stop the thoughts tumbling in her brain. If she was going to face the lawyer tomorrow, she needed her wits about her.

Her last conscious thought was that she was very comfortable in Jean-Paul's bed. Very comfortable.

"We've had a full day, haven't we, Angeline?" Jean-Paul stole a glance at her. Her head rested on the seat back, and she looked dead tired.

"I hope we accomplished a lot," she murmured.

"How can you doubt it? We met with Ted—planned our strategy for the courtroom tomorrow. What more could we have done, *hein?*"

"You are very knowledgeable about the law. Maybe you should have been a lawyer instead of working as a mechanic at Pierre's."

She said it in such a light tone that Jean-Paul knew she didn't mean any insult. Still, it was a reminder of what had been. "You wound me, *chère.* You don't think I can fix your car?"

"I don't know. You haven't gone near it since yesterday."

"Sheathe your claws, little cat. If you'll recall, I haven't had an opportunity to look at it. Something else has kept me occupied."

His teasing response reminded both of them of the circumstances that had forced them to New Orleans. The light went out of Angeline's eyes and she seemed to withdraw into herself once more.

Damn, he didn't want to work through her prickly feelings again. This morning she'd acted colder than the dry ice Pierre used in his cooler. He'd been put off by her attitude, until he realized that she'd been trying to put some emotional distance between them. Of course, once they had stepped into Ted's office, she let down her guard and they'd drawn closer to each other.

If he wasn't careful, things could get out of hand. He'd already gotten too involved with her. Unwelcome feelings and urges were cropping up. He found himself wanting to pull her into his arms and give in to the desire running rampant through his veins.

Illogically, though, her actions irked him. He was a good-looking man and a good lover, he'd been told. So what was it about him that she found so distasteful?

But he knew what it was. All the classic signs were there. She'd been hurt. Some bastard had taken her love and stomped on it. And of course, finding out that her parents and Marianna had lied to her had been rough on her.

The previous night had been torture for him. He'd heard her sobbing into her pillow and wanted to go in and comfort her. But common sense had kicked in, warning him to stay put on the sofa.

"Do you think the court will rule in my favor tomorrow?"

Jean-Paul welcomed the diversion of her question. "I can't see how they could rule against you. Yours is the legitimate claim. Roger's isn't."

She turned toward him, curling her legs under her. "How do you know that the court would've awarded the estate to Roger?"

"Easy. Without a petitioner, the court would have awarded all her property to the state. Then the estate would have been sold at auction. Roger would've offered the winning bid. Probably the only bid."

"Will there be problems?"

"You, Angel, are going to cause a bigger stir than the last hurricane that blew through town. So you best be prepared for the commotion your appearance in court will create."

She rested her cheek on her arm. "I feel like I'm a freak in a carnival sideshow."

His hand grasped hers. Her fingers were like ice. He placed her palm on his thigh, then began to rub some circulation back into her hand. It was a major mistake. All he could think of was how he'd like that delicate hand moving over his heated flesh.

Stop thinking of your zipper and reassure her, imbécile. "You know how small towns are. You'll cause talk for a while, then things will die down and people will get on with their lives." He released her hand.

"Who was that other man you called today?" she asked, tucking her hands into her pockets.

"Edward Dias. He's on a commission to investigate corruption in state government. Marianna had an appointment to see him the day she died. According to Edward, Marianna never showed up at his office. I was calling to see if any other information had surfaced."

"Had any thing more come to light?"

"Not according to him."

She cocked her head and studied him. "Jean-Paul?"

"What?"

"Did you discover something about Marianna's death you're not telling me?"

Oh, yeah, there were a lot of ugly questions that had been raised today, and he worried that if he told her everything he suspected, it would further devastate her. And yet, she needed to know about her *maman*'s death.

"About a week before Marianna's death, she asked me to set up a meeting with one of the members of the task force.

She said she'd come across some information that could prove to be vital to them. So I set her up with Edward."

He and Edward had been appointed to the commission at the same time and instantly had formed a friendship. They had both climbed the ladder of success quickly until that fateful August when Jean-Paul had been indicted. And while Jean-Paul's star fell, Edward's had zoomed to the heavens.

"And?" Angeline prodded.

He snapped out of his morose memories. "Well, a curious thing had happened today. I used to frequent the restaurant we had lunch at today. While you were away from the table, Norman, our waiter and an old friend, asked about Marianna. When I told him of her death, Norman shook his head, saying it was hard to think of such a vital woman gone. He told me that she had eaten there only months before."

"Is that significant?"

"*Oui.* The only time Marianna left town the last month of her life was the day she died. Marianna made it to New Orleans that day." He glanced at her and saw she didn't understand the implications. "When I talked to Edward after Marianna's death, he swore she had not made the meeting. So what happened? Did she make the meeting with Edward, and he lied about it? And why would he lie? Or was she waylaid before the meeting, and killed in New Orleans?"

"But you don't buy that?"

"If she was killed in New Orleans, then why drive her car back to Mirabeau and toss her body into the bayou there? It doesn't make sense."

"No," she quietly responded. "Nothing makes sense." Pain laced her voice.

He gave her hand a reassuring squeeze. "Do you have something appropriate to wear in court tomorrow?" he asked, trying to divert her attention.

"You didn't—"

"It's important for you to look good. The judge will look more kindly upon you if you are dressed correctly."

He felt her gaze upon him, but kept his eyes on the road.

She sighed and righted herself on the seat. "Has anyone ever told you you're as subtle as a frying pan applied to the side of the head?"

He chuckled in spite of himself. There was nothing dumb about this woman. "Some say it's my greatest strength."

She gave an inelegant snort. "They may be right."

He couldn't keep back the laughter. She joined him for a brief moment. When their chuckles died down, he asked, "Seriously, Angel, do you have something to wear?"

"Shouldn't you have asked that while we were still in New Orleans, where I could've gotten something?"

"Add another demerit to my name."

"Two. But in answer to your question, yes, I did throw in a nice dress, just in case. Only this scenario never occurred to me."

"Nor to me, Angel. Believe me, never in my wildest dreams did I imagine anything like this."

They arrived back in Mirabeau immediately after sunset. The frogs and crickets had begun their nightly melodies, with an occasional tugboat whistle or barking dog punctuating their performance. When Jean-Paul drove the truck up to his house and cut the engine, Angie had the oddest feeling of coming home.

She climbed out of the truck and looked around. The night seemed unusually black. Then it struck her. There were no streetlights around, nothing to relieve the darkness.

"Wait by the truck while I turn on a light," Jean-Paul instructed her. "I wouldn't want you stumbling on the steps. Heaven knows the talk that would ensue, if you showed up tomorrow in court with a bruise or scrape."

His concern warmed her. It certainly was going to be enough of a circus without adding anything extra to it.

The instant the yellow porch light came on, Angie squinted. Jean-Paul held open the door for her. Seeing him there, a welcoming smile on his darkly handsome face, made her heart pound. She had to fight against the seductive allure of the setting. If she let her imagination go, she could envision him opening his arms and welcoming her home.

Home.

The vision in her head was that of a man embracing the woman of his heart. His wife.

Angie struggled to break free of the dreamscape.

As she passed Jean-Paul, he caught her elbow. "Are you all right? You look a little pale."

"I'm tired." It wasn't a lie, she told herself. She *was* tired. That could be the only logical explanation for her fantasy.

"That's understandable, since you didn't sleep well last night."

Her startled gaze flew to his face. His smile was soft and understanding.

"The bed creaks."

Angie felt her cheeks flush. "I didn't mean to keep you awake."

He shrugged. "Think nothing of it."

She rested her hand on his arm. "Thank you, Jean-Paul."

He covered her hand with his, squeezing lightly. "I wish there was more I could do for you, Angel."

The heat of his skin on hers acted like a drug, making her feel light-headed and giddy. "There is something else you could do for me."

Surprise lit his features and the muscles in his hand contracted on her hand. "Anything. Ask me anything."

"Would you make me another cup of that wonderful coffee?"

The disappointment on his face made her laugh. It took a moment, but a glint of satisfaction crept into his eyes and his mouth curved into a grin.

"So, I have hooked you, *hein?*" His hand slid around her wrist to grasp her fingers.

It would be easier to think if he'd release her, but she didn't want to lose that wonderful contact. "Well, it was a marvelous cup of coffee."

He brought her hand to his lips and kissed her fingers interlaced with his. "Yes. I'll make a Cajun of you yet." He tugged her into the kitchen.

"Is there anything I can do to help?" she asked.

He pulled out a chair and motioned for her to sit. "*Café Brûlot* is not for novices, *chère.* You rest."

He turned on the radio that sat on top of the refrigerator and hummed along with the song. She didn't understand the words since they were in Cajun French, but from the tone of the song, it had to be about a lost love.

He quickly put together the drink and brought it to the table. "Would you like to sit outside on the steps?" he asked, handing her a cup.

Although it was still hot outside, the idea of sitting in the dark, listening to the night sounds, drinking his special coffee, held such strong appeal that she couldn't refuse. "Yes."

Once they were settled, Angie cupped the mug and sipped the rich liquid. "Oh, this is heavenly."

"I can't think of a more appropriate drink."

She gave him a puzzled frown.

"A heavenly drink for an angel."

"Oh." She shook her head. "I don't know what's the matter with me to miss your meaning."

"It's been a rough two days for you. Not too many people would've handled things as well as you have."

She rubbed the side of the cup with her thumb, thinking of her sleeplessness of the night before and the whirlwind of emotions she'd experienced. "I haven't done a good job."

Cocking his head, he asked, "How did you come to that conclusion?"

"Oh, I don't know. I'm a jumble of emotions. One minute I'm mad at everyone for lying to me, then the next minute, hurt. I feel betrayed and ungrateful all at once." She shook her head.

Jean-Paul wrapped his arm around her shoulders and drew her to his side. "It's understandable that you're confused. But you must remember that they all loved you. I think the reason they lied was to protect you and give you the best life possible. Thirty years ago, having a child out of wedlock held a very bad stigma. And here, in this part of Louisiana that is so much Catholic, such a thing is shameful. Realistically, Marianna couldn't have kept you and raised you here." He set down his cup and tipped her chin up, looking into her eyes. "Bastard is not a pretty word, *mon ange*. And you would have been called that. Marianna did what she thought would give you the best life." He brushed the back of his fingers across her cheek. "Apparently, she was right, *non?*"

"Yes, I had a wonderful childhood. My parents gave me everything. And every summer Marianna would be there, laughing, playing games with me, listening to my thoughts. It just hurts to think I never heard the truth from any of them."

"Perhaps they intended to tell you one day, but they died before they had the chance."

"Maybe."

He looked out into the darkness. "Has the truth helped you? Sometimes the truth isn't the blinding light it's cracked up to be."

"I still believe you're always better off telling the truth."

In the light from the kitchen windows, she could see the sad smile on his lips. "The joy of innocence." Shaking his head, he said, "I'll not be the one to smash that rare jewel."

She looked away from that penetrating and knowing gaze.

The music from the radio drifted out into the night, wrapping around them, creating another world populated only by the two of them. Jean-Paul took the coffee cup from her hand and set it on the porch beside his. He stood and pulled her up with him. "Come, dance with me."

She wanted to claim she didn't know how, but her perfect upbringing had included dance lessons. His strong arm slipped around her waist, and he grasped her right hand in his left and settled it on his chest. Then he pulled her close, so close that a moth couldn't fly between them. His body began to sway with the music, carrying her along with his movements.

This wasn't exactly how Miss Amanda Keyes had taught her students to waltz. "Aren't we a bit close?"

"You must be able to feel the beat of the music and the beat of your partner's heart."

She felt more than the beat of his heart. Pulling back, Angie peered up at him and immediately knew she'd made a mistake. The movement brought her lower body in closer contact with his. He stopped moving and for several moments they stood frozen. With a sad shake of his head, he stepped away from her.

She was grateful that he hadn't pressed his advantage, because if he had, well, there was no telling what her reaction would have been.

"I need to check my truck. Why don't you go on to bed?"

As he walked down the steps, she said, "Thank you, Jean-Paul."

He looked up. "I'm a fool, *chère.*" He disappeared into the darkness.

He didn't need to check his truck. It was just a convenient excuse to put distance between him and Angeline. If he'd stayed a second longer on that porch with her, he would have crushed that sweet body to his and kissed her the way a beautiful woman should be kissed. But that would have been taking advantage of a vulnerable woman.

Not that he hadn't been tempted. He wasn't a saint, just a man who was drawn to a woman. When she'd been in his arms, he'd seriously considered taking her into his room, laying her down on the bed and loving her. It would have kept away the demons that hounded them both.

It had felt right, having her body move with his. It was a glimpse of heaven. And now his body was in hell, twisted into knots of wanting.

He walked around the house and climbed up the front stairs. After turning off the porch light, he stood looking out into the night. The music from the radio floated on the soft breeze.

Everything appeared peaceful. It was a lie. This was just the unnatural calm before a storm.

Chapter 8

Jean-Paul gave up any pretense of sleep, threw back the sheet, slipped on his cutoffs and padded into the kitchen. He opened the refrigerator and pulled out a pitcher of tea.

"May I have a glass, too?"

He nearly dropped the plastic container at the sound of Angeline's voice. He glanced over his shoulder and found her standing at the kitchen door dressed in her lacy white robe. Her hair hung loose, reaching almost to her breasts. Jean-Paul groaned. He didn't need anything to highlight that part of her anatomy. He'd already spent too much time thinking about her body. That was one of the reasons he couldn't sleep.

"Sure."

He retrieved two glasses from the cabinet and filled them with ice and tea. He handed her the drink and leaned back against the counter. "Are you nervous about tomorrow?"

She sipped her tea. "That's the reason I'm awake at three o'clock. I'm worried about the town's reaction. I mean, I've caused quite a stir. Can you imagine the furor tomorrow's revelation will cause?''

Oh, yeah, he could. The truths that would be divulged in that courtroom would tear this town apart with the strength of a nuclear blast. ''There'll be some reaction.''

She laughed. ''An understatement if I've ever heard one.''

The sound was sweeter than the song that the birds brought in the morning. ''You should laugh more, *chère*. It brings such a beautiful sound to this harsh world, where there's too little beauty and too much ugliness.''

There was a need in him to draw her to him, to forge a bond that would survive the coming courtroom battle. He took the glass from her fingers and set it behind her. His thumb traced the bone of her cheek. ''And your kisses bring more joy than viewing the bayou at sunset.''

The large vein in her neck throbbed with her reaction. His finger lightly rested on the pulsing vessel. ''Do you find as much delight in my kisses as I do in yours?''

Her pink tongue darted out, moistening her bottom lip.

''Ah, *ma petite,* what you do to me.'' His lips settled on hers as softly as a butterfly on a leaf. He waited for some sign from her that she wanted him as much as he wanted her. She moaned and opened her mouth. He rejoiced at her invitation by slipping his tongue into the moist heat.

Shyly, she returned the caress. The jolt of electricity nearly knocked him into the next parish. The need to touch her overwhelmed him. He slid one hand through her hair, cupping the back of her head, then wrapped his other arm around her waist, molding her form to his. She fit him perfectly.

His lips trailed across her jaw to the sensitive spot behind her ear. His teeth nipped the velvety soft skin that was rose-petal soft and as fragrant. Her arms slipped around his waist. The heat of her small hands on his back was like hot embers, urging him on.

While he kissed his way down her neck, his fingers undid the belt of her robe. Slowly, he pushed aside the white satin to reveal her beautiful breasts showing through the lace bodice of her nightgown. "You are beautiful," he breathed, leaning down and kissing the generous swell of her breast. A shiver ran through her body.

"Did you like that, little cat?" Before she could respond, he moved his head slightly to the right, his lips capturing her nipple. Her fingers dug into his back.

He found it intolerable that there was anything between his mouth and her skin. His fingers curled under the thin straps of the gown and pulled them down her arms. But before he could reveal the treasure he sought, her hands covered his, stopping him.

"What is it, *chère?*"

She refused to look at him as she fumbled with her nightgown, pulling it back in place, and retied her robe. Finally, she met his gaze, and he read regret in her eyes. "I can't... It's too... Maybe I'd better try to get some sleep," she said, taking a step backward.

"That's a good idea." Not what he wanted, but a damn smart idea.

She paused at the door. "Jean-Paul?"

"Yes."

"I wish—I'm sorry..." She shook her head. "Good night."

He listened to her footsteps going down the hall and the bedroom door closing. Quickly the night sounds returned to normal. Too bad his heart couldn't return to normal, also.

The next morning, Angie emerged from the bedroom dressed in a flowing print dress. She'd pinned up her hair

into a soft bun. Gold stud earrings and a watch were her
only jewelry. She placed an extra dab of makeup under her
eyes, to conceal the dark circles resulting from her sleepless
night. A night spent vacillating between nervousness about
the outcome of the court case and her body's traitorous
longing for Jean-Paul.

She smoothed down her skirt. "How do I look?" She felt
awkward with him, after the heated kisses she had shared
with him the previous night.

Jean-Paul's gaze moved over her with a lazy thorough-
ness. "Like a lady. A very, very beautiful lady."

The frank appreciation in his eyes made her heart beat in
a crazy rhythm. "Would you like something to eat before we
leave for the courthouse? I have croissants and coffee on the
table."

She nodded and followed him into the kitchen, grateful
for the delay. The coffee was hot, strong and a comfort this
morning. She lingered over her second cup, stalling for time.

Jean-Paul glanced at his watch. "We have to leave,
Angeline, or we'll be late."

"I'm scared, Jean-Paul." The words popped out before
she had time to think. Usually, she wasn't so free sharing her
feelings with others, but there was something about this man
that made her act in odd ways.

His hand covered hers. "I'll be with you, Angeline."

The sincerity in his eyes and the warmth of his hand
comforted her.

The first inkling of how things were to go came when they
tried to find a parking spot. There were no places around the
court building or in the parking lot.

Jean-Paul cursed. She glanced at him.

"This is not a good sign, Angel. Be prepared."

He found a spot on the side street and they walked. By the
time they reached the front steps, Angie felt like a wilted

flower. Ted was waiting for them inside the main entrance, in the cool of the air-conditioned hall.

"There's a crowd," Ted said after the exchanges of hellos.

"You've looked in the courtroom?" Jean-Paul asked.

"Yes." He pointed down the hall. Old-style hanging fixtures threw pools of light on the tile floor. "Look for yourselves."

Jean-Paul and Angie peeked in the direction Ted pointed. Several people stood around the open double doors.

Jean-Paul muttered something in French. It didn't take much imagination to figure out what he'd said. Angie took a deep breath, trying to fight off the fear pounding in her brain. Jean-Paul stepped closer and snagged her fingers in his.

"We're here for you, *chère*. Don't let this frighten you. Everything's okay."

She acknowledged his support with a nod.

Ted glanced at his watch. "It's almost time. We need to get in there."

As they approached the doors leading to the courtroom, the whispered conversations of the people outside stopped and everyone turned and stared.

Running the gauntlet of bodies, Angie felt their icy gazes like cold chills up her spine. As they walked down the center aisle, all talking ceased and a tense silence settled on the room. Ted sat down at the table across from the state-appointed attorney. Behind him, in the first row of seats, sat Roger Boudreaux and his son, Guy.

Their startled gazes flew to Angeline.

Jean-Paul nodded to the men. "Roger, Guy. How are you today?" He didn't wait for an answer, but pulled Angie into the first row on the opposite side.

She glanced over at the men. Guy's face took on an unnatural pallor, while Roger's expression turned steely.

Immediately, the proceedings were called to order and the judge asked the appointed attorney administrator if any heir had been found to Marianna Courville's estate.

He rose. "No, your honor. None has been found."

Ted stood. "Your honor, just this past Saturday an heir has come forward."

"And who is this heir?" the judge asked.

"Marianna Courville's daughter."

A murmur raced like fire throughout the courtroom.

The judge had to gavel the audience to silence. "Where is this daughter?"

Ted motioned Angie forward. "This is Angeline Fitzgerald. She is Marianna's daughter."

"And what proof do you have of her claim?"

Handing the documents to the bailiff, Ted said, "There are Angeline's birth certificate and a copy of her adoption by Sarah and Thomas Fitzgerald."

The judge took the documents, scanned them, then handed them back to the bailiff to give to the state attorney. "Have you verified their authenticity?"

"Yes, your honor. I have faxes from the hall of records in Boston and from the courthouse where the adoption was finalized." He handed those to the bailiff.

After studying them, the judge looked at Angie, then at Roger. "I will say that your presence comes as a great surprise to this court, Miss Fitzgerald, but all the documents are in order." He addressed the state's attorney. "Do you have any objections, Mr. Kelso?"

The lawyer looked up from the papers he'd been given. He glanced over his shoulder at Roger. Roger shrugged. "No, your honor."

"Well, since there are no objections and the proof is convincing, I can rule in no other way. I declare Angeline Fitzgerald the heir of Marianna Courville and award her the said estate."

With a final stroke of his gavel, court was dismissed.

Sound and movement exploded throughout the room, as everyone started talking at the same time. Angie sat frozen to her seat, the controversy caused by her appearance swirling around her like a hurricane. And through the din, Angie heard bits and pieces of conversation.

"Illegitimate..."

"A bastard. No wonder Marianna didn't tell anyone. Why..."

"Who was the father?"

She jerked when she felt the heat of a hand on hers. Her gaze flew to Jean-Paul. There, in his eyes, were the comfort and understanding that she so desperately needed at this moment. He leaned close and whispered, "You won, *chère*."

"Did I?" She motioned to the mass of people behind them. "Marianna's name has been damaged. Now the entire population of Mirabeau knows she had an illegitimate child. Her private shame is now public."

"*Non*. You, Angeline, are only a credit to Marianna. She would be proud of you."

Angie had withstood the pointed stares, the public display, the whispered words. But it was his confidence, his obvious pride in her, that brought tears to her eyes. "Thank you," she murmured through the thickness in her throat.

"What a touching scene." The sarcastic words ripped apart the isolated world they'd created.

Jean-Paul stiffened but didn't turn toward the speaker. Angie frowned, then looked up into the intense, cold eyes of

Roger Boudreaux. A hatred, old and powerful, rested in those depths.

Jean-Paul must have seen her reaction, because he turned to face the older man. Roger's attention refocused on him.

"Roger." Somehow Jean-Paul infused the name with such contempt, it sounded like a profanity.

"Delahaye."

The room around them fell silent.

"So, you think you've won?" Roger sneered.

Jean-Paul slowly stood. He towered over the other man. "It was not a contest."

"Hah, what a liar you are. Everything you do is aimed at trying to bring me down. Well, let me assure you, you haven't won."

Jean-Paul's hands knotted into fists. Angie stood and laid her hand on Jean-Paul's arm.

"You're calling me a liar, Boudreaux? You, who've built an empire on deceit and lies?"

"I haven't been convicted of corruption and sent to prison."

Angie jerked as if she'd touched a live electric wire. Roger immediately honed in on her surprise.

"Oh, so you didn't know that the man you've taken up with is an ex-con?" He looked at Jean-Paul. "Tut, tut. You didn't share with this young woman that you once were a hotshot lawyer, until you were convicted of official corruption? How negligent of you, Delahaye."

What this bitter old man was saying had to be a lie. Jean-Paul wouldn't have purposely withheld something that important. Not after all the time he'd spent comforting her. She turned to him, needing his assurance. "Is what he says true?"

All Jean-Paul's attention was focused on Roger in a silent battle of will. It took several seconds before Jean-Paul looked at her. There was a remoteness and resignation in his expression.

Her heart plummeted to her feet. It was true. And for the second time in less than forty-eight hours, Angie knew the bitterness of betrayal.

"I'd be careful if I was you, Ms. Fitzgerald. Jean-Paul only wants revenge. He blames me for his father's drinking. He will use anyone for his own ends. I think you are his latest victim."

With a poisonous smile directed at Jean-Paul and Angie, Roger strode out of the courtroom.

Angie slowly sank down onto the wooden seat. She'd trusted Jean-Paul, opened her heart to him. She peered up at him, hoping that he would somehow negate Roger's assertions.

"Jean-Paul, is what he says true?"

"Which part? Yes, I'm an ex-con. Yes, my father drank himself to death because Roger tricked him into signing away his oil rights."

"And were you using me to get back at him?"

The bleakness and shame that crept into his eyes ripped her heart like steel talons. The pain made her gasp.

"I see." She would not fall apart in front of all these witnesses. Later, when she was alone, she could give in to her grief. Gathering her tattered pride, she stood. "Ted, would you drive me to Mr. Delahaye's house so I can retrieve my things?"

"I—" Ted glanced at his silent friend. Jean-Paul nodded his head in consent. Ted hesitated, then said, "Sure, Angie. I'll take you."

Squaring her shoulders, Angie walked through the milling crowd. Never once did she look back.

* * *

Jean-Paul watched Angeline disappear into the press of bodies. He turned his back on the curious looks thrown in his direction. Grasping the railing that divided the spectators from the court proceedings, he took a deep breath, trying to get himself under control. If he gave in to the rage pounding in his chest, he would grab one of the chairs from the defendant's table and throw it across the room. Of course that would just confirm the general opinion about him, that a Delahaye had no breeding and didn't know how to act in proper society.

He didn't care what the folks in the town thought. What had hurt and caught him off guard was Roger's assertion that he had used Angeline as a tool of revenge. When faced with that ugly truth, Jean-Paul couldn't deny it. Oh, consciously, he hadn't used her. But when he looked deep inside himself, he had to confess revenge was a motivating force in his offer to help Angeline. It wasn't the only reason—but still it was there.

When Angeline had turned to him for a guarantee that his motives had been purer than that, and he couldn't give it to her, it had proved to be the most painful moment of his life. Even through his arrest, conviction and imprisonment, Jean-Paul had known he was innocent of the charges. This time, he wasn't so innocent.

He ran his hands through his hair. What was he going to do now? Could he leave Angeline to fend for herself, against Roger and his minions?

He didn't have to debate the answer. He knew he couldn't turn his back on her. So what if his reasons had been selfish? Wasn't Angeline's safety more important than his impure purpose for helping? If he hurried and got back to his house before she left, maybe he could explain to her the danger she was still in.

Jean-Paul whirled and plowed through the lingering group of onlookers.

Jean-Paul breathed a sigh of relief when he saw Ted's new car was still parked in his driveway. Ted greeted him at the door. His old friend looked uncomfortable. If the situation wasn't so serious, Jean-Paul might be tempted to laugh. Never had he seen such an expression on Ted's face.

"Where is she?" Jean-Paul asked.

"In the bedroom, packing."

"Of course, what did I expect?"

Jean-Paul strode into the room. Angeline paused, glanced at him, then resumed folding the skirt she'd had on the day before. Her nightgown and robe were lying on the bed next to the suitcase. That bed had been his grandparents', then his parents', now his. His grandfather had carved the headboard with long, twisting vines of grape leaves. Seeing Angeline's things there pierced him with a longing.

She grabbed the nightgown and robe and threw them into the suitcase, slammed the lid shut, then yanked it off the bed. She started toward the door, but Jean-Paul didn't budge.

"Move," she commanded through gritted teeth.

"Non."

Their gazes clashed.

"Ask me, *Angeline.*"

"What am I supposed to ask you? Why did you lie to me? Why did you betray the trust I gave you?"

He grasped her upper arms. The suitcase slipped out of her hand, falling to the floor with a thud. "You never gave me your trust, Angel."

She jerked out of his hold. "Then what would you call my spilling out my heart to you? I opened myself to you like I've

never done with another human being. And how did you
repay me? You lied."

"I never lied to you."

A harsh laugh escaped her lips. "That's the answer a
lawyer would give, Jean-Paul."

"That's what I am. Or was."

She went on, as if he hadn't spoken. "You didn't lie out-
right. No, you simply chose not to tell me everything."

"I didn't tell you because I knew you'd react the way you
are now. And you needed my help, Angel. Whether you
want to admit it or not, you needed me. I got you a lawyer,
helped uncover the mystery of who you are. And I pro-
tected you. Do you think you would've fared better without me, against the sheriff and Roger, *hein?* Answer me
that."

A sob caught in her throat, and she turned her back to
him. Seeing her hunched into herself, Jean-Paul reached out
to touch her. She pulled away from him, moving toward the
window.

"You see how easily Roger has divided us?"

"It was you, Jean-Paul. All you talked about was trust.
Over and over again. You cajoled, teased, seduced. And
fool that I was, I began to believe you were right."

He had wounded her, whether intentionally or not. She
was hurting and needed some sort of explanation. But he
was also angry that his actions over the past few days
weighed so little with her that she needed the verbal reassurance. "So you want me to share my sordid past?"

She shook her head. "No, I don't." Moisture glistened in
her eyes. She tried to go around him. Again, he blocked her
path.

"Well, that's too bad, because I'm going to tell you. I was
a fast-rising star in the Louisiana government. I was appointed to a commission to investigate corruption of state

officials. I went after Roger. I'd built a good case and was close to an indictment.''

He rubbed the back of his neck, feeling again the bitter taste of betrayal. ''One day, state troopers came into my office with a search warrant. In my desk they found a stash of cocaine. I was accused of taking it as a bribe from a major underworld figure. I was arrested, convicted and sent to prison.'' He looked directly into her eyes. ''Everyone in this town believed I was guilty. They believed a Delahaye could never amount to anything, and the conviction proved it. Marianna was the only person who didn't give up on me. She never wavered in her belief. And I held on to that trust the entire time I was shut behind those prison walls. Sometimes, that was the only thing that kept me sane.''

She glanced down at her hands.

Disappointment shot through him. He'd hoped she would understand. Apparently she didn't. ''I was set up, Angel. Somehow Roger discovered what I was about to do and stopped it. The evidence I had on him disappeared. No charges were ever brought. And I was disbarred.'' He shook his head. ''Of course, some people might say having one less lawyer in the world is a good thing.''

He tried to bury his pain in his anger. ''I was stabbed in the back by someone who knew about the investigation and was close to me. Do you know how that feels?''

''Yes.'' The word slipped from her trembling lips.

''Aw, hell.'' Of all the stupid questions to ask her!

She darted around him, picked up her suitcase and ran from the room.

He listened to Ted and Angeline get in Ted's car and drive off. When the noise of the car engine faded, Jean-Paul glanced around the room. There on the dresser, he discovered a tube of lipstick.

He picked up the gold-tone container and examined it. The shade was called primrose. Wrapping his fingers around the metal, he closed his eyes and saw the mouth that this lipstick covered.

He should walk away now and leave her to her righteous anger. A bark of laughter erupted from his chest. Who was he fooling? He wouldn't leave her to Roger's machinations now, any more than he could have from the moment she stumbled into Pierre's garage.

"Who's the fool now, Jean-Paul?" he whispered to the empty room.

He was afraid he knew.

Chapter 9

Ted stopped his car at the end of Jean-Paul's drive. After a moment he asked, "Which way?"

To Angie's dismay, she couldn't give him directions to Marianna's house. "I want to go to my mother's house, but we'll have to drive into town and find someone to tell us the way." Her face flamed. "I'm sorry. I was there only once, and Jean-Paul drove me that time. While we are in town," she added, "I can make arrangements to turn on the utilities."

Ted's understanding smile eased her embarrassment. He turned onto the paved road.

"I couldn't help overhearing your argument with Jean-Paul."

The blushing in her cheeks intensified. "I guess we were rather loud."

"This isn't any of my business, but I'll say that I think Jean-Paul was framed. I've known him since we were in law school together. He was a crusader. The white knight trying to slay evil dragons. No matter what anyone says, Jean-Paul is a good, honest man and a damn fine lawyer.''

She glanced at him. ''He wasn't honest with me.''

''He had his reasons. Compelling reasons, I'd say.''

''Maybe.''

''I'd trust Jean-Paul with my life.''

''Yes, but would you trust him with your sister's life?''

''In a minute. I just wish my sister had picked as fine a man as Jean-Paul. Unfortunately she didn't. She picked scum.''

''What happened here?'' Ted asked, setting Angie's bags inside the front door of Marianna's house.

The interior didn't look any better today than it had Saturday afternoon. Of course, who did she expect would clean up the mess—the sheriff? ''Someone broke in and searched the place.''

''Why?''

She wished she knew. ''Who can say? Everyone in town knew the house was vacant. Maybe vandals, or kids looking for something valuable to pawn.''

From his frown, Angie knew what was coming. ''Maybe you should stay somewhere else,'' he said.

Angie picked up the cushions from the floor and put them back on the couch. ''There isn't anyplace in Mirabeau. That's why I was staying at Jean-Paul's.''

''It wouldn't be a bad idea if you went back.''

The man didn't know what he was asking. She turned to him. ''I can't.'' Extending her hand, she said, ''Thank you for all your help.''

''I really didn't do that much. It was Jean-Paul who did most of the work.''

She moved to the front door and opened it wide. Ted took the hint.

"Good luck, Angeline. I'll be in touch. And remember what I said about Jean-Paul."

As she watched him drive away, Angie wished she could forget Ted's words. *Jean-Paul is a good, honest man.*

She fought back the tide of tears. She would not think about what had happened today in court, because if she did, she'd shatter into a million pieces. Maybe later she could deal with Jean-Paul's betrayal.

Turning, she surveyed the mess before her and decided that if she cleaned up Marianna's house, then maybe she'd be too tired to think.

She worked her way through the living room, righting lamps and chairs. Unfortunately, she became a victim of her own success. Her mind was so focused on what she was doing that when she picked up several unpaid bills scattered on the floor, the significance of her work finally hit her.

These were her mother's things that she was touching and holding. And all that was left of the warm, vibrant woman.

Angie glanced down at the envelope. It was a statement from a national department store. With trembling fingers, she pulled out the bill.

Shoes. It was for a pair of leather pumps.

Moisture gathered in her eyes, making it hard to read the print. "Oh, Marianna, why?" she whispered. "Why didn't you tell me? I would've understood and loved you."

A tear splashed onto the paper.

The roar of a car engine and the screeching of brakes broke into her sorrow. She put down the bill and walked to the window expecting to see Jean-Paul's old truck. Instead, a new beige Cadillac was parked in the driveway. She hurried to the front door and opened it the same instant a man emerged from the car. She recognized him as the man who'd been sitting by Roger Boudreaux at the court proceedings.

Walking to the edge of the porch, she asked, "May I help you?"

The man's head jerked up and he froze.

The glazed look in his eyes alarmed Angie. She moved down the steps. "Are you all right?"

He slammed the car door, but the momentum caused him to stumble. She rushed forward to prevent him from falling. The overpowering smell of whiskey nearly knocked her off her feet. Once they were both steady on their feet, he grasped her shoulders.

"I didn't know." His words were slurred and hard to understand. "I swear, I didn't know." Tears filled his eyes.

"Didn't know what?" Angie asked.

Before he could reply, another car, a limousine, came barreling down the road.

"The old witch," he grumbled.

The limo stopped beside them, kicking up a cloud of dust. Angie stepped back, coughing.

From the back seat stepped a well-groomed woman. Angie couldn't tell her age, but something hard in her eyes warned her that this woman had seen and experienced a lot.

"Get in the car, Guy. Monroe will drive you home."

Guy leaned toward Angie. "See, I told you she was a witch. She's got eyes in the back of her head. Sees every time I take a sip."

The older woman's expression never changed, except for a slight tightening of her thin lips.

"Monroe, help my husband into the car."

Instantly, a burly man in a chauffeur's uniform climbed out of the limo and headed straight for Guy. Clamping his beefy hand around Guy's upper arm, he escorted the drunken man into the limo.

"Get his keys," she commanded Monroe.

Monroe wrestled the keys from Guy, locked him in the back seat, then handed them to the woman.

Angie watched in amazement as the limo disappeared around the bend in the road, leaving behind the imposing woman.

"It was quite a shock to learn Marianna had a child. Sometimes old sins and secrets are best left buried."

The haughty tone in which the advice was given made Angie bristle. "I'm not the one who has any secrets."

"We all have secrets."

The comment didn't deserve a reply. Instead, Angie silently studied the woman. From the top of her head to the bottom of her small feet, every inch of the woman screamed money. Old money.

"I think it would be best for all concerned if you go back to where you came from."

Who had died and made her queen? Angie wondered. "Better for whom?"

"This town. If you stayed, you would be a constant reminder of how our dear Marianna fell. Her reputation has been greatly damaged by what happened in court today."

"The only thing that's been damaged, Catlin—" Jean-Paul's voice rang out "—is Roger's plan to get his hands on Marianna's estate."

Both women turned toward his voice. Jean-Paul emerged out of the long shadows cast by the house in the late afternoon sunlight. He strode up to them, stopping before the older woman.

A cold fury darkened Catlin's eyes. "What do you know?"

"I know that Angeline's appearance has foiled Roger's plans."

"You don't know what you're talking about." She drilled Angie with a hard look. "If you're smart, you'll take my advice. It will be very uncomfortable for you, in a town that knows the circumstances of your birth."

She climbed behind the wheel of the Cadillac. Jean-Paul lunged, grabbing the side of the door.

He leaned into the car. "It's an ugly threat, Catlin. But what could I expect out of a cold-blooded woman like you who loves only money and power? I have a threat of my own. If anything, anything happens to Angeline, if she so much as stubs her toe, I'll know at whose feet to lay the guilt. And you'll pay. Believe me, you'll pay."

He stepped back and Catlin yanked the door closed. Dust and gravel rained on them as she sped away from the house. Jean-Paul pulled Angeline toward the steps, out of harm's way.

"Are you all right, Angeline?"

Angie didn't know whether to be grateful for his timely interruption or to be offended that he had come to spy on her. She freed her arm and backed away from him.

"How did you get here?" She hadn't heard his truck, and didn't see it parked anywhere.

"I followed Guy's car weaving through town, figuring he was up to no good. I parked off the main road and walked across the field, so I wouldn't be seen. I suspected the Boudreaux might give you trouble." He leaned his hip against the porch railing. "I'm glad I was here to run off Catlin. She's got a heart of stone, that one."

His assumption that Angie couldn't take care of herself irritated her. What did he think she'd done up until the time she wandered into town? Did he think she went looking for some male to solve all her problems?

"I was handling everything quite well until you charged in."

He pushed away from the railing. "Ha. That old bat was chewing you up."

"Not all of us, Jean-Paul, approach a problem with the attitude that whoever shouts the loudest wins. I was about to tell Mrs. Boudreaux that I don't run from problems." *And that she could take her snooty tone and sit on it.* But not in such delicate wording. Of course she wasn't going to share that with Jean-Paul.

"Her kind doesn't respond to a mild rebuke. Catlin Boudreaux might appear to be the embodiment of a genteel southern woman, but a meaner female hasn't lived in this parish."

"You're exaggerating, trying to scare me."

"You're damn right I'm trying to scare you. I'm trying to frighten you into being careful."

She gazed defiantly up into his eyes. "Well, I'm not scared, and nothing you say is going to make me turn tail and leave this house." Lifting her chin, she gave him a final determined look, then turned toward the door.

Jean-Paul's hand shot out and snagged her arm. "If you have any sense, *chère,* you'll heed my words and be frightened of that den of thieves. They've killed before, for their own personal gain. And will do so again without hesitation." His grim tone made her shiver.

He was succeeding admirably at frightening her, but he had to be bluffing. "Who did they kill?"

His grip on her eased, and some emotion crept into his eyes. "Your *maman.*"

His words were like a slap across her face. The emotions that had gripped her when he first told her Marianna was an only child hit her again. "You think *they* were responsible for Marianna's death?"

"Yes."

"Do you have any proof?"

He jerkily ran his hands through his hair, then shoved them into the back pockets of his jeans. "No. I have suspicions and coincidences. Too many to ignore."

Her heart was yelling for her to believe him. Jean-Paul might have held back certain truths in his own life, but he had not ever been wrong about Marianna. And because she knew how he felt about her mother, Angie was willing to listen to him. "Tell me."

He seemed surprised. "All right." He pointed to the top step. "Why don't we sit?"

She settled beside him. His large form so close to her made her feel safe . . . at least for a few minutes.

He rested his elbows on his knees. "There are a lot of things that don't add up." He held up his index finger. "First, there was no autopsy done on Marianna's body, so we don't know if she drowned or was killed and then placed in her car and pushed into the bayou."

"Is that unusual?"

"Yes. An autopsy should've been ordered on a questionable death like that, unless someone had something to hide. Second, within a day of the doctor signing the death certificate, Marianna's body was cremated."

"Well, maybe she wanted her burial handled that way."

Jean-Paul shook his head. "I never heard her say anything about cremation. She once mentioned a family crypt in the next parish. But, what's questionable here is, why hurry everything unless someone had something to hide and didn't want the body examined?"

His reasoning made sense. "I don't know. But why do you think Roger Boudreaux is behind these coincidences?"

"Because he's the only person in this parish who has the power to override the law."

Was Jean-Paul being paranoid? she wondered.

He rubbed his eyes with the heels of his hands. "Another thing that bothers me is the sheriff claims that Marianna's car probably skidded off the road during the rainstorm we had that night. And I believe him. So that means Marianna was coming back from New Orleans. What if someone followed her and forced her off the road?"

"But she didn't meet with Edward."

"What if she did? What if Edward lied?" A dawning knowledge darkened Jean-Paul's eyes. He slammed his right fist into the palm of his left. "Damn, I feel responsible for her death. If I hadn't arranged that meeting, maybe Marianna would be alive today."

Suddenly, Angie wanted to comfort him. He had given her emotional support over the past few traumatic days. Now she wanted to give in return. She laid her hand on his forearm. "You don't know that. You never would have intentionally hurt Marianna."

"Who can say? But I can help protect you. That you must believe, Angeline. The Boudreaux family do not wish you well. For your protection, I want you to come and stay at my house tonight."

That she couldn't do. The wound of his deception was too new and fresh to allow her to be with him. "I'll be all right, Jean-Paul."

From his look, she knew he wanted more from her. An explanation.

"I don't doubt what you've said. But I need time, Jean-Paul. Time to myself, to think and sort things out." When he looked as if he would press his cause further, she added, "Please."

He relented. "You win. But if anything happens or you hear something you don't like or just get scared, you call me, you hear?"

He sounded like a disgruntled parent. "Yes."

"Bien."

"Jean-Paul."

"Yes, *chère.*"

"That man that was here. His name was Guy?"

He nodded.

"Did you hear what he said?"

"No."

"He was mumbling that he didn't know. What do you think he was talking about? And why did he come here?"

He intently studied her. "I wish I knew. I think it would've answered a lot of questions you have."

"Like who my father is?"

He ran his fingers through his hair. "Yeah."

He stood, then reached down and pulled her up. She could read in his eyes his intention of kissing her and backed up a step, putting herself out of his reach. "Good night."

"Bonsoir."

He'd taken a couple of steps, when he stopped and reached into the front pocket of his jeans. He brought something out, then held out his hand to her.

"This is yours. You left it on the dresser."

He didn't say *in my bedroom,* but that phrase rang through her head. Her lipstick looked ridiculous lying in his palm. She took it, wrapping her fingers around the tube. The metal was still warm from the heat of his body.

"Thank you." It was rather odd to have a man return something so personal.

He nodded.

She watched him walk across the yard and disappear into a growth of tall vegetation. He believed her mother had been killed. His arguments had been sound, his questions valid. And tomorrow she intended to get some answers.

* * *

Jean-Paul didn't know whether to shout for joy that she believed him or curse because the stubborn female thought she could take care of herself when pitted against the Boudreaux family and their minions.

When Angeline had run from his house this afternoon, Jean-Paul knew he couldn't just leave her to her fate. It had taken him a while to get his bearings after their bitter exchange. Once he could think clearly, he knew he'd have to go and check on her. He feared that someone would show up at Marianna's to hassle Angeline.

He hadn't been wrong.

He'd purposely held back, to hear what Catlin would say to Angeline. When the threat spilled from her mouth along with the ugly things she said about Marianna, he saw red. It had taken several seconds for him to control the rage before he could speak.

His little northern wren probably thought all her troubles were over. She hadn't seen a tenth of the fallout from today that would come her way. If he didn't miss his guess, Angel was fixing to see hell on earth.

Chapter 10

Jean-Paul pulled the rag from his hip pocket and wiped his greasy hands. He had spent the morning fixing Angeline's rental car. He'd gone by her house first thing, to make sure she was all right and nothing unusual had happened during the night, then he'd come to work. After talking to the rental people in New Orleans and getting their okay, he'd done the repairs. Now all he had to do was drive the car out to Angeline.

He strolled inside to call her.

"Hey, Jean-Paul, how you are?"

"Fine, Jock. How's everything goin' with the taxi business?"

Jock's plain face broke into a large grin. "*Mais* excellent, especially after spending this morning driving that new lady all over town. *Key awau!*" Jock shook his hands. "She paid me fifty dollars for takin' her to the doctor's, then to the funeral home."

Jean-Paul froze, stunned and panicked at what he'd just heard. It couldn't be true. The woman couldn't be so naive as to go around town asking delicate questions and not know she was putting herself in danger. "Hell."

Jock frowned. "What's wrong?"

"What did she think she was doing?" Jean-Paul murmured to himself.

"I don't know. But she seemed upset after she talked with Neil at the funeral home."

Well, why didn't she just take out an advertisement in the newspaper and tell the entire town that they suspected Marianna was murdered? Of course, having Jock drive her anywhere was as good as advertising in the newspaper.

Pierre came around the counter. "Is something wrong, Jean-Paul?"

"I'm going to drive Angeline's car out to her."

"Do you want Martin to follow in the truck to bring you back?"

Glancing at the teenager, Jean-Paul knew he didn't want Martin to witness his meeting with Angeline. Martin was as big a gossip as Jock. "No. I'll let the lady bring me back."

Jean-Paul didn't wait for Pierre's reply, but strode into the bay and got into Angeline's car.

Visions of her lying dead in that house ran through his head as he drove through town. He gripped the steering wheel so hard, his fingers ached when he stopped in front of Marianna's house.

"Angeline," he bellowed as he got out of the car.

No one answered.

"Angeline," he called, leaping onto the porch.

Still, there was no answer.

With his heart pounding, he reached for the doorknob. It was locked. He fished Marianna's key, which he'd kept from the previous day, out of his pocket. It was a good sign, he told himself, that the house was locked. No killer would bother to lock up after committing his nefarious deed. That is, unless he wanted things to look normal.

His mouth dry, fear throbbing in his brain, Jean-Paul walked into the house.

The living room had been restored to its former tidiness. But more important, Angeline was *not* lying on the floor dead, in a pool of her own blood.

He crossed the room and glanced into the bedroom. It also had been straightened up. Then he heard it. The most wonderful sound to ever reach his ears—a running shower. After a moment the water shut off, letting Jean-Paul know she was alive.

The relief sweeping through him made him so light-headed, he sank down onto the corner of the bed before he fell flat on his face. He held out his trembling hand, watching in amazement the reaction of his body.

The bathroom door opened and his gaze flew to the woman emerging from the steamy interior. She was wrapped in a towel that barely covered her from breasts to hips. Like a bolt of lightning hitting him squarely in the chest, living heat—powerful and sweeping—flowed through every nerve ending in his body.

He jumped to his feet and took a step forward. "What the hell did you think you were doing this morning?" The angry words flew out of his mouth, surprising him.

His outburst startled her as well, and her grasp on the towel faltered and it fell to the floor.

She was even more beautiful than he had imagined—and he'd done his fair share of imagining. There wasn't a single ounce of fat on her sleek body. From the fullness of her breasts to her small waist to her gently flaring hips, Angeline was all woman.

She snatched up the towel. "Would you care to wait for me in the other room while I get dressed?" she asked with icy formality, but he felt the rage beneath the polite words.

Feeling like the backwater Cajun he'd been called at that fancy eastern boarding school, he nodded and walked into the other room, pulling the door closed behind him. Well, he certainly had acted like a grand fool, he admitted to himself. He flopped down onto the sofa. Maybe he should apply for prize fool for the Mardi Gras parade. But, damn it, didn't she understand that the fear he felt for her was still pumping heavily through his veins?

When she walked into the living room a few minutes later wearing jeans and a blouse, the light of battle was in her eyes. "How dare you barge in here like that?" Her civilized tone had evaporated. The lady was hot. "Who do you think you are?"

She had every right to her anger, Jean-Paul told himself. But in spite of that calm logic, the tumult of emotions inside him demanded a release. And the lady was offering a good fight.

"Me?" he asked, rising to his feet. "You're asking me what I'm doing? I came here after Jock told all of Mirabeau where you went this morning. I was expecting to find you dead on the floor, shot or stabbed." He ran his fingers through his hair. "What were you thinking about, to go and question those men?"

"Oh, it's *me? I'm* the one at fault?" She poked him in the chest with her index finger. "Who put those questions in my head, huh? Who filled my head with doubts? I believed you, Jean-Paul. Since I needed answers to those questions, I decided to investigate for myself. And since I didn't have a car, I called the only taxi in town."

"You didn't just call a cab. What you called was our local version of the phone company. Every house will know about your activities by dinnertime. Whoever pressed those men to turn a blind eye to the law will know that you were questioning the procedure surrounding Marianna's death."

She paled, even as she countered his argument with one of her own. "If you'll stop and think, those men will probably tell this person or persons about my visit without Jock's two cents' worth."

"Oh, I've thought of that. I've thought of nothing else since Jock told me about your little trip." He gripped her arms. "Why did you do it, Angeline? Why?" His anguish rang through the room.

"I told you, Jean-Paul. I did it because I wanted answers."

He brushed back a strand of damp hair that had fallen over her eye. "You should've called me. I would have gone with you." He crushed her to his chest. "If anything happened to you, *chère,* I would never forgive myself."

His hands moved over her back. It had never occurred to him that she would put herself in such danger. He tipped her chin up and his mouth covered hers. His tongue slipped into her mouth, wanting to taste the sweetness that was hers. He wanted to reassure himself that she was all right by touching her, tasting her, warming his chilled soul in the living warmth of her body.

His hands came up to cup her head, his thumbs rubbing gently over the strong pulse in her neck. He lifted his head and gazed down into her blue eyes, which had turned indigo with passion.

"Your kiss makes me forget where I am and what I was saying," Jean-Paul whispered.

Her lids lowered, shielding her emotions from him. She cleared her throat and took a step back.

He cursed himself. She looked so alone and vulnerable, standing there, obviously embarrassed by her response to him. She moved around the couch, putting it between them.

He walked to the window and saw her car, and remembered the reason he'd raced over here. The danger she put herself in this morning was his fault.

"I'm sorry I barged in here. But last night when I told you of my suspicions, I only meant to scare you into being cautious. Never in my wildest dreams did I think you'd take it upon yourself to go and talk to those men. The idea frightens me spitless."

Her brow arched. "So, you admit you meant to scare me."

"Of course. There's nothing wrong with caution, *chère*. But my suspicions are not made up." He held up his index finger and shook it at her. "Apparently, you didn't heed my warning."

Her fingers picked at the loose weave of the couch. "Then you don't want to know what I learned from the doctor and mortician?"

Oh, she was a cutie, this one. She was smart, too. She knew she held all the cards, and was seeing if he'd call her bet. "You know I want to know what they said."

She motioned for him to sit. When he complied, she came around the sofa and sat next to him. Leaning forward, she said, "Well, I went to the doctor's first. He seemed surprised that I would ask why an autopsy wasn't done. But when I pressed him, he said that there was no need to do one." The gleam in her eyes told him she wanted him to ask what she did next.

"And what was your reply?"

"I asked about the law. Since Marianna's death was suspicious, didn't the law require an autopsy? He turned pale and said he only followed the sheriff's order and signed the death certificate.''

Jean-Paul cursed. ''Why am I not surprised? And what did the mortician say?''

''He claimed that Marianna wanted to be cremated. When I asked why they did it so soon, he said that there was no reason to wait—since they didn't know Marianna had any living relatives. But do you know the funny thing?'' She didn't wait for his reply. ''He acted so nervous, like he had something to hide.''

''*Mais sho'*, they all have something to hide. The question is, what? And who are they covering up for?''

There was something here that he was missing. What?

Angie watched Jean-Paul turn over in his mind the things she'd just said. When she'd come out of her shower and found him sitting on her bed, her mind had gone blank. Then when he started yelling at her, her anger had surged. But as quickly as her temper flashed, it died, when she heard the fear in Jean-Paul's voice and his words of concern.

She laid her hand on his forearm. ''Who do you think they are covering up for? What do you think my mother discovered, that caused someone to murder her?''

He looked down at her hand, then up into her eyes. When she started to pull back, he laid his hand over hers. Little prickles of electricity raced up her arm.

''I've racked my brain over that. When Marianna came to me, I asked her why she wanted to see someone on the state corruption panel. She said she'd come across some evidence that was explosive.'' His thumb absently rubbed across her knuckles, making it hard for her to concentrate on what he was saying.

She tugged at her hand. He seemed surprised that he still held it captive. He smiled and released her.

Angie exhaled, trying to bring herself back under control. "Maybe it had something to do with her job? I mean, being a librarian would bring her into contact with a lot of different information. If she ran across something, it might have set off an alarm in her head."

He shrugged.

"Could we call the current librarian and ask?"

"Sure."

They walked into the kitchen, and he punched in the number for the library. After speaking for a few minutes, the tone of his voice changed. "Thanks, Mattie. And I'd appreciate it if you didn't mention our little conversation to anyone." He hung up.

"Well?" Angie asked, eager to know what he'd learned.

"Mattie says Marianna wasn't working on anything for the library, but several months before her death the historical society asked her to write a history of the parish." He leaned back against the counter. "I've got a feeling, Angel, that we may have come up with a good lead."

She propped her shoulder against the wall, taking in the sight of him. He was tall, well muscled and incredibly handsome. His thick, dark hair fell over his forehead, drawing her gaze to his green eyes, which danced with the vibrancy of life. It was almost too much to take in that he might be attracted to her. And yet if his kisses were any indication, he definitely was interested.

"Tomorrow, we'll go see M'sieu Colton at the society." The wonderful, rich sound of his voice filled the room, making Angie want to close her eyes and bask in its sensual quality.

"Why not today?"

He placed a kiss on her nose. "Because it is Tuesday. The society's center is only open Mondays, Wednesdays and

Fridays. And because M'sieu Colton will not open up the doors on any other day for anyone, not even for the pope.''

His teasing was like a gentle rain falling on a parched earth. She couldn't resist bantering back. "Not even the pope? Are you sure?"

He braced his hands on the wall on either side of her head. Startled by his nearness, she turned, pressing her shoulder blades into the solidness behind her. The heat of his body surrounded her like a cocoon.

"It's rumored that the only time M'sieu Colton left his houseboat on a Tuesday was in 1956 when he voted for Eisenhower. He didn't like Stevenson. Why, it was the talk of the parish. M'dame Eleanor nearly fainted dead away when he showed up at the polling place to cast his vote. It was the only time in the last fifty years anyone's seen him on a Tuesday."

"Really?"

He took a step forward, bringing his thighs in contact with hers. Little sparks of energy zipped over her, making her skin seem too tight for her body.

"I swear. Of course, everyone wonders what that man does out there on the bayou by himself." He leaned down and whispered in her ear, "M'dame Eleanor's convinced he turns into a bat and flies up and down the bayou, sucking the blood out of anything he can catch."

The warmth of his breath on her neck stretched Angie's nerves taut. Her gaze collided with his, and her heart skipped a beat at the passion darkening his eyes. She was tempted to reach up and stroke his cheek, maybe even give in to the desire pounding in her chest. Instead, she ducked under his arm to escape the blinding heat.

"I can't believe that sweet, old woman would say anything that mean about anyone."

Jean-Paul folded his arms over his chest and leaned against the wall. "Don't let her ladylike ways fool you. M'dame is very opinionated and not afraid to voice those opinions."

Her body still churned with the aftereffects of his nearness. Her pulse refused to slow, her heart pounded, and the tingling heat that curled deep in her belly didn't subside. She needed more distance, she reasoned, and the living room looked like the best place.

As she passed by Jean-Paul, his hand shot out, capturing her arm. He pulled her flush against his body, anchoring her in place with his hands behind her back.

"*Angeline?*"

The sweet seduction in his voice made her knees weak. He said nothing more, and she knew he wanted her to look up. But if she did that, she'd be lost.

"*Chère,* look at me."

She'd be a coward if she refused.

The choice was taken from her when he cupped her chin and forced her gaze to his. Just as she knew, the consuming hunger in his eyes threatened to swallow her. All she had to do was give him the slightest indication, and he would finish what they had started.

He lied to you, a merciless voice inside her head whispered. *Don't be a fool and give in to the wanting. You did once before with Richard, and what did it get you? A broken heart, that's what.*

Shaking, she placed her hands on his arms and tried to move them. He resisted her at first, but after he read the determination in her gaze, he allowed her to slip away from him.

"Do you think that whoever searched this house found anything?" she asked, walking back into the living room. He followed.

"Who can say?"

She turned to face him. "Did Marianna ever mention a special hiding place she had in this house?" Angie laughed at her own foolishness. "If she had, you probably would have already checked it, wouldn't you?"

"Yes. When you cleaned up, did you find anyplace that might've served as a hiding place?"

"No."

A horn sounded from outside. Jean-Paul went to the window and saw Pierre in his truck. He turned back to her. "I brought your car back. It's fixed."

She gaped at him.

He shrugged. "In the heat of the moment, I forgot to mention it."

"How much do I owe you?" she asked, picking up her purse from the end table.

"Nothing."

"What? I know you probably had to replace the radiator."

"Don't worry. I called the rental company. We'll settle with them."

He stopped at the front door. "Angeline, I'm sorry I didn't tell you about my prison record. But I wanted to help you, for Marianna's sake. I was afraid if you knew, you wouldn't accept my help."

She nodded stiffly. "I understand. Thank you for all you've done."

But, really, she didn't understand. She wanted him to help her because... What? she asked herself. *Because he is wowed by your beauty and sex appeal? Get real, Angie.*

The horn sounded again. "Jean-Paul," Pierre bellowed. "We got a wreck on the highway. Come."

Jean-Paul opened the door and waved at Pierre. "In a minute. Keep your shirt on." He turned back to Angie.

"Tomorrow morning we have a date to go to the historical society, yes?"

"Yes."

"And I will come and pick you up and drive you there, since you don't know where it is?"

"I could get directions."

He shook his head. "*Non.* I'll throw in a hot breakfast at the diner as a bribe."

Pierre blasted them again with the truck horn.

"I'll stand here until I get the right answer, Angel."

"All right. You win this time."

He waggled his eyebrows. "A war is fought a battle at a time. *Bonsoir.*"

She should have been annoyed by his insistence. Instead she was comforted. And that worried her.

Angie pushed away the half-eaten bowl of granola. She wasn't hungry. Her trip into town had robbed her of any appetite. After Jean-Paul had departed, she'd raced into town for some groceries.

As she walked through the market she wondered if she'd grown another arm, with all the stares she'd received. The experience brought home how much she'd come to depend on Jean-Paul these past few days.

She placed her bowl in the sink, then wandered to the back door. The sky was streaked with the fading reds and golds of the setting sun.

Something dark and sensual tugged at Angie, begging her to come out into the gathering night. This time she gave in to the urge. The instant she pushed open the door the moist heat surrounded her, bringing with it memories of Jean-Paul.

The thought of him invoked a dozen different images. His anger at her claims. His strength as he held her when she cried. The passion in his kisses and the warmth of his smile.

She wrapped her arms around her waist. Jean-Paul tapped into that wild part of her nature that she had striven so hard to control, and he brought things to life in her that she hadn't known existed. The Angie she knew and had striven so hard to become was changing before her eyes.

And that was what frightened her the most.

She could deal with the revelations of the past few days. They only changed the outward circumstances of her life. But Jean-Paul was changing the inner person into a stranger she didn't know and was afraid to trust.

Chapter 11

Jean-Paul pushed aside his plate, his appetite gone. He glanced outside at the gathering darkness. An unexplained tension gripped his shoulders and neck. It was nothing, he told himself. Just the aftereffects of the bad accident that he'd help sort out this afternoon. He shook off the odd mood, collected his dishes and went to the sink.

After washing up, he wandered outside. This was his favorite time of the day, when the heat eased and the salty breeze from the Gulf of Mexico caressed fevered skin. His nightly ritual of sitting on the steps and relaxing in the cooling wind was one of the things he'd missed the most while he was in prison.

A neighbor's hounds began baying at something that had caught their attention, setting off a chain of howls that ran through the parish.

Yet in spite of the familiar smells and sounds, there was a nagging apprehension in Jean-Paul. And he could pinpoint the source—Angeline.

Why was he courting trouble by helping her? And make no mistake about it, helping Angeline would result in trouble. His debt to Marianna was part of the reason. But there was more.

He wanted Angeline.

A harsh laugh escaped his lips.

There it was, bald-faced and unadorned. He wanted to make love to the woman who had no idea of her own beauty. Of course, that would be refreshing after all the lovely society ladies of New Orleans, who only considered a man's social standing and his bank balance. Those genteel ladies made a distinction between little flings and social alliances. He had fallen into the former category.

When he'd met Charlene Dilhurst, he thought he'd met a woman who was different from the rest. Their courtship had been whirlwind. Then, days before they were to announce their engagement, he'd been arrested. By the time he got out on bail, Charlene had discreetly visited his apartment and left her engagement ring on the kitchen table along with her key to his place.

Now he found himself saddled with a woman who had no idea of her own power and seemed to go to great lengths to deny her true nature. And every impulse in his body screamed for him to help her discover her true sensual self. He could be such a devoted teacher, if she would allow him.

But this was Marianna's daughter. Could he repay his friend by seducing her daughter? Even if Angeline hadn't been Marianna's child, Jean-Paul knew he couldn't use her and walk away.

Then what, Jean-Paul? Do you have something more permanent in mind for the two of you?

He stood and pushed aside the thoughts. Going inside, he turned on the television and stretched out on the couch, intent on watching the baseball game. But his thoughts pursued him.

Why did Angeline fight the fire in her soul? Who was the man who had made her doubt herself? Had she loved him? Had she gone wild in his arms, yielding to the heat she kept carefully hidden?

The TV announcer announced that after thirteen innings this game would go down as game of the year, and Jean-Paul realized he couldn't recall one play. He turned off the set and went to bed, amazed that his little northern wren had outranked his most indulged passion—baseball.

Jean-Paul woke with a jolt. He was wet with sweat and breathing hard. Something was wrong. Bad wrong, as his *maman* would have said. Glancing at the clock on the nightstand, he saw the time was close to one.

He took a deep breath and tried to concentrate on what it was that was giving him this feeling of urgency.

Angeline.

He threw off the sheet and grabbed his jeans, not bothering with his briefs. There wasn't time. He slipped on running shoes without socks, snatched his key ring from the dresser and raced out to his truck.

He shoved the key in the ignition and turned it. Nothing happened.

He cursed, found his flashlight and jumped out. The ignition wire on this old heap had probably come loose again. He opened the hood and turned on the flashlight. It took him several minutes and two scraped knuckles, but he attached the wire.

Fingers crossed, he tried to start the engine again. It cranked on the first try.

Jean-Paul floored the accelerator and careened down his drive. It seemed as if it took hours to cover the short distance between his house and Marianna's, but it couldn't have been more than five minutes.

In the headlights of his truck Jean-Paul caught sight of a man racing away from Marianna's house. His heart tightened with fear. He slammed the truck into park and jumped out, leaving the motor running.

The smell of smoke hit him. He jumped onto the porch. "Angeline," he bellowed.

Reaching for the front door, he found it ajar. He fought the panic, knowing he needed to think clearly if he was going to find Angeline.

"Angel, where are you?"

Smoke and the dancing light from the fire came from the back of the kitchen. With one glance, Jean-Paul knew he wouldn't be able to put it out. He ran into the bedroom. Angeline lay at a strange angle across the bed.

"Angel." He shook her. She didn't wake, and there was no time to rouse her. Scooping her up, he raced out of the bedroom.

Black smoke filled the living room, making it hard to see and breathe. He bumped into the end table, sending the lamp crashing to the floor. He stumbled for several steps, running into the wall. Angeline moaned.

"Hold on, *mon ange,*" he said, shifting her. Straining to see, Jean-Paul made out the frame of the open door. In three steps he was out, breathing in the fresh night air.

He hurried to his truck and gently placed her inside. In the dim glow of the overhead cab light, he saw a stream of blood behind Angeline's left ear. Carefully, he examined the wound. It was obvious she'd been hit with a heavy object.

She moaned again and began to cough. It was the sweetest sound Jean-Paul had ever heard.

His first inclination was to try to ask her if she knew what had happened. But the lady needed a doctor before anything else.

He hopped in beside her and slid his arm around her shoulders, bracing her against his body. Awkwardly, with his left hand, he put the truck into drive and took off.

"Jean-Paul." With her lips pressed against his flesh, he felt her say his name more than he heard her. Coughing accompanied her effort.

"Shh. Don't try to talk. I've got you. You're safe, *chère.*" She relaxed against him.

He passed the fire engine on the way, but didn't slow down until he reached the parish hospital in the next town.

The longest hour of Jean-Paul's life was waiting for the doctor to examine Angeline. Not even the time he spent waiting for the jury to come back with its verdict had been more torturous than this.

He ignored the disapproving glances directed at his bare chest from the couple sitting in the waiting room with him. Too bad if they thought he lacked manners. He didn't give a damn what anyone thought. He just wanted Angeline to be okay.

Finally, after sixty-three minutes and thirty seconds, the doctor appeared.

"How is she?" Jean-Paul asked, grabbing the doctor by the arm and hauling him out into the hall. He didn't care to discuss Angeline's condition in front of strangers.

"She's doing fine. She is suffering from smoke inhalation and a slight concussion. We're going to keep her here for observation. But you can probably take her home tomorrow afternoon."

Jean-Paul sagged with relief. "May I see her?"

"Sure. This way."

With shaking knees, Jean-Paul followed the doctor down the hall to Angeline's room. Her eyes fluttered open and tears spilled down her cheeks when she saw him. She held out her hand to him.

That simple act of trust sealed his fate. Whatever happened, Angeline would always be in his heart.

The doctor looked from Angie to Jean-Paul, smiled, and left the room.

"I'll confess, Angel, I've imagined seeing you in bed. But this isn't exactly how I envisioned it."

She started to chuckle, but it came out a choking cough.

He moved to her side. "Easy, *chère*. I meant only to make you smile, not cough."

She relaxed against the pillow and gave him a weak smile. "I know."

His fingers curled around hers. "Can you recall what happened?"

"I thought I was dreaming. I heard a sound and started to get up, when this dark shadow appeared and hit me with something." She fell silent for a moment, then asked, "What happened, Jean-Paul?"

He didn't want to be the one who told her, but then again maybe he could ease the blow. "Someone broke into Marianna's house and set it on fire. When I drove up, I saw him fleeing. Although I pulled you out in time, I doubt that the house survived the blaze. When I was rushing you here, I saw the fire truck on its way to Marianna's."

"But you don't know for sure if it's all gone."

"Pretty sure. It was an old house. The wood—" He shrugged. There was nothing else to say.

She closed her eyes, forcing the tears in her eyes down her cheeks. "What's going on, Jean-Paul? What could be of so great an importance that someone would kill my mother, burn her house to the ground and try to kill me?"

"I don't know, but I plan to find out."

Her fingers played along the edge of the sheet. "I guess someone didn't like the questions I was asking this morning and wanted to stop me. The fire could've been set to make my death look like an accident."

He soothed back the hair from her face. "That is why I acted like a crazy man today. There's an evil here, Angel. I've been on the receiving end of its wickedness and seen too many others suffer not to know it would reach out and try to touch you."

He leaned close and brushed a kiss across her lips.

"Is that why you were at my house, Jean-Paul?"

"Your guardian angel woke me and whispered you were in trouble."

She laid her palm on his cheek. "You are my guardian angel, Jean-Paul. Thank you."

"That, *ma petite,* is something I don't wish to be." He captured her hand and pressed it to his chest. "My thoughts go in a different direction."

Her eyes widened and a blush rose from her throat to her cheeks.

"My, what a touching scene." The words were an ugly parody of what they should have been.

Angie gasped and her gaze flew to the man standing in the doorway.

Jean-Paul straightened slowly and turned. He recognized Dennis Mathers's voice. He heard it in his nightmares. "What do you want, sheriff?"

Dennis arched his brow. "Are you always so rude, Jean-Paul, at this time of the night? No wonder the ladies prefer to spend the night with me and not with you."

Jean-Paul's jaw tightened so hard, he was fortunate he didn't snap the tendons. Ignoring the tawdry comment, he asked, "Why are you here?"

Dennis sauntered to the end of the bed. "Did you forget, Jean-Paul? I'm the sheriff, and this lady's house burned down. I need to ask her some questions."

A bitter laugh burst from Jean-Paul's mouth. "Why even bother to show up, Dennis? We all know that if you didn't set the fire yourself, you probably hired the man who did."

Out of the corner of his eye, Jean-Paul saw Angeline push the call button on the remote lying on the bed, summoning help.

"You think you're something special because you went to that fancy eastern school, don't you, Jean-Paul? But all that education didn't help one little bit when you were in prison. Did it?"

"Anytime, anywhere you say, Dennis, I'll meet you and beat the cr— We'll settle the score. Of course, I know what a coward you are. You'll probably try to have the courts do your dirty work. Or if that fails, you'll hire someone to do the deed."

"Why, you bastard," Dennis growled, taking a step toward Jean-Paul.

"Sheriff," the doctor said, rushing into the room. He was followed by a deputy and an orderly. "My patient is in no condition to answer any questions tonight."

"When will she be able to talk?" Dennis asked, still glaring at Jean-Paul.

"I plan to release her tomorrow, if everything goes according to plan."

Dennis pointed his finger at Jean-Paul. "You bring her by my office tomorrow." He strode out.

The doctor turned to Jean-Paul. "That wasn't a smart move."

"Don't I know," Jean-Paul murmured, rubbing his jaw. "But sometimes, Doctor, you have to stomp on the snake, even if it bites you."

"Yeah, well, I hope I don't have to treat you for a knife or gunshot wound in the back."

"I hope so, too."

From her hospital bed Angie watched the sky brighten with the new day. She had only dozed during the night, wakening every few minutes, frightened that whoever had tried to kill her hours before would try again.

Each time she thought of those few horrific moments when she'd seen a form hovering over her, her blood ran cold.

What did he want?

She swallowed hard. Her throat protested, sore from the smoke and rounds of coughing. If it hadn't been for Jean-Paul, she would have perished in that blaze. How had he known? According to him, her guardian angel woke him. In spite of how farfetched it sounded, Angie had the oddest feeling that it somehow was true. He knew she needed him and had come.

"Good morning, *chère*. How do you feel this morning?"

Jean-Paul stood in the doorway. And although he didn't look any better than she felt, he was a welcome sight. His hair looked as if he'd run his hands through it constantly. His clothes were wrinkled, but at least he had a shirt on this morning. The memory of resting her head on his naked shoulder brought an odd sort of contentment to her heart. And embarrassment.

He glanced down at his shirt and then at her. "Is something wrong? I know I look like I'm coming off a four-day drunk, but at least I have a shirt on. It's an improvement over last night, yes?"

She smiled and lifted her shoulder.

He walked across the room and set a brown grocery sack on the bed by her feet. "I had more important things on my mind last night, like making sure you were okay, to be worried by my dress or lack thereof. As I told you, after your guardian angel woke me I grabbed my jeans and ran."

Yes, she knew. "What's that?" she asked, pointing to the paper sack.

"M'dame Eleanor showed up on my front porch this morning, a pile of clothes in her arms that she collected for you. She refused to say where she got them, but I have my suspicions." He took the items from the bag and set them on the bed. "Here's a skirt and blouse," he said, holding them up. "And something for, uh—underneath." He pointed to the remaining items. "And sandals."

Angie nearly burst out laughing at his avoidance of the underwear. Well, who would have thought so sensuous a man would be embarrassed by a lady's unmentionables?

She picked up the blouse, noting the delicate scalloped edging of the collar. It reminded her of a similar blouse she'd found in Marianna's closet.

"Is there anything left of Marianna's house?" she softly asked.

His expression hardened. "No. It was gutted before the fire department could get there."

It was like learning of Marianna's death all over again. She bit her bottom lip, trying to keep her composure. "All her letters . . . pictures . . . were in the house."

He sat on the bed and pulled her into his arms. "I'm sorry, *chère*. The most important thing is you're all right." He pulled back and studied her face. Gently, he smoothed a tendril of hair from her cheek, but inadvertently he grazed the bump above her ear.

She tried to bite back the moan.

"Let me look," he softly commanded. As he inspected the injury, he mumbled a threat under his breath. He quickly got himself under control and cupped her cheek. "Why don't you get dressed and we'll leave?"

"Okay."

When she didn't pick up the clothes, Jean-Paul frowned. "Don't you like them?"

"They're fine. I'm waiting for you to leave so I can get dressed."

"Oh."

Angie grinned to herself as she changed, recalling the comical expression on his face. As soon as she had finished, the doctor came in and examined her and signed her release papers.

The morning air was still cool and felt wonderful on her skin as they drove back to Mirabeau.

"I'd like to stop by and thank Miss Eleanor for the lovely clothes."

"She was glad to help. But I think it would be best if you just called her. M'dame Eleanor speaks her mind, but there's no reason to bring her grief." He glanced at her. "Do you understand what I'm saying, *chère?*"

Oh, yes, she understood, and it made her sick. "You mean whoever did this to me wouldn't hesitate to take out their displeasure on her."

"You got it. The scum we're dealing with have no problems hurting little, old ladies. There's a better class of folk in the state prison than these guys."

That assessment of their enemy was foremost in Angie's mind when they pulled into the parking lot of the sheriff's office. Jean-Paul caught her arm before she got out.

"If you get tired, say the word and we'll leave."

"But what if the sheriff's not done questioning me?" she asked, worried that Jean-Paul would get himself in more trouble than he had last night.

"If Dennis doesn't like it, he can go jump in the bayou. You're not the suspect, and he has no right to hold you."

"Jean-Paul—"

He ran his hand down her arm and clasped her fingers. "Believe me, *chère*. Even if I'm not practicing law right now, I know the limits of the sheriff's authority. I won't let him step across them."

She placed her finger over his mouth, silencing him. "I'll be all right. Now, let's get this over with."

The next hour was torture for Angie. Dennis and Jean-Paul acted like two wolves circling, each waiting for an opening to lunge in and wound the other. But true to his word, the moment her energy began to wane, Jean-Paul stood up, helped her to her feet and escorted Angie to his car. His parting words to Dennis were rather crude.

"Couldn't he arrest you for that?" Angie asked, glancing over her shoulder, through the rear truck window, to see the fuming sheriff standing outside his office.

He shrugged. "He could try, only I'd demand a jury trial, and everyone in this parish agrees with my evaluation of Dennis's character. So I'd be acquitted, and he knows it."

His statement was so outrageous that she could only gape at him. And then, from deep inside, a laugh bubbled up.

Hearing her, his grin grew more mischievous. "You think I'm teasing, *hein?* I swear to you that Dennis couldn't find twelve people in this parish who would convict me."

Angie shook her head. She didn't know how the man could slip past all her natural reserve and make her laugh at the strangest things. Of course, since she'd met Jean-Paul, she had experienced so many intense and varied emotions that she no longer recognized who she was. And although he was not responsible for the situation, he had touched things in her that until now had lain dormant.

Love.

That wasn't it, she told herself. But then again, how did she know what love was? The last time she'd thought she was in love, she'd been taken for a fool.

So what did she know of love?

She stole a peek at Jean-Paul. She sensed that he felt something for her, but what if she was wrong? The last time, she'd barely survived the humiliation and shame when she discovered her fiancé had swindled her out of ten thousand dollars and skipped town.

What she felt for Jean-Paul was stronger, deep, richer than anything she'd felt for Richard. If she was wrong this time, she wouldn't survive.

Jean-Paul recognized the beige Cadillac parked in front of his house as belonging to Guy Boudreaux.

"Dammit—" Jean-Paul swallowed the rest of the descriptive phrase. "Why can't they just stay away?"

He shut off the engine and looked around for Guy, before getting out and coming around the front of the truck to help Angeline out.

They had just climbed the steps, when Guy appeared from around the side of the house.

"Hello," he quietly greeted them.

Jean-Paul slid his arm around Angeline's shoulder. "Are you sober this time, Guy?"

The older man flushed and dropped his gaze to the ground.

Angeline elbowed Jean-Paul. He glanced down, surprised at her action. The militant set of her jaw warned him against further rudeness.

"Why are you here, Guy?" Jean-Paul asked.

"I came here hoping to talk to Angeline. Will you talk to me, child?"

"Yes."

Jean-Paul unlocked the door and motioned the others inside. He followed, then sprawled beside Angeline on the couch. Guy sat stiffly in the rocker. He looked uncomfortable and lost.

"I don't know quite where to begin."

"Start with why you're here," Jean-Paul shot back.

Angeline sighed. "Please, let him talk."

Her plea on behalf of a Boudreaux irritated Jean-Paul. How could she even consider listening to the tripe that Guy would spew out? Didn't she understand about the Boudreaux men?

The older man smiled at Angeline. "Thank you, *chère.*"

Jean-Paul nearly came off the couch and threw the old coot out of his house. How dare he call Angeline *chère?* So what if the term was used loosely by everyone in these parts as a substitute for everything from "you" to "sweetheart." Hearing a Boudreaux say *chère* to Angeline chafed.

"I came today for several reasons. First, to apologize for showing up the other night drunk. And for my wife's behavior. She is rather overprotective of me."

"She watches you like a hawk because you're a sot," Jean-Paul grumbled under his breath. Angeline must have heard, because her elbow found its way into his side again. He frowned at her.

"Why did you come to see me the other night?" Angeline asked.

"For the same reason I'm here today. To explain." He stopped and again he seemed lost, unable to find the right words.

"To explain what?" Angeline prompted.

"About Marianna and me."

That brought Jean-Paul up straight. "What?"

Guy looked distinctly uneasy.

"You're my father?" Angeline asked, her voice barely a whisper.

Relief flooded Guy's face. "Yes."

Jean-Paul felt the fine trembling in Angeline's body. Glancing at her, he saw her bite down hard on her lower lip.

"But I never knew about you until yesterday morning when you walked into the courtroom," Guy hastily added.

"I find that hard to believe," Jean-Paul snapped.

"Stop it." Angeline's command rang through the room. "Please allow him to explain what happened." Her voice softened and her eyes pleaded with him.

Jean-Paul crossed his arms over his chest and settled back. After a long moment of silence, he motioned for Guy to continue.

"I had just finished law school and come home to Mirabeau. That summer Marianna and I fell in love. But we kept it a secret because I knew my father wouldn't approve. We planned to get married after I passed my bar exam." He paused, lost in some memory.

"When I came back from New Orleans after taking the bar, my engagement to Catlin had been announced in every newspaper in the state and an engagement party was scheduled for that night. Marianna was gone and no one knew where she was. I tried to find her, but . . ."

He reached out his hand, then let it drop. "I know it sounds like I could've done more. That's true."

Jean-Paul started to comment, but one glance at Angeline told him the only thing he'd accomplish was to further alienate her.

"When Marianna finally returned to Mirabeau, I was already married to Catlin. I went to her and asked her why she'd left. She told me never to seek her out again. That I was married and she would never involve herself with a married man. She never spoke to me again." He shrugged, and at that moment he looked much older than his fifty-some years. "I occasionally saw her in town. We would exchange glances, nothing more."

Guy stood. "I never stopped loving Marianna, Angeline. I did my duty to my family, but I could never give my heart."

Jean-Paul had had enough of this drivel. What Guy had failed to mention to Angeline was that he'd married Catlin for her family's power in this state, and for the past thirty years he'd drowned his sorrow in the best Kentucky mash that money could buy.

"What do you want from Angeline?" Jean-Paul baldly asked.

Guy shook his head. "Nothing. I only wanted to explain. Maybe ask her forgiveness."

Jean-Paul shot up to his feet. "Oh, please, Guy. You see an embarrassing situation here and you're doing damage control. You don't want anything to interfere with your drive to the governor's mansion."

"Jean-Paul," Angeline admonished, standing. A small cry of distress escaped her lips and she staggered sideways into him. Jean-Paul's hand shot out and grabbed her arm before she could fall.

"You got up too fast, *chère.* Sit." He gently pushed her down onto the cushions.

She slapped his hands away. "I know why I stumbled."

Her outraged reaction puzzled him.

"You're being rude, Jean-Paul."

"What?"

Her chin came up. "Your evaluation of my father's motivation for coming here is very insulting."

"Yeah. And it's also true, Angeline. Believe me, I've lived with the Boudreaux family all my life and I know their patterns."

Clearly uncomfortable with the drift of the conversation, Guy coughed. "I didn't mean to come here and stir up trouble. I hope, Angeline, that you'll think about what I said." He took her hand and kissed it.

Jean-Paul choked. Angeline threw him a glare.

"I'd like to see you again," Angeline told her father.

"Yes, I want that, too. You're a beautiful woman and your parents must be very proud of you. You give them reason. I know Marianna would have been proud."

She followed Guy outside and waved goodbye to him before turning to Jean-Paul. "You were unforgivably rude to him. He came here to explain what happened and ask my forgiveness."

"No, that's not why he came. His father sent him because Roger wants to make sure you don't make any waves and ruin Guy's chances at the governorship."

"Perhaps your past is coloring your judgment in this case."

Jean-Paul wanted to put his fist through the wall. From the expression on her beautiful face, she was buying Guy's line. "Maybe I can see what's behind his pretty words."

She gasped.

"You know, Jean-Paul, you can't see anything beyond that chip on your shoulder." She turned her back on him and walked into the house.

Jean-Paul ground his teeth. Angeline hadn't seen through the little gutless wonder's lies. And, sadly, neither had Marianna.

Chapter 12

Angie paced the living room, livid with Jean-Paul. How dare he? How dare he imply her father's only motive in coming to see her was damage control?

She stopped and glanced out the window. The object of her wrath sat under a large magnolia tree, his elbows resting on his up-drawn knees. Despite the fact he'd acted like a boor, Angie felt a flare of attraction. She shoved the feeling aside, in no mood to listen to her body's signals.

Jean-Paul's obnoxious behavior toward her father was rude and inexcusable. Guy had obviously come to tell her about himself and her mother, and to imply anything else, as Jean-Paul had, was outrageous. She didn't know how she felt about what her father had told her, but she knew Jean-Paul shouldn't have behaved like a heathen.

Over the past few days Jean-Paul had proved himself to be a reasonable and clever man. And very perceptive. But in this instance, why was he so far off base?

Or was he?

Angie shook her head. It was obvious Jean-Paul's feelings toward the Boudreaux family were colored, which might explain his misinterpretation of Guy's motives.

Angie walked into the kitchen and looked at the clock over the stove. Three-thirty. Giving her statement to the sheriff had taken longer than expected. That meant she had only an hour and a half to get to the historical society and start searching for whatever Marianna had been working on.

She refused to ask Jean-Paul to take her. And since her rental car was at Marianna's and had probably been trashed by the fire, that left only one option—Jock and his taxi.

After she called, Angie realized she had one tiny, little problem. Her cash had burned along with her clothes. She hoped Jock would take an IOU.

Jean-Paul rested his head against the trunk of the magnolia and glared at the house. What was the matter with Angeline, not to see Guy Boudreaux for what he really was? Why, even the story he'd told Angeline pointed out how spineless he was. Guy should have stood up to his father and told him he loved Marianna and was going to marry her. Instead, Guy had buckled under, married Attila the Hun in skirts and drunk his way through the past thirty years.

Jean-Paul ran his fingers through his hair. But would Angeline believe him, *hein?* If she spent any time with Guy, she'd discover his true nature. But if Jean-Paul continued to oppose Guy, it would drive Angeline closer to her father—and probably closer to danger.

The sound of a car coming down his drive drew Jean-Paul's attention. He glanced over his shoulder and saw Jock's old Chevrolet station wagon.

"Hallo, Jean-Paul," Jock called out as he rolled to a stop.

Jean-Paul stood. "Jock, what are you doing here?"

Jock's eyebrows rose in surprise. "Why, the little northern lady called and said she wanted to go to the historical society, would I come and pick her up? *Mais sho'*, I told her. I figured you were at Pierre's working. She never mentioned you."

Jean-Paul grinned. So his angel was so mad at him that she wouldn't ask him to take her? His attitude toward Guy really must have made her mad.

Perhaps it was time for him to apologize.

"Me, I was surprised when she called." Jock clicked his tongue several time. "I heard what happened last night. It was the talk of the diner today, with everyone guessin' what happened. We all thought she'd be in the hospital today for sure. I'm glad she be fine."

"You're not the only one, Jock."

Jock winked. "I understand how it is. This Angeline Fitzgerald is a mighty fine-looking woman, yes?"

"Yes." Jean-Paul rested his arms on the open window. "I'll be honest with you, Jock. Angeline is a little stubborn, and I made her very angry. So she called you to drive her."

"Ah, I see."

"So, if you don't mind, I'll take her over to the historical society."

"I understand, Jean-Paul. But you must understand that I need the money she will pay me. Nothing personal," Jock added.

Jean-Paul shrugged. "All of Angeline's things were burned in the fire, including her wallet."

Jock stared at Jean-Paul. "You're pullin' my leg, yes?"

"Ask her yourself."

At that moment Angeline emerged from the house onto the porch. She looked like a lost angel fallen from heaven. The usual peach color of her cheeks was gone and the strain of the past twenty-four hours showed in her eyes. She looked as if one strong gust of wind off the bayou would sweep her away.

"Good afternoon, Mr. Mason," she said, pointedly ignoring Jean-Paul.

"Call me Jock, *chère.*"

Her smiled looked forced. "Jock. Thank you for responding so quickly." She reached for the back door and got into the car.

"You better ask her now, Jock," Jean-Paul prompted.

Turning and resting his arm along the top of the seat, Jock asked, "I hate to be so rude, *mamselle*, but Jean-Paul claims that you don' have any cash to pay my fee. Is that so?"

"Temporarily," she murmured, blushing down to her toes. "In a few days I should have money and can pay you then."

The sheepish expression on Jock's face almost made Jean-Paul laugh. "I—uh—that is—"

Angeline raised her hand, stopping Jock's tripping excuse. "It's all right. I understand." After shooting Jean-Paul a killing glance, she slipped out of the vehicle. "Thank you for coming." She walked back into the house, her spine straight, her head held high.

"I think that little *fille* is gonna cook your goose, Jean-Paul, and have it for dinner."

Jean-Paul feared Jock was right.

He waited until the station wagon had disappeared around the bend of the driveway before he headed for the house. He found Angeline sitting in the rocker. She didn't look at him but simply continued to slowly rock.

Guilt hit him hard for shaming her. He went down on one knee in front of her and pried her hand away from where it was wrapped around her waist. Holding her delicate fingers in his, he rubbed the back of her hand.

"I'm sorry, *Angeline,* for embarrassing you in front of Jock. But I simply couldn't allow you to drive off with him. Someone in this town is out to hurt you, and I won't let you go out unprotected. If you want to go to the historical society this afternoon, I will take you. All you had to do was ask."

She looked at him then. "I didn't want you to take me."

He cupped her cheek with his free hand. "Ah, *chère,* I know I behaved badly with Guy. I'm sorry." He leaned toward her and lightly brushed his lips across her cheek. Her skin was as smooth as the petal of a magnolia flower and as flawless. "The only defense I have is that I worry that Roger will use Guy to hurt you. The old bastard isn't above doing that."

He slipped his arm around her waist and pulled her toward him. "I have this driving need to protect you. I don't know its source, but I can't deny it any more than I can stop the Mississippi from flowing into the Gulf. And I don't want to. To go against that flow would be to drown."

His gaze locked with hers and he allowed the passion inside him to show. He wanted her to see what he felt for her. He wanted to seduce her with the heat that burned him each time he saw her, touched her, thought of her.

The stiffness in her posture melted under the flames of his stare, as a candle melts under the heat of fire. The sky blue of her eyes turned dark and stormy as they focused on his lips. The invitation was exactly what Jean-Paul had been waiting for.

He lowered his head and covered her waiting mouth with his. An explosion of sparks and lava engulfed Jean-Paul. Her lips were warm satin, molding to his, seeking his, begging more from him. He tilted her head back to gain a better angle to the sweetness of her mouth. She moaned and his tongue slipped inside to taste heaven.

Her arms slid up around his back, bringing her breasts flat against the wall of his chest. The exquisite feel of her pebble-hard nipples touching him through the fabric of her blouse and his shirt bordered on pain.

She broke off the kiss and pulled back as a wave of coughing overtook her. When it subsided, she gave him an apologetic smile. "I'm sorry—" she began.

"*Non, chère,* it was my fault. In the heat of the moment—" he gave her a very Gallic shrug "—I simply forgot."

A smile played around her kiss-swollen lips. "You're not the only one." She glanced down.

He caught her chin, forcing it up. "I meant what I said, Angeline. I don't want to see you hurt by Roger—or by me. I'll try to behave around Guy."

"Only try?"

His heart sank at her stern tone, but then the corners of her mouth quivered. Her teeth sank into her bottom lip, stopping her from grinning. Jean-Paul's jaw dropped open as the implications of her action hit him. She was teasing him. And if she could tease him, then hallelujah, she wasn't mad at him.

"I'm afraid so. It would take a saint to promise to behave around the Boudreaux. And I am no saint, as you well know. And I refuse to make promises I can't keep. So the best I can do is to tell you I'll try. Is that enough?"

She ran her finger along his lower lip. In one quick movement, he caught the pad between his teeth and lightly bit it. Then his tongue stroked over the abused flesh. The surprise in her eyes quickly turned to hunger. With a final swipe of his tongue, he freed her.

"You didn't answer my question, *Angeline*." Purposely, he murmured her name, giving it the full silky French pronunciation.

"Question?" Her eyebrows crinkled. After a moment her mouth opened silently in an *O*. "Yes, Jean-Paul, your trying will be enough."

The tension seeped from his spine with her answer. He rose and held out his hands to help her up. She placed her palms on his, and he gently pulled her to her feet.

She walked to the front door.

"Where are you going?" he asked.

"Since you sent Jock away, I assumed you were taking me to the historical society."

She was in no condition to be running around the countryside. Jean-Paul glanced at his watch, praying it was too late in the day to go. "It's four now. By the time we get there, we'll have less than twenty minutes to begin looking." He crossed the room and laid his hands on her shoulders. "Besides, you have had too much excitement today and need your rest."

"But you said the historical society was closed on Thursdays. It would be Friday before we could begin. What would we do tomorrow?"

He had an answer for that—one he didn't think she wanted to hear.

Make love all day. Slow, glorious, heart-stopping love.

The same thoughts must have occurred to her, because suddenly there was a riot of color in her cheeks. He wondered if she was embarrassed that the thoughts occurred to her, or if she was mortified by the fact that she wanted to make love with him. It was food for thought.

"If you will lie down and take a nap now, I promise that tomorrow morning I will drive you out to M'sieu Colton's houseboat. Together we'll try to talk him into letting us into the society on Thursday."

"You said he never came off his houseboat."

"I swear that's true. But if anyone can charm that old Cajun into opening up, it's you, *chère.*"

Her index finger tapped lightly against her pursed lips as she studied him. He tried to keep his expression honest and open in an effort to convince her. There wasn't a snowball's chance in hell that the old codger would reconsider his position, but Angeline needed rest more than she needed honesty.

"All right. But I'll hold you to this promise."

A grin spread across Jean-Paul's face. "It's one I'll gladly keep."

When Angie woke, darkness had settled around her. It was amazing what a little sleep could do. Her body felt restored, her mental balance reestablished. If she had ever doubted what a clever lawyer Jean-Paul had been, his manipulation of Jock left no doubt of his skill. The poor man had been putty in his hand.

The analogy made her smile. If anyone was putty in Jean-Paul's capable hands, it was she. The memory of his earthshattering, ground-moving kiss came roaring back in all its intensity. Her behavior was mortifying. It was as if an alien had invaded her body and had taken control of it. Suddenly, she didn't know who she was and didn't have a clue how to act as each new situation arose.

She glanced at the clock on the nightstand. It was a little after nine. Her stomach growled, reminding her she hadn't eaten since breakfast. She threw back the crocheted afghan and sat up. The room tipped and swayed. It took a moment before things settled into their rightful places.

She was grateful Jean-Paul had promised to take her to Mr. Colton's tomorrow, because she didn't think she would have made it to the historical-society building and back without swooning or disgracing herself in some other way.

The hum of the window-unit air conditioner drowned out the other sounds of the house. After a quick trip to the bathroom to wash her face and finger-comb her hair, Angie went looking for Jean-Paul.

The lights were on in the living room and the kitchen beyond. "Jean-Paul?" she called.

Nothing.

She walked into the kitchen. The table was set for dinner. Several pots sat on the stove; the fire was on underneath the huge silver-colored pot.

"Jean-Paul?"

Still nothing.

Curious, she peeked into the pot. Potatoes and ears of corn were cooking in the boiling, spicy water. She lifted the lid on one of the other pots. Red beans. In the other was rice.

A sound—a whistled note—came from the yard. She stepped out onto the porch. She could hear a man whistling but couldn't see him.

"Jean-Paul? Is that you?"

"Yes, Angel." He came striding into the light cast from the outside floodlight, carrying a mesh sack.

"What do you have there?" she asked, pointing to the bag.

He held it up in triumph. "Crawfish. Jock felt so bad about what happened this afternoon that when he went out in his boat and caught these *bébés,* he brought some by for us. So you and I are going to have fresh crawfish for dinner."

He looked pleased with his treasure. Setting the bag on the porch, he pulled out a truly ugly creature that looked like a small lobster.

"Have you ever seen anything so beautiful, *hein?* And taste—" He closed his eyes, brought his fingers to his lips, and blew a kiss. The look of rapture on his face caused her heart to beat faster. "The taste is outta this world."

Personally, the thought of eating those nasty, little things didn't bring rapture to her heart or stomach. But for Jean-Paul, she'd give it a try.

Careful, a voice in her head whispered. *Remember when Richard wanted you to try dirt biking and you fell and broke your arm? This time it will be your heart.*

He transferred the crawfish from the sack into a pail sitting by the back door, then took it inside. Angie sat at the table and watched him scoop out the potatoes and corn, then throw the crawfish into the pot.

"Is there anything I can do?" Angie asked.

He shook his head. "Just sit there and relax." He put the lid on the pot and turned off the fire. "All that we have to do is let the crawfish steam."

As he put the bowls of food on the table, he looked right at home.

"You've done this before."

He laughed. "All my life. When I was a boy and my *maman* was working all day long, I would go down to the bayou, catch some of these critters and have dinner waiting for her." He shook his head. "She hated crawfish, but they were free, and when we didn't have anything else—" He lifted one shoulder.

Angie could see the small boy in ragged jeans running down to the bayou to catch his dinner.

"Did your father like them?"

"He didn't like anything that wasn't whiskey."

The starkness of his statement ripped at her heart. So his father had been an alcoholic. What had it been like for him, growing up poor with a mother who worked and a father who drank? It shed a new light on his personality.

He placed bowls of rice, beans, potatoes, corn and a salad on the table. Then, with a flourish, he set a platter of cooked crawfish before her. They were beet red and utterly unappealing. She glanced up at him.

He waved at all the foods. "I started the beans and rice before Jock hailed me from the river. And you can't have crawfish without the potatoes and corn."

He retrieved the newspaper from the other room and opened it out on the table. "When you finish with your crawfish, just toss the remains on the newspaper."

He put several of the little creatures on his plate, pinched the head off one, then peeled away the shell from the tail. He pulled the small amount of meat from inside and popped it into his mouth.

"Ah, that's good. They don't cook them this way in Boston."

"I'm sure they don't," she agreed, wondering why anyone would bother.

"Try it."

She reluctantly picked up one and followed his lead. The meat tasted like lobster.

He then picked up the head of the crawfish and sucked out the insides.

Angie's eyes widened and her stomach threatened to rebel. "Yuk."

"It's the way we eat them," he explained, as if that would convince her of the wisdom of the action.

At that moment, she reached the end of her adventurous spirit. She wasn't going to follow his lead, no matter what.

"I believe that's quite enough seafood for me." She daintily placed her discarded pieces on the newspaper.

He threw his head back and laughed. "That Yankee upbringing is showing, Angel. But don't worry. Stay here long enough, and we'll take the starch out of that pretty body."

Her heart leapt at the thought of staying. Did he want her to stay? Was he asking her to? Visions of how he would take the starch out of her crowded into her mind's eye, causing her to blush.

She filled her plate with salad and began munching on a lettuce leaf.

"How are you feeling, *chère?*" The concern in his voice wrapped around her heart, comforting her.

"Better. My headache is almost gone."

He paused, the head of a crawfish in one hand, the body in the other. "You look wonderful. That soft peach color is back in your cheeks."

If he only knew the real reason she had color in her cheeks! She latched onto the first thing that she could think of. "You've been to Boston?"

He stilled and she could read nothing in his face. "Yeah." Brushing the broken shell from his plate, he reached for another crawfish.

"Did you visit the city?"

He sighed. "No. I went to boarding school in a little town north of Boston."

"B-but, I thought you said..." Her voice trailed off as she realized what she'd been about to say.

"Oh, yes, we were dirt-poor. After my dad took off, my mother vowed that I would be a success. So she took as many cleaning jobs as she could get, to make enough money to send me away to a fine school where I could learn to speak like an 'educated' man. She even worked for Catlin Boudreaux, to pay for my tuition." He paused, lost in some memory. "She got what she wanted. My grades were good enough that I won a scholarship to Harvard."

As he talked, his entire being seemed to change from that of the passionate man she knew into a cold, shuttered stranger. "You hated it, didn't you, Jean-Paul?"

His eyes locked with hers, and the burning intensity of his gaze gave her her answer.

"With every breath I took. The winters were bitter cold beyond anything I had ever imagined. And the other students had no use for a poor Cajun boy. But I knew if I ever wanted to return and win against Roger Boudreaux, I needed to be educated."

"The oil on this land. Roger owned the rights."

"You got that right, *chère*. It ate my dad up. To deal with the pain, he drank."

She laid her hand on his arm, her heart aching with his. "I'm sorry, Jean-Paul."

"Maybe now you'll understand why I feel the way I do about the Boudreaux."

"You can't hold Guy responsible for his father's sins."

"Guy has enough sins of his own. Deserting Marianna, for one."

"That's not fair. He didn't know."

"So he says."

She wanted to leap to her father's defense, but Jean-Paul had just given her a part of himself, and she didn't want to throw it back in his face. She stood. "I'm tired. I think I'll go to bed."

"Angeline," he said, catching her before she could take a step. "I've done it again. Forgive me."

Peering down into his handsome face, his dark hair falling over his forehead, Angie knew much to her despair that she'd forgive him anything. She leaned over and placed a soft kiss on his lips. "Good night, Jean-Paul. I'll see you tomorrow morning." She hurried out of the room.

"'Night, *chère*," he called after her. "Sleep well because tomorrow we'll go see M'sieu Colton, and you'll need all your wits about you."

M'sieu Colton wasn't the only male in this town that she needed all her wits to deal with. A handsome Cajun mechanic was at the top of the list.

pull him to his feet. "We're leaving, Jean-Paul. I say you
have lost enough. Could you drive us to the lodge."

"Of course." He started shaking his head and wincing.
Somehow such as my she slipped an arm and held and as
you're about now.

"If you don't want to come behind the wheel so
please drive you with it. Take me to Jean-Paul. Tomas the
Angie was at his side of the bed.

Chapter 13

The pounding headache woke Angie. She moved her head
to the side, but the lump behind her ear protested the
movement. It was obvious she needed something for the
pain.

Throwing back the sheet, she carefully got out of bed,
slipped on her robe and went into the bathroom for the aspirin she knew were in the medicine cabinet. After retrieving two pills, she walked to the kitchen for a glass since there
wasn't one in the bathroom.

As she tiptoed into the living room, she glanced at the
couch. Jean-Paul wasn't there, but from the wrinkled condition of his pillow and sheet it looked as if he'd tried to
sleep and failed.

The moment she entered the kitchen she saw him through
the screen door, sitting on the porch steps. After she got her
glass of water and swallowed the pills, she padded to the side
door.

He didn't turn, move or in any other way indicate he had heard her walk up.

"Couldn't you sleep?" she asked.

He glanced over his shoulder. "*Non.* What about you, *chère?*"

"A headache woke me."

He clucked his tongue in sympathy. "Come and join me."

She really didn't want to go back to bed and stare at the ceiling, trying not to think about her throbbing head until the aspirin kicked in. Instead, she took his invitation and pushed open the screen door. She froze halfway across the wooden deck. All Jean-Paul had on was a ragged pair of cutoffs. She swallowed. The previous time she'd been in no condition to appreciate the well-honed muscles of his chest and arms. If she had a lick of sense, she would turn around and march right back to bed, headache be damned. Her only problem was how she was going to explain her sudden urge to go inside. *Sorry, Jean-Paul, it's just too much for my nervous system to sit next to your beautiful body so amply displayed.*

Of course he'd ask why it bothered her, and she wasn't going to answer him.

He turned and looked at her. "Anything wrong?"

"No," she quickly replied. Ignoring her nervousness, she hurried to his side and sat. "What do you have there?" she asked, pointing to the fine silver chain and medal wrapped around his fingers.

"The Saint Christopher my mother gave me before I went to boarding school." The utter sadness in his voice drew her to him, making her forget her earlier disquiet.

"You didn't have it on last night."

He raised his brow. "I didn't have on a lot of things. I was in a hurry."

Her cheeks turned hot pink as she visualized what else he'd forgotten to put on. "Did it protect you when you traveled?" Because he gave her such an odd look, she hurried to explain herself. "I mean since Saint Christopher is the patron saint of travelers, I wondered if it had worked."

His fingers closed around the medal. "Yeah, I guess so. I never had an accident going to or coming from school." He opened his hand and let the disk hang free. "Too bad he couldn't help once I was there."

She wanted to reach out and touch him, but wisely kept her hands to herself. "Was it that bad?"

"A frozen hell." He stared at the medal. "It was as if I were an alien from another planet. I could barely understand anything said. The boys at school made fun of how I talked, dressed, my ways of doing things. I learned quickly to conform, to bury who and what I was. But I blew it at the end of my first year. I had an argument with a pompous jerk and he called me a dumb Cajun. I beat him to a bloody pulp. Unfortunately, he had friends, and they took out his beating on my hide for years after."

Angie's heart ached for him. She knew what it felt like to be a foreigner in your own hometown. That was how she'd felt all her life. Oh, she'd lived up to everyone's expectations, but at what price? She'd shut up part of herself and ignored it, because strong passions like hers were frowned upon. Things like swimming in the stream in the middle of the night, romping through the autumn leaves and singing at the top of her voice were thought inappropriate for a young woman of good breeding.

He looked at her. "You know what was really strange, *chère?*"

She shook her head, emotions clogging her throat, making it impossible to speak.

"It was as if I ceased to exist, those years. The place was too cold, the pace too fast, the world was either black or white. When I came home to Louisiana, something inside eased." He lifted one tan shoulder. "Maybe it was the heat that thawed me. But I saw colors again, felt life curling around me, tasted again the Louisiana hot sauce on craw-fish."

His words echoed the feelings in her heart. She had finally found another human being who understood, who had experienced the same alienation from his environment that she had. Here, sitting beside her, was a kindred soul.

He grinned and turned to her. "Ah, Angeline, I didn't mean to make you cry." His fingers brushed away the moisture from her cheek. The medal tangled in his hand and fell against her neck. "I was just feeling sorry for myself."

She tried to speak but couldn't bring her chaotic thoughts into line. Wanting to share his sorrow and offer him comfort, she slipped her arms around him and brought her mouth to his.

He took the tender offering like a starving man. His lips ravaged hers, giving as much as he took. She met his wildness, wanting and needing the contact.

The burning heat of his body imprinted itself on her. It was heaven to feel his solid strength pressed against her. She ran her hands over the smooth skin of his back. Warm satin over steel. The perfection was ruined when her fingers came across a long scar just below his shoulder blade. She wanted to ask him about it, but his fingers untied the belt of her robe and pushed it from her shoulders.

Jean-Paul quickly undid the button running down the front of her nightgown. He pulled the straps down her arms and she felt the cool breeze on her breasts.

"You are so beautiful. Perfect." His gaze burned brightly in the moonlight. His hand covered her breast. The stark contrast of his dark hand resting on her white skin was startling. Their gazes locked, and in the deepest part of her she felt Jean-Paul lay his claim on her. She was his. Gently, he pushed her down onto the deck.

His mouth replaced his hand and Angie cried out with the overwhelming joy of his touch. His tongue laved the nipple, then he raised his head and watched the soft wind make it pucker. Her fingers threaded through the dark strands of his hair, urging him back.

His hands cupped her head, brushing against the lump behind her ear. Pain shot through her brain and she groaned.

Jean-Paul stilled, his eyes searching hers. "Damn, what was I thinking?" he asked. "You're in no condition to..."

He sat up and pulled her with him. He slid the gown's straps back into place, then helped her with the robe. As she tied the belt, he unwrapped the chain from his hand and slipped it over Angie's head. His fingers ran down the links to where the disk rested between her breasts.

"Go back to bed, Angel, before my nobility turns to ashes in the heat of my lust. *Va-t'en.*" When she didn't move, he growled, "Go!"

She scrambled to her feet and headed for the door.

"Angeline."

She stopped.

"Make no mistake about it, *chère,* you and I are meant to be lovers. Tonight wasn't the right time. But soon it will happen."

With a single glance back at him, she hurried to bed, knowing in her heart he was right.

"Jean-Paul, are you sure this is the right road?"

Angie peered out at the dense foliage snaking across the lane.

"According to Pierre, this is the right way."

Angie fought the panic rising in her throat. "You mean to tell me you've never been out here before?"

"I told you that no one knows exactly where M'sieu Colton's houseboat is located. All I know is that we take this road until it stops, then hopefully there will be a boat on this side of the bayou that we can use to ferry across."

"What if there isn't a boat?"

"You certainly got up on the wrong side of the bed this morning, *chère*. Are you usually this grouchy in the morning? If you are, tell me, so I'll know what to expect."

From his words, Jean-Paul sounded as if he was planning on spending his mornings with her. And after what had happened between them the previous night, to be held in his strong arms through the night and be loved by him held infinite appeal to her. It was the very reason she was so crabby this morning. She hadn't fallen asleep until the wee hours because her heart and body were longing for him.

"Why didn't you tell me yesterday this would be your first visit?"

Angie watched in amazement as he blushed.

"I didn't mention it because I knew you would worry. But I promised you we'd come, and I've kept my promise."

All her irritation with him evaporated. He was keeping a promise, no matter how bad it made him look. And a man who kept his promises in this day and age of lost personal honor was worth his weight in gold. And it was one more reason to trust him in every way.

Suddenly the bushes and trees thinned and she could see a forties-model car parked at the edge of the bayou.

"We're at the right place," Jean-Paul told her. "That is M'sieu Colton's Buick."

They got out of the truck and walked down to the water. There was no boat. Jean-Paul pointed to the pirogue tied to the houseboat on the other side.

"There's M'sieu Colton's house, *chère.* But I don't think he's wanting company. The welcome mat isn't out."

She wrinkled her nose at him. "Very funny. Maybe he wasn't expecting company. Why don't we call to him?"

He gave her a look that said he thought she was nuts. "Go ahead. Be my guest."

She took a step closer to the water and cupped her hands around her mouth. "M'sieu Colton. My name is Angeline Fitzgerald. I would like to speak to you."

Silence answered her.

Jean-Paul leaned down and whispered in her ear, "Maybe he didn't hear you."

She wanted to punch him in that oh-so-clever mouth of his. "M'sieu Colton, I want to speak to you about my mother, Marianna Courville."

A wizened old man with a shotgun appeared on the opposite bank next to the houseboat. Her eyes widened when she saw the gun.

"Jean-Paul, you keep that little girl there until I pole across and get you. You hear?" The command rang throughout the woods.

"Yes, sir. I hear."

Angie glanced up at Jean-Paul. "Is that how he greets everyone?"

Jean-Paul grinned. "Can't say. I've never known anyone who's come out here." He leaned close and murmured, "And lived to tell about it."

She wanted to kick him. "You're not funny."

His smile didn't fade.

They watched as M'sieu Colton placed his shotgun in the pirogue and poled across. For such a shrunken, little man, he had amazing agility.

"You're seeing history, Angel," Jean-Paul said. "That's how everyone got around in these parts a hundred years ago. That old man could probably beat any of the young pups in this parish poling his pirogue."

"You got that right," the other man replied as he brought the tip of the boat to the shore. Before Jean-Paul could haul the pirogue onto the bank, M'sieu Colton stepped forward and hopped out onto the land. He laid the pole across the seat, next to his shotgun. Angie's gaze remained on the weapon.

"I was out huntin'," M'sieu Colton explained.

Angie flushed to the roots of her hair.

"Introduce me to the young and beautiful lady, Jean-Paul," the old man ordered.

After introductions, M'sieu Colton leaned over Angie's hand and kissed it. "My name, *chère,* is Henri."

Jean-Paul made a strangled sound and Angie glanced at him. From his expression, she guessed this was the first time he'd ever heard M'sieu Colton's given name.

"I can see why everyone in the parish is talking about you," Henri said. "You cause even this heart to skip a beat. Me, when I saw you I thought I see an apparition. But, no, you are real. Who would've thought." He shook his head and muttered something in Cajun French. "Come. We'll talk on my houseboat."

Henri went first, then helped Angie in. Jean-Paul followed. Gingerly she sat on the seat, afraid of rocking the flat-bottomed boat.

"This is safe, isn't it?" She glanced up at Henri. "I mean, it won't tip, will it?"

He laughed. "*Non*. My pirogue, she won't tip. She's the best."

Angie eyed the cloudy water, wondering what lurked beneath the surface. Much to her relief, in less than five minutes they were standing on the deck of M'sieu Colton's houseboat.

He ushered them inside and pointed to the table. "Sit, I'll get us some tea to drink." He disappeared into the small galley.

The furniture in the combined dining-and-living room was simple and well worn with time. A sketchbook lay open on the table, the drawing of a bird detailed with a careful hand.

The illustration drew Angie. She started to touch the magnificent work, then pulled her hand back, afraid she might smudge it. Jean-Paul stared down over her shoulder at the pad.

"Isn't it beautiful, Jean-Paul?"

"Indeed. And a great surprise. I don't think anyone knows of Henri's talent." He turned his head so his mouth was a breath away from her ear. "Maybe we've discovered what he does with his Tuesdays and Thursdays, instead of changing into a bat like some say."

She wanted to elbow him, but resisted the temptation. "Do you know the name of this bird?"

Jean-Paul shook his head. "I studied law, not ornithology."

"A compassionate and informative answer." She turned the page and another wonderfully illustrated bird appeared.

"You like my drawings, yes?" Henri asked, setting three glasses of iced tea on the table.

"They are exceptional. I've seen some reproductions of Audubon's original drawings. These are as good." She glanced down at the page. "Are the birds local?"

"Yes." He moved to a hutch, opened the bottom door and withdrew several more pads. Laying them on the table, he opened them for her inspection. "I've also drawn the plants and trees of the bayou, and the animals."

Angie sank onto the kitchen chair, stunned by the research before her. This man had chronicled in painstaking detail the wildlife that claimed this land as its own.

She looked at Henri. "I don't have words to tell you how marvelous these are. Have you ever shown them to anyone?"

The old man's brow crinkled into a deep frown. "Why would I want to do such a thing? This I do for me."

"Because, Henri, they are a living history of this place, precious knowledge that should be shared. I bet any university in this state would love to have them." She leaned forward to emphasize her point. "They probably would even send students to you to teach them about the ecosystem of this bayou."

"Bah," he replied, but Angie saw a glitter of interest in his eyes.

"She knows what she's talking about, M'sieu Colton," Jean-Paul said. "She's *un prof d'Anglais* at some university in Vermont."

The old man shook his head and clicked his tongue. "A shame. And so beautiful a woman."

Angie threw Jean-Paul an I'll-get-you look, then turned back to the old man. "I have a friend who teaches biology, who would love to see your work."

Henri perked up. "You're fooling me, yes?"

"No. I'll call her today and tell her about you. That is, if you're agreeable to the idea."

He leaned back and stroked his chin. "Let me think on this. Now, why are you here with me? You didn't come to see my drawings. You mentioned something about Marianna."

Angie realized that she'd been stalling, wishing she could forget the reason she'd come out here and talk of birds and flowers to this eccentric but delightful man all day. "Yes. I guess you've heard about what happened on Monday."

He glanced at Jean-Paul.

"We need the truth, Henri," Jean-Paul told him. "Angeline needs to hear the whole truth."

"Yes, I heard. Claire, who works at the society, talked about nothing else this week. I would fire the busybody, but her *papa* gives much money to us."

"Jean-Paul thinks my mother was murdered."

Henri's eyes widened. "Truly, Jean-Paul?"

"Yes, we think so. What we want to know is what Marianna was working on for the society."

He shrugged. "A history of the parish. What else?"

Jean-Paul leaned back in his chair. "Did she mention running across anything unusual?"

"No."

"Would you allow us to go through the things Marianna used?" Jean-Paul asked.

"Of course, and I can show you what she wrote, too."

"Could we see it today?"

Henri looked at Jean-Paul as if he'd asked him to walk down the main street of Mirabeau stark naked. "No."

"But—" The protest burst from Angie's mouth.

Henri held up his hand. "This is Thursday. I have my reputation to think of. Besides, if I came into town today, Eleanor would have a stroke. The last time I came to town on a Tuesday, she pitched such a fit that I still haven't heard the last of it.'' He moved closer to Angie and whispered, ''And I can't let the old girl get the best of me.''

For a moment, Angie stared at him in stunned surprise, then she laughed. ''Why, you old rascal. I think you like Miss Eleanor.''

Henri looked offended, but the corner of his mouth turned up.

Jean-Paul gripped the steering wheel and fixed his eyes on the road ahead. He didn't know quite how to feel. Poleaxed most accurately described it. In one afternoon he'd learned M'sieu Colton's given name, been inside his house and discovered he was a talented artist. Angeline had charmed more information out of the old man in the span of an hour than the rest of the people in the parish had done in almost seventy years. Jean-Paul bet there weren't two other people in the entire state of Louisiana who knew what they knew about Henri.

''Can you imagine that?'' Angie's voice broke into his thoughts.

''What?'' he groused.

''I think Henri has a crush on Miss Eleanor.''

Here was another thing that came as a shock. Was he that unobservant? Maybe that's why Roger had been able to outmaneuver him. ''On what evidence do you base this startling conclusion?''

''The sound of his voice when he talked about her, the way he tried to hide that mischievous smile of his. He was acting like a boy with his first crush.''

Jean-Paul grunted.

''I think Henri is shy. So shy, in fact, that he's never been able to work up enough nerve to approach Miss Eleanor.''

''*Henri. Henri.*'' His temper flared. ''Why is it, *chère*, that he is always *Henri?* And me, I'm John-Paul?'' He gave his name a noxious English pronunciation. "Can you answer me that?"

He knew he sounded childish, but it made him see red that she so willingly used the French pronunciation of the old man's name. But she put him through hell before she said *Jean-Paul.*

He glanced at her and immediately regretted his outburst. She sat rigidly on the seat, her lips taut.

"He didn't call me a liar when we first met."

The dagger plunged into his heart. What was the matter with him, attacking her like that? "Your point is well taken."

She mumbled something else.

"What did you say?" he asked.

"Nothing."

She turned her head and stared out the window. But he could have sworn she said, "I wasn't attracted to him."

Silence settled on the cab of the truck, but Jean-Paul savored her answer as he drove the rest of the way home. His mood soured at the sight of Guy Boudreaux sitting on his porch, obviously waiting for them.

"Now what?" he grumbled.

Angie faced him. "You promised, Jean-Paul, you would try to be nice to him."

He noted she gave his name the proper inflection.

"And as you told me earlier, you always keep your promises."

She didn't need to remind him. "I remember, Angeline."

Guy stood and walked down the steps to greet them. He nodded to Jean-Paul and kissed Angeline on the cheek. Jean-Paul was tempted to push Guy away from her, but he restrained himself.

"I tried calling you, Angeline, but got no answer. I became worried and came over to make sure you were all right."

"I'm fine. Jean-Paul was with me. We went—"

"Out." Jean-Paul didn't want Guy to know where they'd been, because Guy would turn around and tell Roger.

Angeline frowned at him, but he shook his head, silently telling her not to say anything more. And although he knew she didn't agree with him, she complied.

"Uh, yes, out."

A warm feeling wrapped itself around his heart at her show of trust in him. Even her comment to Guy that she'd been with him, said with a confidence that implied she'd been safe, made him proud.

Guy cleared his throat. "Well, the reason I was calling is I wanted to invite you to dinner tomorrow night. I know your impressions of my father and my wife are somewhat colored, but they're sorry for their earlier actions and want the opportunity to get to know you and have you know them."

Jean-Paul wanted to scream to the heavens that Guy was lying through his teeth. That the only reason those two rats wanted Angeline to come was so that they could ferret out any weakness she might have and use it against her. But one look at Angeline's face and he knew he couldn't tell her that. Given time and opportunity, Angeline would discover that truth herself.

"I'd be delighted to come. May I bring Jean-Paul with me?"

Guy looked as if someone had kicked him in the pants. "Of course. We'd be delighted to have him accompany you."

Like hell you would. But he'd give Guy this, he was a smooth liar.

Angie touched Jean-Paul's arm. "Will you go with me?"

He'd rather eat with snakes, but he wouldn't allow Angeline to walk into that pit without him. "Yes. I'll go." *And protect you.* His gaze locked with the other man's, and silently Jean-Paul promised him that if anything happened to Angeline, Guy Boudreaux would pay—in blood.

Chapter 14

"I want to thank you, Jean-Paul, for being polite to Guy this afternoon," Angeline said, sitting back in the rocker.

Jean-Paul, who was sprawled on the couch watching TV, sent her a disgruntled look. From the instant he'd agreed to go with her, he regretted the decision. But there had been no other choice short of ordering Angeline not to go, and he knew she wouldn't sit still for that kind of high-handedness from him.

She ran her hands up and down the curved arms of the wooden rocker. "I know you're not pleased about my going, but I feel I have to take this opportunity to get to know Guy and his father."

He sat forward and rested his elbows on his knees. "Sugar, a gator is a gator. And when he's out on the bank sunning himself, he looks like a lazy, old critter. But you get close enough and give that gator the opportunity, you're goin' to be his lunch."

"I knew it." She sounded like a mother who'd just caught her child stealing cookies from the cookie jar. "I knew you were upset."

"I'll admit that I'd rather eat with gators than Roger Boudreaux, but I made you a promise. And I plan on living up to it."

She stood. "I think you're blaming Guy for the sins of his father."

If he told her how he really felt about the situation, it would appear he was attacking Guy, and that would drive Angeline right into his hands. Jean-Paul shrugged. "Could be."

She walked over to where he sat. Her chin came up and the light of battle entered her blue eyes. "You're just saying that to make me happy. You don't believe that."

Why was she trying to pick a fight with him? Slowly, he rose to his feet. "How do you know that, *chère?*"

"Because I feel it here." She laid her hand over her heart.

His larger hand covered hers and his fingers rested on her breast. "I can believe that, because it's the same for me." His fingers contracted, bringing a small gasp from her lips. Blood pounded through his brain and his jeans suddenly became too tight. "Why is it that way for us?"

"I don't know." She backed away from him, her eyes reflecting her confusion.

"Why won't you trust your heart, Angeline?" he asked, stepping toward her. She scooted around the couch. "Tell me, *chère,* why you don't give in to your passion?"

Her lips trembled. "You want to know why?"

"Please, help me to understand."

She wrapped her arms around her waist in a protective gesture. "I'd been teaching a year when the college invited this actor with wonderful credentials to come and help put on several Shakespeare plays. Richard was charming, dramatic and could coax a snake out of its skin. He certainly charmed me.'' She paused, swallowing several times.

"And you fell in love with him?"

She nodded. "When he asked me to marry him, I was flattered, excited and immediately said yes. He found a lovely, little house right outside of town for us to live in.''

Jean-Paul knew what was coming next and braced himself.

"Richard was embarrassed that he didn't have the cash for the down payment, but he told me the owner wanted to sell and someone else had bid on the house. I gave him the ten thousand he needed. He skipped town with the money.''

Hearing the tears in her voice, Jean-Paul moved around the couch and pulled her into his arms. "The fault wasn't yours for loving, Angel.''

She turned her face into his shirt and burrowed deeper into his embrace.

"Did they ever catch the man?"

"Yes."

There was a tortured quality to her voice that warned him he hadn't heard the worst. "Tell me the rest, *mon coeur.*''

"Richard had done the same thing to another woman in the next county at the same time. When he was caught fleecing a third woman in upstate Vermont, they prosecuted him and called me as a witness. I had to sit there and tell all my neighbors and friends what a fool I'd been. Several had cautioned me about him, and there I was admitting I didn't have the sense of a turkey.''

The pain her words brought surprised Jean-Paul. He knew exactly the humiliation she'd endured. And he knew how that could scar a heart. He'd lived through a similar experience.

His hand cupped the back of her head and he tilted it up to gain access to her mouth. He tasted the saltiness of her tears on her lips. Her hands grasped handfuls of his shirt, bringing her closer to him.

She needed him, almost as badly as he needed her.

Suddenly, she pulled away. Anguish and regret turned her eyes the color of a storm-darkened sky. "I can't. I almost didn't survive the pain the last time, Jean-Paul." She held out her hand. "Please understand."

"You didn't survive, Angeline. You've allowed him to rob you of your heart."

"You don't understand."

"You're wrong. When I was arrested, I was engaged to a very well-connected lady. It didn't take her two hours after hearing about my arrest to break off the engagement. Her excuse was, How would it look to be associated with a criminal? It was *her* heart that was shallow. Not mine."

"What of the grudge you hold against the Boudreaux family?" she shot back. "That rules your life, just as Richard's actions rule mine."

Her words were like a slap in the face. "You are a Boudreaux after all."

He turned and walked out the front door.

Angie collapsed onto the sofa, ashamed at what she'd said to Jean-Paul. Her trembling hands covered her face and she bent over her knees. The Saint Christopher medal that he'd given her the previous night slipped out of the neck of her blouse.

She clasped the disk and looked at it. "I'm sorry, Jean-Paul," she whispered to the empty room. "So very sorry."

Hot tears ran down her cheeks. Her only excuse for being so hateful was that she'd been fighting for her very existence. If she'd surrendered her heart to Jean-Paul, yielded to the pulsing beat of life that he called forth, and then he turned from her, she knew she would never recover. What she'd felt for Richard paled in comparison to what she felt for Jean-Paul. She would never survive his leaving her. So wasn't it better not to give in to her feelings for him, than to risk losing it all?

The phone rang, causing Angie to jump. After taking a deep breath, she picked up the receiver. "Hello."

"I'm sorry," the woman said. "I must have the wrong number. I was calling for Jean-Paul Delahaye." She started to hang up.

"Wait," Angie cried. "You have the right number."

"Oh ... May I speak to him?"

"He isn't here right now. May I take a message?"

The woman at the other end paused. "Yes. My name is Nancy Wells. Tell him that I have the information on the Boudreaux case that he asked for."

"What did he ask you to find?"

"I can't share that with you."

"Please. I'm the reason Jean-Paul is trying to find out who took the case. The answer may tell us who killed my mother."

Angie had given up hope Nancy would answer, when she said, "Tell Jean-Paul that Edward Dias was the only attorney in the Boudreaux case. John Kirby never saw the file."

"Edward Dias?" She couldn't believe her ears.

"You know him?" Nancy asked.

"No, I don't." But the implications were stunning. "Thank you for the information." Her hand shook so badly that it took two tries to hang up the phone.

The news was explosive. And she was afraid of how Jean-Paul would react. She turned off the TV and sat back on the couch to wait for his return. Her mind raced with a dozen different ways to break the news to him. When she heard his footsteps on the porch, she sat up straighter.

He seemed surprised to see her, but he didn't say anything. He started toward the kitchen.

"Jean-Paul."

He stopped, but didn't turn around to face her. She ached for him, wanted to wrap her arms around him and comfort him. But how could she do that when she was the major cause of his pain?

"Nancy Wells called."

"What did she say?" he asked, turning toward her.

"She said Edward Dias was the only attorney on the Boudreaux case after you left."

"Not John Kirby?"

"No."

It was as if she'd laid a whip across his back. His face tightened with pain. "And I sent her to him." The moan that ripped from his mouth came from the deepest part of his soul.

She stood and took a step. He moved back, away from her.

"Go to bed, Angeline." He turned and walked into the kitchen, then out the side door into the night.

Angie glanced at the clock on the nightstand. It showed two minutes after two. It had been four hours since Jean-Paul had walked out of the house. She had changed into her nightgown and robe, but hadn't bothered going to bed. She knew she couldn't sleep.

She looked out the bedroom window, searching for him among the trees and tall grass. The ache in her chest expanded, robbing her of breath. Her fingers worried the Saint Christopher medal.

He was out there, hurting and blaming himself for Marianna's death. And he needed her.

The pull of that need overwhelmed all her fears and she hurried through the house out into the night.

Angeline.

She heard the cry as clearly as if he'd shouted it. She paused on the bottom step, scanning the area beyond the house. Through the leaves of a pecan tree, she saw him sitting on the ground, his back braced against the trunk.

The moonlight filtered through the rustling leaves making odd shapes of light dance over his extended legs, but his face was buried in the shadows of the night. She didn't need to see his expression. She felt it. Felt the blame he heaped on himself, and the despair.

She slowly approached him. "Jean-Paul."

He said nothing, but watched her approach. She held out her hand to him. "Come back inside with me. Please."

He didn't move and she couldn't simply turn around and leave him out here in his anguish. She knelt beside him and took his hand. His eyes were black with pain. "It wasn't your fault. How could you have known? And if you had, you never would've sent Marianna to him."

"I called him a friend," he whispered, his voice raw. "How could he have betrayed me like that? After I got out of prison, I called him and asked who'd taken over the case. He swore up and down it was John. That by the time the case was turned over to him, all the evidence had disappeared." His head fell back against the tree trunk.

She scooted closer and rested her other hand on his cheek. "Didn't you just tell me that my heart wasn't the one at fault, when I loved and lost? The blame isn't yours, Jean-Paul. It's Edward's."

He moaned, and buried his face between her breasts. His arms wrapped around her waist and she felt the violent tremors that shook his body. She closed her eyes, relief washing through her that he had given in to his sorrow.

Her hands held his head, her fingers lightly stroking the rich strands of his dark hair as the grief roared through him.

Her poor Jean-Paul. He had cared too deeply to guard his heart. And had paid the price. But she didn't doubt he'd love again. And oddly enough, his pain gave her the courage to risk her own heart.

She felt his lips press against the inside slope of her breast again and again in a series of small kisses.

"Angeline," he moaned, his voice dark with need. "My sweet angel."

His hold slackened and she pulled back to look into his eyes. Through the hurt, Angie saw something that drew her. A yearning. A love. She answered by settling her mouth on his. Her tongue plunged past his teeth, reveling in the unique masculine taste of him.

He pulled her across his lap, then cupped the back of her head, angling it so she had better access to his mouth. The heat and smell of him surrounded her and filled her senses. But more than that, there was a wildness in Jean-Paul, a natural joy in the pleasures of life that called to her. And that heat and passion melted the cage that held her soul.

The solid wall of his chest pressed against her side. Her fingers went to the buttons of his shirt. His hand stopped her.

"Are you sure, *chère?* Because there will be no turning back once we become lovers. You're not doing this simply to comfort me? You want this as much as I do, don't you, Angeline?"

Tears filled her eyes. That he would consider her feelings and needs at this time proved to her he was a man of honor. At that moment, she knew without doubt she loved Jean-Paul.

"Yes, Jean-Paul. I want this. I want you."

He released her hand. He didn't move or make any other gesture to further the intimacy, and she knew he was giving her one final chance to back out.

She leaned up and ran her tongue over his lower lip, and her fingers resumed their task of unbuttoning his shirt.

"Such a clever little tongue," he whispered. "Give it to me."

He settled his mouth over hers and allowed her to lead the dance. Angie's fingers got to the last button and pulled his shirt from his jeans. He helped her slide the material off his shoulders and down his arms.

Her hands skimmed up his arms and down over the muscles of his chest. "You are so beautiful," she breathed, laying her palms against the hardness of his belly.

He gritted his teeth and threw his head back.

"Jean-Paul, what's wrong?"

His laugh was a cross between a bark and a moan.

"Those sweet, little hands of yours are killing me. But it's a death I gladly welcome." He picked up each one and placed a kiss in the center of the palm.

His reaction made her giddy.

"I want more, Angel, but not out here. The sheriff's been known to snoop around people's homes. I think we should go inside."

Angie blushed and scrambled to her feet. The very idea of making love out in the open was scandalous. But oh, so appealing.

"Someday," he said as he stood, "I promise we'll come to this very spot and love the night away." He picked up his shirt and threw it over his shoulder, then swept Angie up into his arms.

"What are you doing?"

"Carrying you inside. I don't want to lose you now."

"You won't, Jean-Paul." She laid her head on his shoulder. "I promise."

As he carried her insignificant weight, Jean-Paul thanked heaven above for the miracle that had been dropped into his lap. He'd been lost in a pit of despair and anger, his heart crying out. Then suddenly his angel had been standing over him, holding out her hand to him.

He'd remembered silently calling out her name in his head. And until his dying day, no one would ever convince him that she hadn't heard that cry of anguish.

He felt the fine trembling in her body and promised himself that soon her tremors would be from pleasure and not fear.

He walked through the house to his room. Gently, he set her on the bed and threw his shirt on the chair. When he looked back at Angeline, her head was bowed and her hands were folded primly in her lap. She looked like a nervous bride.

And he could think of her no other way. His. She was his. He would fight Roger and Guy Boudreaux to his dying breath to protect her.

With his knuckle he lifted her chin, almost afraid of what he'd see in her eyes.

"Have you changed your mind?" He had to ask the question. His heart demanded it.

Her gaze traveled down his chest to his jeans, then back up to his face. She swallowed. "No."

He wanted to shout his victory to the night sky. He settled for a wicked smile. Crouching before her, he untied her robe and slowly peeled it down her arms. His lips followed the material.

"You taste like the sweet cream we put on strawberries," he murmured. Sitting back on his heels, he paused to study her. The Saint Christopher medal he'd given her rested between her breasts. He lifted the chain over her head. "You won't need this tonight." He kissed it and put it on the nightstand.

When he turned back to her, she soothed her fingers over his brow, then rested her hand on his cheek. "Love me, Jean-Paul. Show me what is meant to be between a man and woman."

She had just handed him the moon and stars. And the glory of the night sky rested within her eyes.

He stood, stepped out of his shoes, unsnapped his jeans and stepped out of his remaining clothes. He pulled her to her feet and helped her discard her nightgown. Resting one knee on the bed, he held out his hand to her. She took it and he pulled her down on top of him as he stretched out.

He laughed at her stunned expression.

"You're not quite so adventurous this time, *hein?*"

She gave him a shy smile. "Well..."

He turned, rolling them onto their sides, facing each other. This time he would take her slowly into that realm of the joining of hearts. And souls.

He ran his hand down her side and up her back. His mouth took hers while he caressed her with strong, sure strokes. He cupped her breast, his fingers finding the nipple, lightly playing with it.

She moaned and shifted her legs restlessly.

"Touch me, *mon coeur.* Your touch is like living fire eating me."

Shyly at first, then more boldly she moved her hands over his body. And the heat of her touch burned him.

He turned her onto her back and his mouth replaced his fingers on her breast. The little sound of surprise and pleasure plunged Jean-Paul further into a fiery furnace.

His fingers moved down her belly to the core of her. Angeline's eyes flew open and sought his. He settled himself between her thighs. His hands cupped her face. "Am I the first?"

Her body stiffened and her gazed slipped away. He had his answer, but at what price? He captured her chin and brought her gaze back to him. "Angel, listen to me. The reason I ask is because I'm concerned with how gentle to be. Nothing else."

His fingers played along her jaw. "But if the truth be told, *mon coeur,* I really am your first. The first to touch your heart." He smiled tenderly. "And you're my first."

Her body, under his, relaxed as his mouth sought hers. He felt her passion begin to build again. He kissed his way across her cheek to her ear. His tongue traced the whorls of her ear, then he lightly bit the lobe.

"Jean-Paul." He heard in her voice her need. Yet he continued to build the fire inside her. She would know completion, if it killed him. Her hands stroked up and down his back.

His mouth returned to hers, his tongue preparing her for the final act to come. She rolled her hips under him and he positioned himself at her woman's core and drove home.

"Jean-Paul," she panted as he moved in and out of her. He felt her tension building, building, and then she screamed as she convulsed around him.

The feel of her heat around him plunged him through the final barrier. As he came back to reality, Jean-Paul knew he'd come through the fire, died and come out the other side a different man. A whole man.

Chapter 15

With her head resting on Jean-Paul's chest and her body curled around his side, Angie listened to the beat of his heart. She watched the first rays of dawn wash across the sky. When she woke minutes earlier, a sense of well-being she hadn't experienced since childhood had surrounded her.

She now knew what heaven on earth was. Jean-Paul had shown her that place last night. What she'd shared with him in no way resembled what had passed between her and Richard years before. She tried not to remember, but those other, more distant memories came flooding back.

She and Richard had gone back to her apartment after spending the evening at a friend's party. She'd had several drinks, and Richard had had even more. After a few uninspiring kisses, Richard talked her into seeing if they were sexually compatible. The brief, hurried encounter on her couch left her wondering what all those romance novels touted. She'd found the experience totally negligible.

That is until now. Until Jean-Paul.

Her hand idly stroked across Jean-Paul's chest. The pleasure he'd shown her was indescribable. She had reveled in each touch of his hands, each brush of his lips, the feel of his body imprinting itself on her. It was quite a surprise to know she was so hedonistic. It was also very disturbing.

But what had truly shocked her was the feeling of oneness she'd shared with Jean-Paul. What had happened between them went beyond the physical. They'd touched souls and exchanged secrets. And Angie knew she'd given him her heart. The implications of that terrified her.

"Ah, Angel, what a wonderful feeling to wake to. Your soft fingers on me."

Her hand jerked away as if burned. He captured her wrist and placed her hand back where it was.

"*Non, chère.* I like your touch." His accompanying wicked smile left no doubt as to what he meant.

Her hand slipped down his body to close around his manhood. His eyes widened and his body convulsed.

"This is what you had in mind, *hein?*" she asked mischievously.

He threw his head back and laughed. "I've made you a Cajun, yes?"

The fleeting thought danced through her brain that maybe he had. "Perhaps. You've certainly shown me how to appreciate, uh, things."

"Is that right? Well, because you're such a perceptive *pichouette,* and such a fast learner, I want to reward you."

Indeed, she was *so* fast a learner, she didn't recognize herself. But he pushed her back into the pillows, leaving her no time to worry about it.

Later. She'd worry later.

"Your choice, Angel. Shower or make coffee?"

She slipped out of his hold and ran to the bathroom.

"You make the coffee," she called out over her shoulder, then shut the bathroom door.

After viewing her charming backside on her dash from the bed to the bathroom, Jean-Paul was tempted to join her in that shower. He discarded the notion. His angel was tender, and to take her a second time this morning would be greedy.

Throwing back the sheet, he slipped into his jeans and padded into the living room. As he walked by the telephone, it rang, and he lifted the receiver.

"Jean-Paul, this is Nancy. Did you get my message last night?"

The subject he had purposely avoided thinking about came roaring back. He steeled himself against the pain. "Yes, Angeline gave it to me."

"I was nervous about giving it to her."

"There was no need."

"Good."

He could see his former secretary, a tiny woman with blue-black hair and an infectious laugh. He had probably been the only male in the office who had not tried to hit on her. That was probably one of the reasons she felt a loyalty to him.

"Jean-Paul, Edward caught me in the file room and asked me what I was doing. I made up a story about getting some background information on another case. I don't think he believed me. He's watched me like a hawk ever since, and this morning I was notified I was being transferred to another office."

That's just what he needed, to put someone else in danger. "I'm sorry, Nancy."

"Don't worry about it. I was getting uncomfortable in that office. Odd things were starting to happen. I called to warn you, and tell you if you need any more information I won't be able to help.''

"You've helped more than you know." He hung up the phone and took a deep breath. The bitterness of Edward's betrayal came roaring back, leaving a bad taste in his mouth. He didn't know if Edward had sold him out after he'd been set up or if he'd been in on it from the beginning, but Jean-Paul vowed he was going to find out.

He picked up the phone, called Ted Peters and related the conversation he'd had with Nancy. "If you still have any friends on that commission, Ted, I think you need to suggest they investigate Edward. Something's going on."

"I will," Ted answered. Ted had left the commission six months before Jean-Paul's arrest. Ted had been fed up with the bureaucracy and the dealings that went on. "How's Angie?"

"Someone burned down her house, Ted."

"They what?"

Jean-Paul sighed. "Someone hit her on the head, then set fire to the house."

Ted cursed. "Is she okay?"

"She's fine, but she's staying with me until we find out who's behind all this. Call me and let me know how things are progressing in New Orleans."

"I will. You keep that little girl safe."

"With my last breath."

Angie rushed through her shower, afraid Jean-Paul would join her at any minute, disappointed when he didn't. She hurriedly dressed in another borrowed skirt and blouse. Today, sometime, she needed Jean-Paul to take her shopping to replace some of the items she had lost in the fire.

A wave of anger and sorrow washed over her. Marianna's house was gone. The pictures, letters, her birth certificate and adoption records gone in the blaze.

A knock on the door interrupted her thoughts. "Angeline."

She checked herself in the mirror and wiped away the tear on her cheek. Fixing a smile on her face, she threw open the door. Jean-Paul's grin faded when he saw her. He placed the cup of coffee on the sink and rested his hands on her shoulders.

"What's wrong?"

She shook her head, not wanting to discuss it. "Nothing."

"What is it, Angel? And don't say nothing again. I see it in your eyes."

His perceptiveness only added to her confusion. It was as if Jean-Paul could see clearly into her soul, and she had no shield against his knowing gaze. "I was thinking we need to go and buy me some clothes today."

His hands ran up and down her arms in a soothing motion. "And?"

Suddenly, it was too much effort to try to hide anything from him. Besides, she wanted to share her pain with him. "I was thinking of the pictures and letters that burned."

He gathered her into his arms and rocked her. "It's all right, *chère*. You're safe, and that's all that matters."

As his heat sank into her, she knew he was right. Physically she was safe. But what of her psyche, her emotions? What had happened to the Angie Fitzgerald who came to Mirabeau less than a week ago? That woman no longer existed.

They arrived at the historical society's building at ten. Henri Colton was waiting for them at the front door.

"Bonjour," Henri called out as he hurried down the steps. "How are you this fine morning, Angeline?" He clasped her hands and kissed her on each cheek.

"Wonderful, Henri," she answered.

An odd twinge of jealousy assaulted Jean-Paul. It was a common enough greeting and he knew Henri had no designs on Angeline. Still, it irked him.

The old man turned to him. "And you, Jean-Paul? How you doin'?"

"Fine," Jean-Paul answered.

"Well, come. Let me show you what Marianna was working on."

They followed Henri into the building that at one time had been the home of a prosperous planter. The ground floor of the two-story structure had originally been used for storage. It now contained exhibits of farming tools and clothing worn at the time the house was built. The second story had been restored to its pre-Civil War glory.

Henri took them on a quick tour of the facility, then led them outside to the bachelor quarters. "What did your friend the biology professor say when you called her?" Henri asked.

Angeline gasped. "Oh, Henri, I forgot to call. Guy was waiting for us when we got back and—it was very confusing. And one thing lead to another." She touched his arm. "I promise I'll call Sharon today."

Henri threw Jean-Paul a look of mutual understanding of what those other things were. Pulling the keys out of his pants pocket, Henri unlocked the door. "This is where Marianna worked. We keep old journals in here, papers that local residents have donated, anything that is a record of the people who lived in this parish. We also have copies of many early parish deeds, birth and death certificates. And several diaries."

Angie stepped into a thoroughly modern room. Bookshelves lined the walls. Several filing cabinets were back-to-back in the center of the room, separating two desks. A small computer sat on one of the desks.

"That's where Marianna worked." Henri pointed to the computer.

"Then there should be a disk around here where she kept her work," Angeline said, stepping forward.

"That Marianna, she sure did like that computer. Me, I know nothin' of this. I'm too old for such nonsense." He turned to her. "But you are welcome to use this machine and search through her things."

She smiled at him, and Henri straightened his slumped shoulders and sauntered out, whistling.

"I don't know why everyone said he was such an old...uh—"

"Coot?"

"Character. He's been nothing but wonderful to me."

Jean-Paul leaned down and stole a quick kiss from her. "You, Angel, definitely have a strong effect on men. I've never seen that old Cajun act like a schoolboy. But you worked one of your miracles on him."

She sat at the desk and he leaned over her shoulder. "Do you know how to work one of these things?" he asked.

"Of course," she replied, glancing up at him. "What do you think I kept my lecture notes on? And my grades, and—"

"I get the idea."

Angeline turned on the machine and reviewed the files.

"Anything?" he asked.

"Jean-Paul, why don't you—" she glanced around the desk and spotted a stack of files "—go through these and see if there's anything important."

"You're trying to get rid of me, aren't you?"

She gave him a blinding smile. "You are such a perceptive man. Here." She picked up the files and dumped them in his arms.

He took the folders and sat at the other desk. He could see her over the metal cabinets. She was in her element here. She looked comfortable, even relaxed as she went through the disks on Marianna's desk.

They worked all morning. The folders contained notes on various families, interviews that Marianna had done with the living relatives. Several times, Marianna referred to different diaries and journals in the historical society's archives.

"Jean-Paul."

Angeline's voice brought his head up. "Yes."

"Something's wrong."

He stood and came around to see the computer screen. "What is it?"

She pointed to the screen. "You see the listing of files? It's part of a book. Chapters one to thirteen."

"So?"

"But look." She brought up the file labeled: Outline. "You see. She'd planned twenty chapters. Fourteen through twenty were to cover the years 1920-present. Now where are the other chapters?"

"Did you go through all the disks?"

She gave a quelling look. "Yes. And I've searched her desk. There are no other disks."

How come he had never noticed before how her nose crinkled when she was irritated? Suddenly, he wanted to hustle her out to his truck, drive back to his house and spend the rest of the day making love to her.

Immediately, on the heels of that impulse, came guilt. Guilt that all he could think of was his wants, when they were close to discovering why Marianna was murdered.

"Maybe she put the disk in a safe place away from this site."

"That's an idea. Henri might know something." She turned off the machine and they walked back to the main house. Henri was talking to a young woman in her twenties, who wore a sullen expression. When he spotted them, he excused himself.

"Finished already?" Henri asked.

Angeline shook her head. "No. We came to ask you if Marianna left a disk with you."

"Disk? Disk? What kind of a disk, *chère?* One you throw or play on a phonograph?"

Jean-Paul watched Angeline's bewilderment change to amusement. She reached out and touched Henri's arm. And much to his astonishment, Henri grinned right back at her.

"No, that's not what I meant. The disk I'm referring to goes into the computer. It's flat and square." She held up her hands to show him the size. "And about so big."

He clicked his tongue. "*Non,* me, I don't mess with that nonsense. That's for the young'uns, not for the likes of this one."

"Could she have left it with your assistant over there?"

Henri glanced over his shoulder. "That busybody," the old man mumbled under his breath. "Claire, come here."

The haughty angle of Claire's chin set Jean-Paul on edge. He had the feeling this wasn't going to be a pleasant exchange.

"Yes, M'sieu Colton."

"Did Marianna leave anything with you?"

"No."

Henri turned back to Angeline. "See. Marianna didn't leave anything with us. Is there something missing?"

"I'm not sure, Henri."

Claire's eyes widened and her jaw dropped. "Henri," she gasped.

Henri frowned at the young woman. "Isn't a tour arriving soon?"

"Yes."

Henri waved her off with his hand. "Then go. Prepare."

Claire hesitated before turning to Angeline. "I didn't believe everyone when they said you looked exactly like Jacqueline Boudreaux. You do. But you know what they say, blood will always tell."

If she'd yelled the ugly phrase "You're a bastard, Angeline Fitzgerald," her meaning couldn't have been clearer.

Angeline's lips tightened, but she didn't defend herself. Jean-Paul felt Angeline's anguish and shame as surely as if it had been his.

He opened his mouth to reply, but Henri launched into a diatribe of French. Jean-Paul didn't understand it all, since Henri's Cajun accent was pronounced, but he did pick out "ungrateful child" and several other descriptive words about Claire's character.

Henri finished his tirade in English. "I don't care if your *papa* gave much money. You won't insult a guest of mine. Apologize."

Claire's eyes shot sparks of loathing at Angeline, as if it were Angeline's fault she had no manners. "I'm sorry."

"Go," Henri commanded. He turned to Angeline. "I regret that rotten child was rude. Her *papa* bought her this job. Come." He walked out of the building. "Claire's *papa* thinks that his money can buy anything. Too bad it don't buy graceful children."

Jean-Paul thought he couldn't have stated it better. As they walked down the pebbled path, Jean-Paul grasped Angeline's hand and gave it a gentle squeeze. She smiled at him, but he still detected a trace of hurt in her eyes.

Once inside the office Henri said, "Now tell me, Angeline, what you think has happened."

Jean-Paul noted that Henri addressed his question to Angeline and not him. He didn't take offense, because if she could get the information from the secretive old man, the better for them.

Angeline explained what she had found. "I don't know if we're on a wild-goose chase. Do you know if Marianna wrote those missing chapters?"

Henri nodded. "She sure did. She told me she'd almost finished the book. I know she'd written up through World War II."

"And she put that on the computer?"

"Yes. I watched as she started chapter sixteen. It was the beginning of the Depression and Huey Long. Did you know Roger was a good friend of Huey's?"

She sat down in the desk chair. "Then there's a missing disk."

"And if I don't miss my guess," Jean-Paul said, "it contained evidence that got Marianna killed."

Henri frowned. "Maybe she hid it here in this room, yes?"

"The only way we'll know is to search," Jean-Paul replied.

They spent the balance of the day searching through the bookshelves and filing cabinets. Henri noted that several journals and a box of documents were missing. All items were from the early twentieth century. The old man huffed and puffed about the missing material.

"Who would do such a thing?"

"The same person who killed Marianna."

Claire appeared at the office door. "I've locked the house, M'sieu Colton, and I'm going home."

Henri held out his hand for the keys, which Claire surrendered.

"Are you the only one with a key?" Jean-Paul asked after Claire's departure.

"Yes. But I leave the keys in my desk, in the small office I have in the main house."

Jean-Paul rubbed his chin. "So it wouldn't be hard for someone to take the keys and make a copy, then put it back in your desk without you knowing about it? Right?"

The old man seemed reluctant to agree. "Yes," he finally said. "You want to take home Marianna's files so you can look at them this weekend?"

"Yes," Angeline answered.

Jean-Paul shouldn't have been surprised at Henri's offer, but he was. Henri Colton, who wouldn't so much as let a piece of paper be taken off society grounds, had offered Angeline an entire box full of important papers. Another miracle he attributed to Angeline.

"Thank you, Henri. That will be very helpful."

The old man beamed.

Jean-Paul returned the folders he'd reviewed to the box and picked it up. Henri locked up after them and followed them to Jean-Paul's truck, then took Angeline's hand. "I look forward to seeing you on Monday. If you need anything else, *chère*, come to my houseboat. I will get it for you."

As they watched the old man drive away, Jean-Paul said, "Angeline, this is a grand day in parish history. Henri Colton invited someone to his house. M'dame Eleanor will not believe this."

"Maybe we should invite Henri and Miss Eleanor to the house at the same time. Something tells me they would be interested in seeing each other."

Jean-Paul started the engine. "Are you matchmaking?"

Snapping on her seat belt, she said, ''After all this time, someone should.''

As he pulled out of the parking lot, he saw the sheriff's car sitting across the road. A chill raced up his spine.

Chapter 16

Jean-Paul parked his truck in front of Miss Sophie's dress shop. The whitewashed building, circa 1940, with a green cloth awning, also housed the only hardware store in town.

Angie gave him a puzzled frown. "Why are we stopping here?"

"You need clothes for tonight," he explained. "Something elegant."

It amazed her that he had remembered such a mundane detail, when she hadn't. "That's right. Dinner with the Boudreaux. I'll need a dress."

The reminder of the coming event made his mouth flatten into a thin line. "Come."

She followed him to the front door of the shop and glanced at the decals for bank cards on the glass pane. Grabbing his arm to stop him, she whispered, "I don't have any money or credit cards to buy anything. I mean, with everything that's happened, I simply forgot." She looked around and saw a bank sign down the street. Suddenly it was important that she maintain this small amount of independence. Pointing, she said, "We can go there and have my bank transfer funds."

Jean-Paul looked at his watch. "It's four-thirty, Angeline. Your bank in Vermont would be closed."

Her spirit fell.

"I'll pay, then you can repay me on Monday when the bank is open."

She didn't want to take more from him. And yet, his solution made the most sense. "All right."

Jean-Paul held open the door for her. The saleswoman behind the counter saw them enter but made no move to help them. Angie didn't know if the insult was directed at her or Jean-Paul, but no matter who it was intended for, the action annoyed her. She glanced at Jean-Paul. The expression on his face was closed, but from the set of his shoulders Angie knew the woman's behavior angered him.

Another woman entered the shop and immediately the saleswoman jumped up to help her. As Angie looked through the dresses, she heard the women whispering.

"That's her."

"And with him. 'Course it figures."

Angie's hands gripped the plastic hanger she was holding so hard it broke.

Jean-Paul circled the rack of clothes and planted himself between the two women. The saleswoman lifted her chin. "Do you need something?"

Angie immediately knew she had to defuse the situation before something awful happened. "Jean-Paul, I don't see anything here I want. Let's go."

He hesitated a moment, then nodded. With a parting glare at the women, Jean-Paul escorted Angie from the building. Apart from her own embarrassment, she felt protective toward him. How dare those women talk about Jean-

Paul that way? She was tempted to go back in there and give them a piece of her mind.

"There's a place in the next town where we can go," Jean-Paul said.

She let the swell of emotion she felt for him fill her eyes. "What I have on will be fine."

He took in the simple white shirt and blue straight skirt. "No. We'll get you something that will do justice to an angel."

She leaned up and brushed a kiss across his lips. The look of surprise on his face made her chuckle. Her impulsive action shocked her, too. Kissing a man in public was definitely out of character, but the gratitude and warmth in Jean-Paul's green eyes eased her doubts.

"Well, well, what do we have here?" Dennis Mathers's voice intruded into their isolated world.

Angie closed her eyes, hoping the sheriff would go away. She felt Jean-Paul's entire body tense.

"What do you want, Dennis?" Jean-Paul asked, turning to the sheriff.

"Why, nothin'." Dennis slid his hands into his front pockets and rocked back on his heels. "I just saw the little lady walk out of Sophie's and came over to see if she's recovered from the fire."

"She's fine," Jean-Paul answered tersely.

"I got a call from the rental company today," Dennis casually said. "They wanted to verify if your car was really destroyed in the fire."

Angie stopped and looked at him. "How did they know about the car?"

"I called them before I came to get you at the hospital," Jean-Paul replied. His gaze drilled Dennis. "What did you say?"

"I told them sure, it was true."

The piercing whistle Jean-Paul gave made her jump. "I'm surprised, Dennis. Without any cash crossing your palm, you told the truth."

Dennis surged forward, his beefy fist pulled back. Before he could throw the punch, a cane came down on his knuckles.

"Behave, you two," Miss Eleanor commanded both men. "It's a disgrace to see two grown men taunting each other like boys in short pants."

Jean-Paul and Dennis looked chagrined. Neither man had the gall to meet the little, old lady's gaze. The sight of two big, powerful men being put in their place by a little bitty woman was almost comical. Miss Eleanor summoned the deputy from his squad car. "Come and drive the sheriff—" she waved her cane "—wherever he needs to go."

She said nothing until the sheriff had left. Miss Eleanor turned to Jean-Paul, a expression of reprimand on her face. "What do you have to say for yourself, *hein?* Scrapping like a naughty boy in the street. Shame."

He shrugged. "The man's an ass."

"That may be, but you don't have to stoop to his level."

Jean-Paul grinned. "You are right, M'dame."

She lifted her chin. "Of course. Now, what were you doing in Sophie's?"

"Trying to buy Angeline a dress for dinner at the Boudreaux mansion tonight. She refused our patronage."

Eleanor waved her hand. "Sophie never had a lick of sense. Come, take me home. I think I can solve your problem."

He leaned down and kissed her wrinkled cheek. "You are heaven-sent."

"You can be a smart boy when you want to be."

He laughed as he helped the women into his truck. "On the way, I'll tell you about our visit to Henri's houseboat."

Miss Eleanor's eyebrows disappeared into her hairline. "Henri? Henri who?"

"Henri Colton."

"What?" the old woman shrieked.

"It's a long story, M'dame. A long story."

Jean-Paul glanced at the closed bedroom door, behind which Angeline was getting dressed for their dinner engagement with the Boudreaux family. He fiddled with the tie around his neck. He hadn't worn a suit since his trial, but for Angeline he would endure the heat and humidity in this getup.

He sat down, throwing his suit jacket over the arm of the couch. A smile played around his lips as he remembered M'dame Eleanor's reaction to their tale about the trip to Henri's houseboat. The little, old lady had kept a running commentary in Cajun French as Angeline related their experience. Angeline's theory about M'dame having a certain softness for Henri was lent credence by her actions.

He leaned forward and pulled several folders from the box they'd brought from the historical society. If he was going to have to wait on Angeline, he might as well put the time to good use.

He closed his eyes and offered up a silent plea that he'd have enough patience and common sense to endure this evening. It would take a major stroke of luck, if he made it through the night without crossing swords with Roger and Catlin.

He glanced at the name on the first folder, Roucheaux. He opened the file and read about his former schoolmate Émile's grandparents and great-grandparents. The notation at the end of the notes puzzled him.

"Jean-Paul." Angeline's voiced floated down the hall.

He heard the tap of her heels on the wooden floor and glanced up. She was a vision in the dress M'dame Eleanor had given her. As soon as the old woman heard what had happened at Sophie's, she went to her closet and presented Angeline with a dress she called her tea dress. The pleated bodice ran past Angeline's tiny waist to the tops of her hips, then flared out in a skirt of soft, gauzy material that flowed around her shapely legs. A fine lace collar framed her lovely neck and delicate collarbone. The shoes and hose they had purchased on the way home. The champagne color of the material gave it the appearance of a wedding dress rather than a tea dress, and Angeline looked like a bride. He could think of her in no other way.

She fiddled with one of the ivory combs that held back her hair from her face. Her hands smoothed down her hair, then toyed with the silver chain that disappeared into the neckline of the dress.

"How do I look?" She sounded unsure of her appeal.

Jean-Paul had no qualms about how good she looked. He felt the effect like a hard jab in his middle. Coming to his feet, he drew her into his arms and took her mouth with his. She moaned in surrender, her arms sliding around him.

His natural inclination was to take her back into the bedroom and undo what she had spent so much time and effort doing, but common sense intruded. He stepped away. "Does that answer your question, Angel?"

She looked thoroughly kissed and overwhelmingly tempting. "I would've believed you if you'd simply said I looked okay."

He cupped her face, his fingers spreading over her cheeks and neck. Her skin was soft, smooth, and made him ache to touch more. "*Non*. You don't simply look 'okay.' You are breathtaking, as beautiful as the first magnolia blossom in the spring."

Her hand came up, grasped his and brought it to her lips. "Thank you." Warmth and passion filled her eyes.

"The hell with the Boudreaux. Come back in the bedroom with me, *chère.*" When he reached for her, she danced away from him.

She wagged her finger at him. "No, you don't. Do you know how long it took me to get ready?"

He threw his head back and laughed. "Aw, so you are really not an angel, because only a flesh-and-blood woman would say such a thing."

Wrinkling her nose at him, she said, "Have you found anything in those folders?"

"Background notes on different families, research from other books, things like that. I think if we're going to unravel this mystery, we're going to have to read every one of those folders several times, to find whatever it is we're looking for." He pointed to the last page of notes on the Roucheaux family. "In this file, Marianna referred back to document twenty in file forty-two. I guess that's some sort of bibliography. We'll need to find that on the shelves when we go back."

He closed the manila folder, replaced it in the box, then carried the box into the kitchen.

"What are you doing?" Angeline asked, trailing behind him.

He opened the pantry door, sat the box down and pulled up a trap door in the floor. "Hiding this *bébé*. If we have unexpected visitors, they won't find this evidence."

"Do you really think that's necessary?"

He glanced up at her. "Can you still doubt it?" Her continued innocence amazed him.

Her expression fell. "No," she whispered, then walked back into the living room. Jean-Paul felt lower than a slug.

He quickly secured the box in the hidey-hole, then went in search of Angeline. He found her standing in front of the window, staring out. He came up behind her, slipped his arms around her waist and placed a kiss on her neck.

"I'm sorry, *chère*."

Her hands covered his. "It's all right, Jean-Paul. Sometimes I forget to be cautious."

He nipped her ear. "That's what I'm here for—to think of these things and keep you safe."

Glancing over her shoulder, she gave him a sultry look. "That's all you're here for?"

He patted her on her rear and stepped away. "Saucy *fille*. Come, let's go before I give in to my desire."

On the drive to "The Mansion," as Jean-Paul referred to the Boudreaux house, the mood in the truck turned from gentle teasing to a dark tension. Angie fidgeted with the tissue in her hands, shredding it into little pieces, clueing in Jean-Paul that she was nervous. His somber mood didn't help ease her mind.

He turned his truck onto a brick drive lined with roses and honeysuckle. When the two-story mansion came into view, Angie gasped.

"Quite a sight, *hein?*"

She looked at him, then back at the house. "It's very impressive."

"Yeah. The Boudreaux go in for the big and showy. They want everyone to know just how important they are and how much money they possess." His voice dripped with contempt. Angie threw him a worried frown.

He parked his truck right in front of the massive double doors. "My truck is not exactly the kind of distinguished vehicle these people want sitting out in front of their elegant place." He nodded. "Good." He got out and slammed his door.

Guy emerged from the house. "Angeline." He reached her before Jean-Paul did and helped her out of the truck. An odd expression crossed Guy's face as he examined her from head to toe. "You look exquisite, my dear. Why, if I didn't know better, I'd think you were my dear Aunt Jacqueline come back to haunt us."

Jacqueline has been the only worthwhile one in the bunch, Jean-Paul thought. Her heart was so kind, she never would have come back to disturb her own.

Guy finally released Angeline's hands and turned to acknowledge Jean-Paul's presence. The old boy probably wasn't any happier having Jean-Paul to dinner than he was being here.

"Jean-Paul, how are you this evening?" Guy said in well-modulated English.

The whiskey lacing Guy's breath confirmed Jean-Paul's guess. He felt only contempt for the man standing before him. It still amazed him that Marianna and Angeline saw anything admirable in this coward.

Angeline laid her hand on Jean-Paul's arm and gently squeezed. He understood the silent message. He plastered on his most charming smile.

"I'm just grand, Guy," he said with forced cheerfulness.

After a long, awkward silence, Guy said, "Why don't we go inside? Father and Catlin are waiting." He offered Angeline his arm. Much to Jean-Paul's disgust, she took it and entered the house.

"Only for you, Angel," Jean-Paul muttered under his breath as he followed, "would I endure having dinner with these snakes."

Guy led them inside to the formal living room. Catlin sat on a white French-provincial couch, a cocktail in her well-manicured hand. Roger stood by the window, his hands folded behind his back, an appraising look in his eye.

"Angeline, you remember my father, Roger," Guy said, escorting her to Roger's side.

"Yes." She nodded, but offered no other gesture of polite meeting. No smile, no extending of her small hand.

Good girl, Jean-Paul cheered in his head. *Make him squirm.*

"I'm glad you consented to join us tonight. It will give me an opportunity to apologize for my outrageous behavior in court the other day. You came as somewhat of a surprise."

I'll just bet, Jean-Paul thought. *Her appearance shot your plans for Marianna's property all to hell.*

"I'm afraid we've all been surprised by the revelations of this past week," Angeline supplied. "I didn't know until I arrived here that I was adopted."

The muscles of Roger's neck tensed, but the old wolf managed a smile.

Guy guided Angeline toward the couch. "And you've also met my wife, Catlin."

Catlin set her drink on the coffee table. "Of course we've met," Catlin gushed. "And much to my chagrin, it was under the worst of circumstances. I hope you'll overlook my words that night. I was afraid you might try to use your relationship with Guy to enrich your bank balance."

"That's quite enough, Catlin," Guy commanded.

She put on a pouty moue. "But dear, I was only trying to protect you."

"We all know what you were trying to protect," Jean-Paul groused.

The older woman glared daggers at him. He didn't care one whit. It was Angeline's look of displeasure that reminded him that he needed to behave.

A young woman dressed in a maid's uniform appeared at the doorway. "Mr. Boudreaux, dinner."

Angie breathed a sigh of relief. Maybe if everyone was eating, they wouldn't spar with each other. Again, Guy offered her his arm. She glanced over her shoulder at Jean-Paul, silently pleading with him to understand, then looped her arm around Guy's. The other three followed them into the dining room.

A massive chandelier hung over the table, the hundreds of prisms shooting colored rays of light all over the room. Angie stopped, awed by the sight. "That's so beautiful. I've never seen one so..."

"Gaudy?" Jean-Paul whispered as he walked by her.

"You like that?" Roger asked, strolling into the room. "I designed it myself. It was made in Paris and shipped over here right before France fell in World War II."

"It was one of the first things I fell in love with when I came here as a new bride," Catlin remarked. "It spoke of distinction and the uniqueness of this family."

Jean-Paul rolled his eyes but thankfully said nothing. Of course, Catlin's words said it all. The Boudreaux family had money, and Catlin liked that, as evidenced by the enormous diamond gracing her right hand.

Angie shook her head. She was beginning to think too much like Jean-Paul. Her innate sense of fairness screamed that she needed to give these people a chance to prove themselves and not take for granted Jean-Paul's judgment on their character. But when had he been wrong before, *hein?*

Hein? Hein? He really was turning her into a Cajun.

"You're smiling, Angie," Roger said. "Care to share what it is that amuses you?"

"Father, don't put her on the spot like that," Guy protested.

"I want to know, too," Catlin chimed in.

All eyes were fixed on her. "I'm pleased to be here, that's all."

Sweet liar, Jean-Paul mouthed.

Her words seemed to smooth over the rough spot and dinner went amazingly well. Guy told Angie about his law practice and mentioned his upcoming bid for the governorship of Louisiana. Angie turned to Roger. "I'm sure you're very proud of Guy."

"Yes. The governorship has been our goal for a long time." The dark hunger in Roger's eyes made her shiver. He wanted power.

Angie glanced at her father. His face showed no emotion, as if he feared he would break down into tears if he let himself feel.

"Yeah, it's amazing what money can buy," Jean-Paul said. "But that's what you use money for, isn't it, Roger?"

"Jean-Paul," Angie gasped, reaching out to him.

"No, Angeline. You need to understand." He pinned Roger with a burning glare. "Why don't you share with your granddaughter how you made your money?"

Roger brought his cup of coffee to his lips, sipped, then set it in the saucer. "I made my money on oil-and-gas leases in this and several parishes around here."

"And?" Jean-Paul prompted.

Roger shrugged. "And my business dealings proved profitable."

Jean-Paul grasped Angie's arm, pulling her around in her chair to look at him. "He ran through the parish, acting like a savior, buying the leases dirt cheap. It was the Depression and people thought he was an angel sent from heaven to rescue them from starving. Within weeks of his buying the last lease, oil was discovered in the next parish." Jean-Paul threw a razor-hard glare at Roger. "He spent the rest of the

Depression getting rich, while everyone else got poorer and poorer.''

Angie pulled her arm free of Jean-Paul's grasp. Roger sat calmly, drinking his coffee. Guy turned pasty white and downed in one gulp the contents of the highball glass in front of him. Catlin's hand tightened around the fork she was using to eat her red velvet cake.

''Is that not so, Roger?'' Jean-Paul demanded.

Roger toyed with his water glass, an air of unconcern resting on his shoulders like a cloak. ''Yes, it's true. I was lucky.''

''I'd bet a thousand dollars that you had a geological report in your hot, little hands before you made any of those offers.'' Jean-Paul's eyes narrowed and he tapped his finger against his mouth. ''Could be you even knew someone with the oil company, and he told you about what they suspected.''

The tension vibrating throughout the room thickened until the air was hard to breathe.

Roger crossed his arms and leaned back in his chair. ''Yours is a vivid imagination. You should write fiction. Or—'' he leaned forward ''—if you think you can back up your lies, have the attorney general charge me with something. Otherwise, quit accusing me of crimes. I could always sue you for slander.''

Jean-Paul stood. His chest heaved in and out like bellows. Placing his hands on the table, he pierced Roger with a look of pure hatred. ''But if I did, you'd simply buy off the state attorney like you did before. Or would you kill me, like you did Marianna? What did she have on you, you old bastard, that you needed to kill her?''

Roger stood. ''I don't have to take talk like that, in my own house, from an ex-con who's the son of a drunk.'' Stepping behind his chair, he ordered, ''Get out.''

Jean-Paul straightened, but the air of menace clinging to him made Angie want to flinch. "You have nothing to fear from me, Roger. Physically, that is. I wouldn't lay a hand on an old man like you. But if I can find evidence to ruin you, I'll do it. That's a vow. And I won't stop until I'm dead or you're indicted."

A deadly silence fell over the room.

Angeline tugged on Jean-Paul's shirt. "Let's leave."

He looked down into her face and seemed to come back to himself. Although some of the roiling anger left his eyes, there remained a burning fire. He nodded, turned and headed out.

Angie shot Guy a look of regret.

"Go," he softly commanded.

With a parting nod, she hurried after Jean-Paul. He was waiting for her in his truck, the engine idling, his hands clenched around the steering wheel, his suit jacket and tie lying on the seat. She barely had time to close her door before Jean-Paul hit the accelerator and careened away from the curb.

Angie clamped her mouth closed to keep from shouting at him. She wanted to be in control of herself, not a raving lunatic, when she took him to task for his behavior at dinner.

He raced through town a good thirty miles over the speed limit. The second corner he skidded around broke Angie's control. "Stop!" she yelled.

He didn't react. She grabbed the sleeve of his shirt and tugged. "Stop, right this minute."

After a quick glance at her, he slowed the truck and stopped by a curb. Immediately, Angie jumped out and slammed the door with enough force to make the old Ford rattle.

"What do you think you're doin'?" he asked, one hand on the seat bracing him so he could see out the passenger window. "Get back in the truck."

"No." She began to walk.

She heard him get out. "Angeline, it's another two miles to the cutoff to my house. You can't walk, *chère*. It's dark and someone might not see you on the road."

She whirled on him. "You're worried about my safety?" She poked him in the chest with her finger. "I'm probably safer walking than riding with you, Mr. Delahaye. I'd have been safer going over Niagara Falls in a barrel than riding with you." She spun around and started off.

Jean-Paul snagged her wrist, whirling her back to face him. "I'm sorry, Angeline. I was driving like a madman. Come back to the truck. I promise to drive at a normal speed."

Angie looked around at the dark and unfamiliar landscape. Her anger at Jean-Paul's behavior hadn't lessened, but it would be stupid to wander around blindly on this road. "All right," she reluctantly agreed.

"Good." He tried to slip his arm around her shoulders but she stepped away from him. He studied her in the beam from the headlights. "So, I'm gonna catch hell from you for my conduct at the mansion, *hein?*"

"Don't you agree that your manners were sadly lacking? To insult your host like that was inexcusable. Last I heard, Emily Post didn't condone accusing your dinner host of murder."

"*Non, chère.* What is inexcusable is how Roger Boudreaux feeds on the misfortune of others. He's an evil man and so far he has been rewarded for his wickedness. *Non*, I don't apologize for standing up to wrong. If more people did it, this world would be a better place. Then men like Roger wouldn't get away with murder."

The rage burning her brain ate up all her caution. She took a step toward him, her hand resting on her hips. "Are you saying that I'm one of those people who allow evil men to rule? That I just turn a blind eye to their wrong deeds? Is that what you're saying to me, Jean-Paul? Tell me, is that what you're saying?" She shook with the tremors of anger and hurt.

He ran his fingers through his dark hair. "*Non, chère.* Me, I'm just crazy with the fury that man creates in me."

"He baits you, you know that?"

Jean-Paul kicked a rock out of the road. "*Mais sho'*, I know. 'Course, he likes a good fight now and then. It's sure that Guy don't give him no back talk."

"Why are you always down on my father?"

"Because Guy is a gutless wonder. He's never once in his lifetime stood up to his *papa*." He spat the last word, as if it left a bad taste in his mouth.

"Maybe if he had someone to believe in him, he could."

"He had Marianna, and he threw his chance away."

A car sped by, honking its horn.

"Come, let's get in the truck before someone runs us down."

Silently she followed him and got into the cab. They said nothing else until they were inside Jean-Paul's house. He took a sheet and pillow from the hall closet and set them on the couch.

"I think I'd better sleep here," he said.

"I think you're right."

But as she walked to the bedroom, an overwhelming sense of loss clutched her heart. She had every right to be enraged over his behavior. Too bad her heart didn't agree.

Chapter 17

Jean-Paul punched his pillow in a vain attempt to make it more comfortable, then lay back down. Fed up with sleeping with his knees under his chin, he straightened his legs. His feet hung off the end of the couch.

Folding his hands behind his head, he stared at the ceiling. Well, he had certainly handled tonight's engagement with all the finesse of an ape. No, that was wrong. He'd read somewhere that apes were very social creatures and acted according to a specific code. Which meant he'd acted worse than an ape. And look where it had landed him—out on the couch, aching for the woman in the next room.

He groaned and covered his eyes with his arm. Why couldn't Angel see her father for what he was? And why did she insist on defending him?

Maybe because Guy was her last living parent, logic told him, and she wanted to hold on to him no matter what. Or maybe she was the kind of person who judged others on their actions, and so far she had no basis on which to judge Guy. The thought comforted him.

He turned his head to the side and saw the box containing Marianna's files. There was something bothering him about that missing disk. Wasn't it standard practice to make backup disks?

Jean-Paul heard the floorboard in the bedroom creak. So Angeline couldn't sleep either. He got up and padded to the door.

"Angeline?" he called through the closed door.

He heard her walk to the door, then pause. He held his breath, praying that she would give in to her heart. Slowly the door opened and she peered out at him. Her gaze slid down his body, stopping at his briefs. Her eyes widened when his body stirred to life.

The darkening of her blue eyes gave him satisfaction, and he had to hold himself in check not to snatch her into his arms and kiss their disagreement into oblivion.

"Yes, Jean-Paul?"

He leaned against the door frame and gave her a smile. "Since I couldn't sleep, I got to thinking about the missing disk. Don't you think Marianna would've made a backup disk of her work? I mean, wouldn't you?"

Her expression perked up. "Yes, I would have made a backup. Maybe that's why her house was trashed. Someone was looking for the disk."

"It's my guess that whoever searched her place didn't find the disk. And since they couldn't afford for you to run across such damning evidence, they set fire to the house."

She pulled her robe tighter around her waist, the brief flare of hope in her eyes dying. "If it was hidden in the house, it's gone now."

"Or Marianna could've hidden that disk at the historical society, knowing it was risky to keep it at her house. Why don't we retrieve the key from Henri tomorrow and search that office again."

"Okay." Angie started to close the door but Jean-Paul grasped the edge, holding it open.

"Angeline—"

The lamp on the end table exploded, sending shards of glass flying down the hall. Jean-Paul felt a slight sting on his cheek. He dragged Angeline to the floor as another shot tore through the window screen and slammed into the living room wall.

"You're hurt," she gasped.

Jean-Paul wiped the blood off his cheek. "It's just a scratch. You stay here," he commanded her.

"Where are you going?" she asked, laying her hand on his back as he started to crawl away.

"To get my shotgun and level the bastard shooting at us."

"Be careful."

He gave her a short, hard kiss. "You bet, *chère*."

On his elbows and knees, he crawled to the hall closet and pulled out his shotgun and shells. He shoved several rounds into the breech and pumped one into the firing chamber. He scooted across the floor and peeked through the damaged screen. In the moonless night, he couldn't see anything. Their sniper wasn't out in the open.

Jean-Paul fired through the opening, hoping to get the coward to return fire so he could get a bead on the man's position.

Immediately, his shot was returned and Jean-Paul honed in on the area. He squeezed off three rounds, peppering the area around the pecan tree in front of the house. A yelp split the night air. Jean-Paul reloaded the shotgun and waited. He strained, listening as the shooter retreated.

He sat at the window, ready to send anything that moved to his Maker. He heard Angeline move. Turning, he watched her crouch, then run across the floor. She sat down behind him, silent for a few moments.

"Do you think he's gone?" she asked, a tinge of fear in her voice.

"Yes, but I'm gonna wait here for a few minutes more to make sure we're safe."

She nodded and he focused his attention on the yard beyond. After several moments of silence, she rested her cheek on his bare back. Jean-Paul nearly jumped out of his skin, stunned by her action, yet welcoming it. Her perfume, soft and flowery, floated up to tantalize him. He remembered how good she tasted, how sweet her kisses were, how her body had welcomed his.

"Who do you think was shooting at us?" she whispered. "And why?"

"Damned if I know, but I'll bet my last dollar it's connected somehow, some way, with our little visit to the historical society this afternoon."

"Why do you say that?" Her warm breath fanned over his bare back.

"The sheriff's car was parked across the street from the society when we left this afternoon."

"Oh."

They fell silent again.

It was torture for Jean-Paul to sit here and watch the yard and not give in to the urge to turn and pull Angeline into his arms. The minutes seemed to stretch into hours and the torture escalated. His want turned to need, and his need turned into a driving force.

She rubbed her cheek against his back, like an affectionate kitten. Her action proved to be his breaking point. Jean-Paul carefully laid the shotgun on the floor, then turned. Before he could reach for her, she launched herself into his arms, tumbling them to the floor. Angie ended up sprawled across Jean-Paul's chest, their legs tangled. They stared at each other for a moment, then started laughing. Tension and fear evaporated.

After their chuckles died down, Jean-Paul cupped the back of her head. "I'm sorry, Angel, for acting like a jackass tonight. You don't need me adding to your troubles."

"It doesn't matter," she murmured, kissing her way up the side of his neck. "You're okay, that's all that matters." Her fingers lightly touched his injured cheek. "Oh, Jean-Paul."

The need to reassure herself that he was all right overwhelmed her. She had been unable to sleep, missing him, wanting to come to him, but telling herself that she had a right to her anger. Jean-Paul's actions had been reprehensible, but when the first shot shattered the darkness, their earlier fight faded into nothingness. Priorities fell into place. All that was important was that he was alive and unharmed.

She brushed a kiss across his wounded cheek, then settled her mouth over his. The warmth of his body and the liquid heat of his lips comforted her.

He lifted his head and looked down at her. "We're fine, *chère,*" he whispered tenderly, his fingers stroking through her hair. He sounded as if he thought fear was her only reason for her actions. Well, the only part fear played was helping her know what was important.

Her fingers outlined his lips. "I know." She leaned up and kissed each eyelid. "Love me, Jean-Paul."

He grasped her wrists, holding her hands away from his body. The fire of passion burned brightly in his eyes. "Are you sure, *mon ange,* this is what you want?"

He was such a good man. He could have taken advantage of the situation, capitalized on her fear, but he gave her the opportunity to think about the decision and back out.

"Let go of my hands, Jean-Paul."

His eyebrows shot up in surprise, but he complied. Angie wrapped her arms around his neck. "This is exactly what I want." Her mouth met his and he returned her kiss with hunger that burned into her bones.

Jean-Paul's hands roamed up her back, molding her curves into the hard plains of his body. His arousal pressed intimately against her belly, sending rivers of liquid fire through her body. He tugged at the hem of her nightgown and she raised up to allow him to slip the garment over her head. The action pressed her hips deeper into his.

She started to lower herself again when his hands cupped her buttocks, pressing her further into him. "Ah, Angel, that is heaven."

His lips caught the tip of her breast and sucked greedily. Angie's hands clutched his upper arms. Her head fell back as the piercing pleasure engulfed her.

"Do you like that, *mon coeur?*"

She could only moan her answer. He transferred his attention to her other breast. She wanted to return the pleasure he was giving her. Sinking her fingers into his midnight-dark hair, she pulled back his head and her mouth melded with his.

He hooked his fingers in the waistband of her panties and pulled them down her legs. She returned the favor by peeling off his briefs. His fingers wrapped around her hipbones and settled her over his waist. She looked at him in surprise.

He threw his arms wide. "I'm yours, *chère*. Do with me what you want."

The notion was totally foreign to her. He wanted her to take control. She liked the idea. A saucy smile curled her lips as she leaned down and kissed him. When he tried to deepen the kiss, her mouth moved down his neck to the flat male nipples. She nipped and sucked.

She felt the muscles of his chest quiver and jump. It gave her an odd sense of power that she could affect this man as deeply as she did. Her mouth moved lower, her tongue flicking into his navel.

When she made a move to go lower, Jean-Paul's hands caught her around her waist. "You learn quickly, Angel," he panted. He dragged her up to straddle his hips and with a single thrust entered her.

The fire that had been building in her veins flared high. She began to move with him, her hips moving in counterpoint to his. With a last single thrust, the fiery ecstasy consumed them both, melting the two and making one.

As Angie drifted in the sweet aftermath, she finally admitted to herself that she'd fallen in love. Hopelessly in love.

Jean-Paul stirred under her. "Come, Angel. This floor is a little too hard for my old bones."

She smiled at him. "I kind of like where I am."

He turned, pinning her beneath him. "Maybe you'd like to be on the bottom this time. I believe I have slivers in some rather unusual places," he added, rubbing his buttocks.

She grinned up at him. "Try me."

He shook his head. "You certainly have blossomed, *chère.*" His finger ran lightly over her jawbone. "And I like the rose." Before she could wind her arms around his neck, he stood, then scooped her up into his embrace.

"Where are you taking me?"

"To bed. I like that little backside of yours so much, I don't want to see it hurt."

She kissed the side of his neck. "I love you, Jean-Paul." The words slipped out before she could think.

He glanced down at her, a sad smile on his face. "I wish it were so."

"It is."

He shook his head. "Tell me the same when all this is over and life has settled back to normal. Tell me then, Angeline. Tell me then."

He didn't give her any more time to think. He tumbled them onto the bed and he loved her with a desperate intensity that made her wonder why he didn't believe her.

Jean-Paul studied the sleeping woman in his arms. He still could taste the fear that had raced through his veins when the lamp exploded. Their trip through the historical-society files had riled someone, Roger Boudreaux being the prime suspect. Or maybe it was Jean-Paul's actions at dinner that had set him off.

He curled a strand of Angeline's hair around his finger as he recalled the words she had whispered so sweetly. They had wrapped around his heart, firmly catching him as a fishing net caught crawfish.

He wished to heaven that she meant the words, but she had been through so much hell in the past week that it would have been natural to confuse her feelings of gratitude for something more than they were.

Oh, she'd been generous with herself, giving him her support when he'd learned of Edward's betrayal, but he couldn't allow himself to grab on to that thin thread of hope that she really loved him. Because if he did, and she later came to realize her mistake, it would rip apart his life. And this time he knew he wouldn't survive.

Angeline leaned back against the truck seat and let the wind blow her hair loose from the barrette holding it at the back of her neck. "Henri didn't act at all surprised to see us."

"I think, *chère,* he was secretly hoping you'd come today and visit."

She laughed, the sweet sound caressing his mind and bringing his body to life. At that moment Jean-Paul could no longer deny the truth. He loved Angeline.

"Don't tell that to Miss Eleanor. I think she would skin me if she knew that."

The shrill siren of a police car sounded behind them. Jean-Paul glanced in his rearview mirror and cursed. He pulled his truck over to the curb and stopped.

Dennis stomped up to the truck, looking as mean as a wounded bear. "You were speeding, hotshot. Give me your license."

Jean-Paul fished his wallet out of the back pocket of his jeans, then handed the sheriff his driver's license. Dennis flinched when he took it from Jean-Paul's hand.

"How fast was I going, sheriff?" Jean-Paul asked.

"Three miles over the limit."

"That fast. My, my, a real crime wave breaking out here."

"Shut your mouth, Delahaye," Dennis snarled. "If I had my way, you would've never made it out of prison." Dennis handed him the tablet of tickets. "Sign."

Again Jean-Paul noticed a grimace on Dennis's face as he moved his arm. "Something wrong with your arm?" Jean-Paul asked as he penned his name.

Dennis's beady eyes hardened. He ripped off the ticket and gave it to Jean-Paul. "I'm gonna get you, boy," Dennis threatened, pointing the tablet at Jean-Paul. "And that's a promise. You just keep looking over your shoulder. I'll be there."

Jean-Paul waited until the sheriff drove off before he pulled away from the curb.

"What was that about?" Angeline asked.

"I think I know who was shooting at us last night."

She gave him a puzzled frown, then suddenly her eyes widened. "You don't mean the sheriff, do you?"

"Did you see the way he flinched every time he moved his arm? I nicked our shooter last night. And today Dennis has trouble moving his arm. I would've loved to have seen what was under his shirt. Besides, he was wearing a long-sleeved shirt. Now why would anyone wear a long-sleeved shirt on a day when the temperature's gonna hit the high nineties, if he didn't have something to hide, *hein?*"

She visibly paled. He reached over and took her hand. He refrained from mentioning that he didn't doubt that after the blowup he'd had with Roger last night, the old goat had called the sheriff and demanded Dennis take payment out of his hide. Unfortunately, it was Dennis who had paid.

For the next few hours, Jean-Paul and Angie combed every inch of the office of the historical society. They checked every shelf, every drawer, even banged on the paneling to make sure there were no hidden compartments, but they found no backup disk. What they did discover missing were several of the files and journals Marianna had mentioned in her notes. Document file forty-two, which they needed, was one of the missing items.

Jean-Paul sat on the corner of the desk. "Well, whoever took the disk did a thorough job."

Angie closed the old journal she held and placed it on the desk. "Why didn't they take it all? Her files and the other disk?"

He rubbed his hand over his chin. "Maybe they didn't want to cause too much suspicion. Who'd miss one disk and a couple of those document boxes? But if they took everything, then even Henri would've questioned the disappearance."

"Which leaves us where?"

"That means, *chère,* we're gonna have to read through all of Marianna's notes and see if we can come to the same conclusion she did."

"That sounds like a long shot, considering we don't know what we're looking for and we're missing vital pieces of information."

Jean-Paul pulled her into his arms. "You're a sharp cookie."

"Let's hope so."

He kissed her nose. "I know so."

She wasn't so sure by noon the next day. They'd read through most of the files and discovered nothing earth-shattering. Document file forty-two had been mentioned in reference to two other families in the parish.

Jean-Paul threw down the folder he'd been reading. "This is hopeless. I don't see anything that would send Marianna to Edward to talk about corruption. Whatever was in forty-two is the key."

Angie glanced at the stack of manila folders littering the coffee table. "We could go back to the historical society and see what files forty-one and forty-three contain. That might give us a reference point, to look at all these records again."

He closed his eyes and laid his head on the sofa cushion. "That sounds as good as anything I can come up with." His hand snaked out and he tumbled her onto his lap. "Are you ticklish?" Before she could answer, his fingers went to work on her rib cage.

"No," she gasped, squirming and wrapping her arms protectively around her waist. "I'm not."

His hands stilled, but there was pure devilry in his eyes. "Liar." He whispered it so sweetly that he lulled her into a false sense of security and she relaxed her arm. His lips hovered over hers, then his fingers struck, tickling her on each side.

"Jean-Paul," she squealed. "Stop." She playfully slapped away his hands. "Stop it or I'll—"

His hands slid up from her waist to rest beneath her breasts. "What will you do, *chère?*" He leaned forward, his mouth resting against her ear. "I hope it is very naughty."

She pulled back and opened her mouth to reply.

"Excuse me. I hope I'm not intruding."

Angie immediately recognized Guy through the screen door. Jean-Paul muttered a low curse, and she wanted to faint from embarrassment at being caught in such a position.

Her cheeks flaming, Angie jumped off Jean-Paul's lap. "Of course not. Please come in." She hurried across the room and opened the door.

The slight flush on Guy's face told her he was as flustered as she was.

"I came by today to tell you how sorry I was about how things turned out at dinner."

He looked so lost and forlorn that Angie couldn't be angry with him. He wasn't as strong a man as Jean-Paul or Roger. That much had been made painfully clear the other night. But that didn't mean Guy was a bad man. Angie felt sorry for him, caught in a power struggle between the other two men.

"Don't worry about it." She started to say it wasn't his fault, but she didn't want to point a finger at Jean-Paul. He had his reasons for acting as he had.

"I was hoping you'd allow me to redeem myself with lunch today." Guy glanced at Jean-Paul. "You are invited too."

Jean-Paul shook his head.

"You don't have to worry," Guy hastily added. "My father has gone to Morgan City for a friend's birthday bash, and Catlin is in New Orleans shopping."

Jean-Paul looked from Angie to Guy, then back again. "You two go on. You need to get acquainted without any interference or interruptions."

Angie knew he was giving her the chance to talk to her father one-on-one. She also realized how much it cost Jean-Paul to yield. She walked over to him and kissed his cheek. "Thank you for understanding," she murmured in his ear. "And don't worry. I have on the Saint Christopher medal. I'll be safe."

Jean-Paul let himself in the office of the historical society and went straight to the shelf that held the document file boxes. He pulled out box forty-one. Miscellaneous documents filled the box. Marriage certificates, birth and death records, deeds and various legal papers from the ninteen-twenties.

Forty-three held the same sort of items from the nineteen-forties. Which meant box forty-two must have held papers from the thirties. He replaced both boxes on the shelf. What had happened in this parish in the thirties? And what did the Roucheaux, McKays and Saddlers have in common except that they were poor?

Poor with oil pumps on their land.

Excitement raced through Jean-Paul. Roger Boudreaux had signed everyone in the parish to leases in the thirties.

Damn, why hadn't he thought about that before? Whatever Marianna discovered, it had to do with those leases.

He had to get his hands on copies of those leases, and the logical place to find them was in the office of conveyances, where all mineral and oil leases for the parish were filed.

He took a deep breath to clear his head. He needed a strategy. It was Sunday and the courthouse was closed. Also, he didn't trust Lawrence Rush, who was in charge of the office of conveyance. The man liked money more than personal honor. So where did that leave him?

M'dame Eleanor. She would have a key and would let him in without alerting Roger or his cronies.

Amazingly enough, M'dame Eleanor eagerly embraced Jean-Paul's idea.

"That Lawrence." She clicked her tongue in disgust. "He goes whichever way the wind is blowing," she said as she opened the office door on the registry of conveyances. "Who knows what he's hiding?"

Jean-Paul closed the door behind them and turned on the light.

"All right, young man, what do you wish to see?"

"I want to see the oil leases on the Roucheaux, McKay and Saddler land. Also, I should check the lease on the Courville land."

M'dame Eleanor retrieved the black ledger where all the leases were recorded. "This J-Book will tell us in what file the leases are located," she said, setting it on the counter that separated the reception area from the work area. Pulling her reading glasses from her skirt pocket, she opened the book and quickly located the oil leases Roger had filed in the thirties. Her finger ran down the page.

"Here we are. McKay. File 334. The Roucheaux and Saddler leases are in the same file, according to this."

As Jean-Paul waited for her to find the file, he silently read through the information on the page. Owner of the land: McKay. Length of the lease: eighty years. Person taking out the lease: Roger Boudreaux.

Eighty years...that didn't seem right. Twenty-five, fifty, maybe even one hundred years, but eighty?

He looked closer. The shape of the eight looked odd. It looked as if someone had tried to make the number five into an eight.

"Ah, here it is," she crowed with delight, holding up her find.

"M'dame, if you were negotiating an oil lease, how many years would you make it for?"

She put the file on the counter. "Who can say?"

"Just guess."

Shrugging, she said, "Fifty years."

"Not eighty?"

"Non."

Jean-Paul pointed to the entry in the ledger. "Do these numbers look like they've been doctored to you?"

Squinting, she studied the numbers. "Yes. That's not how Lilly made her eights. Look." She flipped back several pages until she came across entries made in August. "See," she said, pointing to the number. "Lilly was the clerk who recorded leases in the twenties and thirties. See how the top circle ends with a little comma on the inside? Nothing like this—" she turned back to the original page "—forgery."

"Let's compare it to the file."

Jean-Paul eagerly opened the folder and spread the leases on the counter. In addition to the three leases he wanted to see, there were ten more leases on property that had proven to be unproductive. They all were for eighty years.

"Something is foul here, Jean-Paul."

"Why do you say that, M'dame?"

"Because these duplicate leases are typed. At that time, there was not a typewriter here in the courthouse. If you'll look at other documents done during that time, you will find they were handwritten. We got our first typewriter in 1934."

"Roger could've had them drawn up by his attorney."

"Perhaps, but I think no. Look at Lilly's signature at the bottom. It's the same on each lease."

Damn, if she wasn't right. "So, these are probably forgeries. Roger must've gotten Lawrence to make up these new documents."

She tapped her index finger against her lip. "As I recall, Lawrence started driving a grand car about ten years ago. I wondered how he could afford a new Cadillac every two years."

"If it's true, that means Roger's been collecting money from the oil company for over a decade that he isn't entitled to." He banged his fist on the counter. "This has to be what Marianna discovered." He shook his head. "Can you imagine the scandal this revelation will cause? One big enough to keep Guy out of the governor's mansion."

"You need proof, Jean-Paul."

He leaned against the counter. "You're right. I need to find someone who has a copy of the original lease." He rubbed the back of his neck. "The lease on my land was destroyed years ago, when my dad ripped it up after a binge of drinking. And we can write off the Courville lease. Roger probably has it."

"What about the Roucheaux family? Aaron, Émile's *papa,* was a stickler on keeping records."

Jean-Paul grinned. "You, M'dame, are a jewel."

"But of course."

A noise came from the hall. Jean-Paul walked to the door, opened it and peered into the corridor. Nothing.

He turned back to M'dame. "We'd better clean up before someone catches us."

"Pshaw. If someone comes in and asks me what I'm doing, I'll tell them."

He had to smile at the woman's spunk.

Now that he had the key to the mystery, he needed proof. He prayed Émile Roucheaux still had the original lease, but if he didn't, Jean-Paul vowed to interview everyone in the parish who had oil discovered on his land and find out if Roger had had the leases doctored. And if he found any discrepancies, he'd have the evidence to bring down Roger Boudreaux.

As they headed out of the courthouse, the hairs on the back of Jean-Paul's head stood up. He glanced around to see if anyone was watching them. Although he didn't see anyone, he couldn't shake the feeling someone had seen them.

Chapter 18

"You will call me, Jean-Paul, after you visit the Rou-cheaux, and tell me what you have learned."

"Yes, M'dame. I promise to call." Jean-Paul leaned down and kissed her cheek.

"I still think I should go with you," M'dame Eleanor insisted.

He shook his head. "I worry that I've put you in too much danger as it is. If Roger discovers what we suspect, we might also have fatal accidents."

She waved away his concern. "Too many deaths cause questions. And Roger has always been too smart for this town's good."

He had to smile at her gumption. "And I, M'dame, am still as hardheaded as ever. I will go alone."

"If you forget to call me, I'll have your hide, *jeune homme.*"

"I swear to call."

"*Bien.*"

Jean-Paul climbed in his truck and headed for the Roucheaux place on the far side of the parish. He'd just turned onto the main parish road when the sheriff's car raced up behind him, his lights flashing, his siren going. Jean-Paul pulled over.

What now? he wondered as he waited for the sheriff to approach the truck.

"Get out," Dennis commanded.

Resting his wrist on the steering wheel, Jean-Paul asked, "Why?"

"Because I said so, Delahaye. Now, out."

"Am I under arrest, sheriff?" Jean-Paul asked.

Dennis drew his gun and pointed it at Jean-Paul's chest. "Get out."

A chill ran down Jean-Paul's back. "What do you plan to do, Dennis? Shoot me right here on a frequently traveled road, in broad daylight? Why, that isn't your style, is it? You like shooting your opposition from behind a tree."

Dennis shoved the gun in Jean-Paul's face. "Leroy," he called to the deputy in the sheriff's car. "Get out here and put the cuffs on this man, then put him in the back seat of the cruiser."

Leroy immediately complied with the order, cuffing Jean-Paul's hands behind his back. Jean-Paul didn't fight because he didn't have any doubt that Dennis would blow him away and have some plausible excuse as to why he did it. Leroy stuffed him into the back seat and slammed the door.

"Now, get rid of that truck," Dennis commanded his deputy.

As Jean-Paul watched Leroy climb into his truck, a knot formed in his stomach. Dennis slid behind the wheel of the sheriff's car. He threw Jean-Paul a wicked smile. "Why don't we go see Roger? He might like to know how you spent your afternoon."

"So that was you I heard in the hall," Jean-Paul replied.

"That's what I'm supposed to do, guard this town and stop lawbreakers."

"No, Dennis, that's not what your job is. Your job is to protect Roger Boudreaux's backside."

Dennis looked into the rearview mirror and grinned. "You got it, which means yours is cooked."

Jean-Paul was afraid Dennis was right.

"You love him, don't you?"

Angie set her fork down and looked at her father. They were sitting in a glass-enclosed porch, green plants growing in abundance all around them. A ceiling fan gently moved the air throughout the room.

She hadn't realized her feelings were that transparent. She felt lost and unsure of who she was. Her calm, ordered life had been tossed to the four winds, and she was acting on gut instinct, which was 180° opposite of how she normally operated. Usually, she carefully considered each decision, weighed the pros and cons, and came to a conclusion. This past week she hadn't had time to ponder anything but had been forced to go on her feelings instead.

But was she any good at gut reactions? Or had she ended up on the short end of the stick yet again?

"Yes, I do," she quietly answered. "And I don't know what to do about it."

"Have you told him?"

"Yes. And he thinks I'm just reacting to the pressure of the situation."

Guy reached over and squeezed her hand. "Don't give up on him, Angeline. I didn't fight hard enough to keep Marianna, and I have regretted it all my life. Don't make the same mistake I did."

A tear ran down her cheek. It was as she suspected. Guy had loved her mother. "Thank you for telling me that."

Out of the corner of her eye, Angie saw the sheriff's car stop in the driveway. She started to look away, but when Dennis pulled a cuffed man out of the back seat, Angie stood.

"That's Jean-Paul!" she gasped. "Why does Dennis have handcuffs on him?" She turned to Guy. "What's going on? If Dennis is arresting Jean-Paul, why'd he bring him here?" She headed for the door.

"I don't know," Guy said, following her.

They ran into the men in the hall. Dennis cursed.

"It's going to be kinda hard to kill me now, isn't it, Dennis?" Jean-Paul quietly said. "You've got witnesses."

"Shut your face," Dennis snarled.

"What's going on, Dennis?" Guy asked, stepping forward.

"Nothing you need to concern yourself about, Guy. This is just something between your papa and this con."

"I've discovered why Marianna was killed," Jean-Paul said, his gaze locking with Angie's.

Dennis's fist smashed into Jean-Paul's mouth. Angie cried out and flung herself at the sheriff. He shook her off as he would a fly and drew his pistol before anyone else could move.

"You just signed the little lady's death warrant, Delahaye," Dennis snapped. He motioned with the gun. "Everyone, get in the library. We're gonna wait on Roger."

Jean-Paul cursed himself for being a fool. He should have kept his big mouth shut, and maybe Dennis would have let Angeline go. Instead, he'd tried a power play and lost. Unfortunately, his Angel would have to pay for his mistake. Just as Marianna had. The thought made him sick.

The four filed into the room. Jean-Paul settled on the leather couch. When Angeline tried to sit beside him, Dennis waved her away. "Sit over there in that chair in the corner."

She obeyed. Guy stood by her side, his hand resting on her shoulder. Jean-Paul prayed that if Guy had any courage, it would surface now.

"What's going on here?" Guy demanded. "Why have you brought Jean-Paul here?"

Before Dennis could do more than open his mouth, Jean-Paul answered, "He caught me before I could blow the whistle on your father." Maybe if Guy knew what was going down, he'd stop the sheriff. "It was a smart move on Dennis's part. If I'd interviewed the Roucheaux family, the cat would've been let out of the bag. Then everyone would know about the oil leases."

Angeline leaned forward in the chair. "What did you learn about them, Jean-Paul?"

"Shut up," Dennis barked. "No talking."

Jean-Paul sat stiffly on the edge of the sofa cushion, his manacled hands making it impossible for him to be comfortable.

"Could you at least take the cuffs off him?" Angeline implored Dennis.

"No. He'd just try to wrestle this peashooter outta my hand, and I can't have that, now, can I?"

"It's the only way Dennis can even the odds," Jean-Paul said.

Dennis backhanded Jean-Paul with the barrel of the pistol, knocking him to the floor. Angie cried out and surged to her feet.

Pointing the gun at her, Dennis ordered, "Stay where you are."

All color fled Angeline's face and Jean-Paul saw the fear in her eyes.

"Dennis, just because you're the sheriff doesn't mean—" Guy began.

"Your daddy needs to explain a few things to you, Junior. Until he does, keep your trap shut." Dennis emphasized his words by jabbing his pistol in the air toward Guy and Angeline.

Jean-Paul sat up, then placed his elbow on the cushion and awkwardly levered himself onto the couch. The gash had opened up on his cheek and bled freely.

Angeline stepped forward. "At least let me stop the bleeding."

"Why?" Dennis asked. "He's gonna be dead pretty soon."

Guy gasped, his cheeks paling, and in spite of his disgust with the man's spineless behavior, Jean-Paul knew Guy had realized for the first time the seriousness of the situation. He could almost feel sorry for the man. Almost.

Jean-Paul looked up at Dennis. "Roger wouldn't want me bleeding all over his expensive carpet and implicating him in a felony."

Dennis gave the words a moment of thought, then nodded his head. "All right, but no tricks."

Angeline turned to Guy. "Is there a towel or something I can use?"

The tremor of fear in her voice hurt Jean-Paul more than the wound on his face.

"You're not going anywhere." Dennis nodded at Guy. "You go get something."

Guy nodded and hurried out of the room. Apparently, Dennis didn't think Guy posed any threat. He couldn't blame Dennis for the assumption. After several minutes Guy returned.

"What took you so long?" Dennis demanded.

Guy handed Angie a white hand towel. "I had to go looking for this. The maid forgot to put out clean towels this morning."

A look passed between father and daughter, and Jean-Paul had the craziest impression that Guy was telling Angeline to hold on and not give up.

She hurried to Jean-Paul's side and pressed the towel to his cheek.

"How are you?" she asked through her tears.

He wanted to pull her into his arms and reassure her that everything was going to be all right. But it wasn't. They were going to be gator bait, and it was his fault. If he hadn't persisted in his belief that Marianna had been murdered, Angeline wouldn't be facing the danger she was now.

"Cut the chatter," Dennis commanded. "Get away from him."

Angie pulled away the towel from Jean-Paul's cheek. Most of the bleeding had stopped. As she stood, Jean-Paul whispered, "Run if you get the chance."

Before she could respond, Dennis stepped between them and pulled Angeline back to her chair.

The minutes ticked by in painful silence. Angie fought to remain calm. She tried to imagine what Jean-Paul had discovered about the oil leases that would sign their death warrants.

Her gazed locked with his. Regret showed in his eyes. Angie wanted to cry out at the unfairness of it all. Just when she had found the love of her life, it appeared it would be snatched away.

They waited for over an hour. Finally, they heard Roger in the hallway. Dennis hurried to the door and opened it. "Roger," he called.

"What are you doing here, Dennis?" Roger asked, strolling into the room. He stopped, taking in the scene before him. Carefully closing the door, his face tight with anger, Roger demanded, "What the hell is going on here?"

Dennis pointed with his gun. "Delahaye and M'dame Eleanor were checking oil leases this afternoon at the courthouse. After he dropped the old lady off, I picked him up before he could talk to Émile Roucheaux."

Roger swung around to face Jean-Paul. "Why were you going to see him?"

"I was going to see if he had a copy of the lease on his land and see if the length on it was the same as the one recorded in the J-Book in the parish records. Those leases were for fifty years, weren't they, Roger? That would mean you've been taking money illegally for more than the last decade."

Guy stepped forward. "What's he talking about, Father?"

Roger pinned Guy with a hard look. "Nothing. He's just blowing smoke."

"Pretty smart of you to have Lawrence Rush forge the length of those leases," Jean-Paul continued. "Too bad Lawrence is such a fool in the way he spends his money. The parade of new Cadillacs he's owned over the last decade was a dead giveaway that he'd been bought."

Angie's heart thudded. So that was the secret that had cost her mother her life. Oil leases.

Roger glared at Jean-Paul, hatred burning brightly in his eyes. If looks could kill, he'd be dead.

"Is what he says true, Father?" Guy quietly asked.

Roger turned toward his son. "Get out of here and don't ask any questions. I'll take care of this."

The brusque tone gave no recognition of their relationship, and Angie ached for her father. It was painfully clear what Roger thought of his son.

Before Guy could respond, Jean-Paul spoke. "Nobody would've ever known, if Marianna hadn't stumbled onto the truth when she was writing the parish history. What did she find, Roger? Was it an unchanged lease, or a letter, or maybe a diary entry stating the length of the lease?"

Something flickered in Roger's eyes at the mention of a diary.

Jean-Paul stood. "Whose diary was it?"

An evil grin split the old man's face. "I donated my sister's papers to the historical society. Imagine my surprise when she mentioned the leases."

"And because Marianna read your sister's diary and knew the truth, you had her killed."

Out of the corner of his eye, Jean-Paul saw Guy stagger and Angeline reach out to support him. Damn. He was hoping Guy would at least be strong enough to save his Angel, even if *he* was a dead duck.

Roger shrugged.

"It must've come as quite a shock when Edward called to tell you what Marianna had discovered." Jean-Paul was making a wild stab in the dark. "What amazes me was how fast you were able to mobilize your cronies and have her killed."

"I'll admit to nothing." Roger shot Dennis a killing look. "This is your fault. You had several chances to stop this."

Jean-Paul turned to the sheriff. "So it was you who torched Marianna's house and shot at us last night."

Dennis responded with a cold smile.

Jean-Paul heard Angeline moan. It was tough facing the man who'd tried twice to kill you.

Guy stumbled forward to grasp his father's arm. "You had Marianna killed?"

"Oh, shut up." He shook off Guy's hand, staring at him with utter disgust. "Crawl back into your whiskey bottle and leave this to me."

"No, dammit. I want an answer. Did you have Marianna killed?"

Roger's control snapped. "Yes, I had that little trouble-maker killed. She'd been a pain in my side ever since I discovered you'd gotten her pregnant. I was lucky Dr. Lewis came and told me about it. I gave her money and the name of a doctor in New Orleans who could get rid of it. I thought she had until *she*—" he pointed to Angeline "—arrived in town."

"You wanted Marianna to abort the baby?"

Jean-Paul shivered at the thought. Roger had once again demonstrated what a bastard he was.

"Marianna couldn't help you. She'd have just dragged you down with her. I was lucky to talk Catlin's father into allowing you to marry her on so short a notice."

Jean-Paul took several steps forward. "Who'd you have kill Marianna?"

Roger's gaze touched Dennis, then returned to Jean-Paul.

Dennis poked his gun into Jean-Paul's stomach. His grin was malicious and gleeful. "I did. It's handy being the sheriff." He seemed to enjoy bragging about his feat. "I ran up behind her with my lights goin' and stopped her. It was nothing to hit her on the head and push her car into the bayou."

Rage exploded in Jean-Paul's head. His lips pulled back and he snarled at Dennis. Lowering his head, Jean-Paul rammed his shoulder into the sheriff's stomach. The gun discharged as the two men fell to the floor.

The pistol fell out of Dennis's hand and slid across the floor. Angie and Roger went for the weapon at the same time. Roger reached it first and immediately aimed it at Angie.

"Stay back." He looked at the men on the floor. Dennis's blows went unanswered and unchallenged, since Jean-Paul's hands were still cuffed behind his back. "That's enough, Dennis. Come on. Get up and let's get these two out of here. Then you can go take care of that old hag who was with Delahaye."

Guy stepped forward. "What do you intend to do with them?"

"That's none of your business," Roger replied.

"This time it is," Guy answered, a determination in his voice that Jean-Paul had never heard before. "Let them go."

Roger gaped at Guy. "Are you insane? If this scandal gets out, your shot at the governorship is gone."

"That was your dream for me, Father, not mine. You've already sacrificed Marianna. You can't have Angeline, too." Guy held out his hand. "Give me the gun."

Jean-Paul thought he heard something outside. Sirens maybe. He prayed it was the good guys.

Roger's gaze hardened. "Get out of the way."

"No." Guy tried to wrestle the gun away from his father. A shot rang through the room and Guy fell to the floor.

Dennis surged forward, but Jean-Paul threw his body against the sheriff, knocking him off balance. They staggered backward.

The library door flew open and several state troopers filed into the room.

"What's going on here?" one of the troopers demanded. He looked at Roger, who was now holding the gun;

then at Guy, on the floor, clutching his stomach. "You want to give me that gun, sir?"

For an instant, Jean-Paul thought Roger was going to bolt from the room. But suddenly, his body sagged and he handed over the weapon.

"Call an ambulance," the trooper told his fellow officer. After he'd left the room, the man asked Roger, "Did you shoot this man?"

"We were fighting over the gun," Roger offered, seeming to come out of his shock. "It accidentally went off."

"He—" Angeline pointed to Roger "—had just ordered the sheriff to kill me and Jean-Paul."

The trooper took off his hat and looked at the individuals in the room. "Who's Guy Boudreaux?"

"That's me." Guy raised his hand, gasped and clutched his side again.

The trooper squatted beside the injured man. "You're the one who called the state police?"

Guy nodded. "What she says is true. The sheriff was going to kill my daughter and Jean-Paul. He's already killed Angeline's mother."

"That's a lie," Dennis yelled. "Who're you gonna believe? Me, the sheriff, or the ramblings of an alcoholic?"

The trooper turned to his colleagues. "Take the sheriff and the shooter into custody. Be sure and read them all their rights. We don't want any complaints."

While the two men were being cuffed and led out of the room, Angie knelt beside her father and cradled his head in her lap.

"Hang on," she whispered.

He gave her a watery smile. "I couldn't let him kill you, too."

She soothed back the hair from his brow. "I know."

Jean-Paul appeared beside her, minus his cuffs. "How is he?"

Guy looked up at him. "You were right, Jean-Paul. I've been a coward all my life. But maybe it's not too late to rectify some of my mistakes. There's a hidden room behind the south wall of this room. Dad didn't know I knew about it. Pull on the last book on the third shelf from the bottom, to open the door. Maybe you'll find the evidence you need in there."

Before he could say more the paramedics arrived, pushing Jean-Paul and Angeline out of the way. Tears ran down Angeline's face as she watched them work to stabilize her father.

"Angeline," Jean-Paul whispered.

She looked at him. Her face was ravaged by the emotions that were tearing her apart. She reached up and touched his injured cheek.

"You're bleeding again."

Jean-Paul didn't care about his damn cheek. He needed to tell her that he was sorry for this mess.

"*Chère—*"

"You were right all along. But I think maybe my father's paid the price for his actions." She sniffed back her tears.

The paramedics placed Guy on the gurney and started to wheel him out. Angeline looked from her father to Jean-Paul. Her indecision as to whether to go with her critically injured father or stay with Jean-Paul was easy to read in her face. The least he could do was ease her burden.

"Go with your *papa*. I need to stay here and answer questions. We'll talk later."

Angie hesitated a moment, then nodded. At the door, she stopped one of the paramedics and pointed to Jean-Paul. "He needs his cheek looked at."

Jean-Paul waved the man away. "I'm fine."

But the truth was he wasn't. He was worried as hell that the fallout from tonight's events would somehow separate him from Angeline.

Jean-Paul parked his truck, which he'd retrieved from the woods where Leroy had left it, in the hospital parking lot and stared at the building. It had taken nearly twenty-four hours to get away from the Boudreaux house. The papers he and the state troopers had found in the hidden room would provide enough evidence to put Roger and Dennis away for the rest of their lives.

Numerous law-enforcement agencies had been called in. Since it wasn't clear if the local district attorney could be trusted, they had turned the information over to the state's DA. Jean-Paul had to guide the man through the tortuous scheme of oil leases. In the process, Jean-Paul discovered papers on his frame-up, and Dennis's and Edward's complicity in the deed. But the satisfaction Jean-Paul thought would come with winning his war against Roger never appeared. Instead, all he could think about was Angeline.

She had changed him, brought him a joy and peace he'd never known before. When she had told him the other night she loved him, he had been afraid to believe her. How could she love both him and Guy when he'd hated Guy most of his life? And now he'd ruined Guy's future and helped put her grandfather in prison. He wouldn't change what he'd done, but he feared Angeline might find it difficult to love him.

In spite of how he'd blackened Guy's name, Angeline had seen something in her father and brought out the goodness in him. But why did Jean-Paul find that so unusual? Hadn't she come into his life and changed him for the better? Hadn't she taught him how to love again?

Angeline had seen something good in her father to believe in. He prayed she saw something in him, Jean-Paul, that would make her want to spend the rest of her life here in Louisiana with him. At least, now with the evidence they'd found, he had a future to offer her.

Angie pulled her hand from Guy's. He'd finally gone to sleep after they'd moved him from intensive care to a private room. He would live. The bullet had missed all vital organs but had caused extensive tissue damage.

She glanced down at her watch. Where was Jean-Paul? It had been nearly a day since they'd arrived at the hospital and still Jean-Paul had not come. She'd called the mansion several times, but each time the officials told her they were still sifting through things.

Fear gnawed at her stomach. After hearing Roger confess to all the evil deeds he'd done, she realized that Jean-Paul's hatred for the Boudreaux family was well-founded and justified. Roger had robbed Jean-Paul's parents of their wealth, destroyed his career and had him sent to prison. Yet, in spite of the bitterness Jean-Paul felt, he'd still given generously of himself and helped her.

He had been there for her through the whole ordeal of discovering who she was, never once abandoning her. He'd believed in that passionate part of her personality and nurtured it until it bloomed. He had taught her how to be at ease with herself. More importantly, he had taught her to love.

But the question that plagued her mind was, Could Jean-Paul forget she was a Boudreaux and love her?

"Angeline." His voice came from the doorway.

She looked at him. He appeared tired, haggard and the most welcome sight in the world. He motioned for her to join him in the hall.

"How is he?" he asked when the door to the room closed.

"He should recover completely."

He looked relieved. "I'm glad."

Was he truly? Did he hold it against her that she'd gone with Guy?

"Did you find the evidence?" Her insides were quaking. She wanted him to take her in his arms.

"Yes. Everything we need to make a case against Roger and Dennis was there. Roger was very maniacal in keeping a record of his deeds."

Her brows knitted into a frown. "But isn't that rather stupid, to document your crimes? Roger struck me as someone shrewder than that."

"I think Roger's ego was so big that he thought he'd never get caught. He kept the records as a snub to society. In his own way he was saying, 'See, I'm more cunning than you.'"

Chills raced over her skin.

"And without Guy's help, we never would've found any of that evidence." Jean-Paul stuffed his hands into his jeans pockets. He glanced down at the floor, then at her. "You made a difference in his life, Angel. Just as you've made a difference in my life."

"How have I made a difference, Jean-Paul?"

"You gave Guy something to believe in and fight for."

She stepped closer to him. "And what about you? How have I made a difference to you?"

"You've taught me to believe again. That what is true and just and beautiful will always win." He cupped her face. "I love you, Angel. And I want to spend the rest of my life with you, seeing the world through your eyes and learning how sweet life can be. Will you marry me, *chère?*"

She wanted to yell *yes* with every fiber of her being, but she needed to know if he could accept her for who she was. "I'm a Boudreaux, Jean-Paul. Can you live with that? Can you live with the fact that I want a relationship with my father? Does your love include that?"

A tender smile curved his lips. "Yes, *chère,* it does. In fact, I would have you no other way, because if you were different I would no longer have my Angeline."

She threw her arms around his neck. "I love you."

"Will you marry me?" he whispered in her ear.

She pulled back and gazed into his eyes. "*Mais sho',* I'll marry you."

His laughter rang down the hall. "I've made a Cajun of you, yes?"

Indeed he had. He'd also given her a home and a love that would last a lifetime.

Epilogue

Angie cradled the five-month-old infant in her arms and rocked him softly, hoping he'd quit fussing.

"Here, give him to me," Jean-Paul said, holding out his arms.

She surrendered the baby to his father's arms. The sight of so small a bundle of humanity cradled so tenderly in Jean-Paul's huge arms brought warmth to Angie's heart.

"He's a happy man," Henri Colton commented.

Angie laughed. "He's not the only one. Your grin goes from ear to ear."

"That's because I'm marrying Eleanor today."

The courtship of Henri and Eleanor had run a close second as a topic of conversation to Roger's trial and Jean-Paul's reinstatement to the bar. Jean-Paul had taken the job of DA of the parish after the previous one resigned.

Angie glanced down at her watch. "It's time, gentlemen, for the wedding to begin."

Jean-Paul handed the baby back to Angie, then gave her a quick kiss on the cheek. *"Viens, mon ange.* Let's go help Henri and Eleanor celebrate."

Angie followed Jean-Paul into the church. Miracles still did happen in this day and age. She held the newest one in her arms.

* * * * *

Take 4 bestselling love stories FREE

Plus get a FREE surprise gift!

Special Limited-time Offer

Mail to Silhouette Reader Service™

3010 Walden Avenue
P.O. Box 1867
Buffalo, N.Y. 14269-1867

YES! Please send me 4 free Silhouette Intimate Moments® novels and my free surprise gift. Then send me 6 brand-new novels every month, which I will receive months before they appear in bookstores. Bill me at the low price of $2.89 each plus 25¢ delivery and applicable sales tax, if any.* That's the complete price and—compared to the cover prices of $3.50 each—quite a bargain! I understand that accepting the books and gift places me under no obligation ever to buy any books. I can always return a shipment and cancel at any time. Even if I never buy another book from Silhouette, the 4 free books and the surprise gift are mine to keep forever.

245 BPA ANRR

Name	(PLEASE PRINT)	
Address	Apt. No.	
City	State	Zip

This offer is limited to one order per household and not valid to present Silhouette Intimate Moments® subscribers. *Terms and prices are subject to change without notice. Sales tax applicable in N.Y.

UMOM-94R   ©1990 Harlequin Enterprises Limited

Now what's going on in

 ?

Guilty! That was what everyone thought of Sandy Keller's client, including Texas Ranger—and American Hero—Garrett Hancock. But as he worked with her to determine the truth, loner Garrett found he was changing his mind about a lot of things—especially falling in love.

Rachel Lee's Conard County series continues in January 1995 with A QUESTION OF JUSTICE, IM #613.

Return to the classic plot lines you love, with

January 1995 rings in a new year of the **ROMANTIC TRADITIONS** you've come to cherish. And we've resolved to bring you more unforgettable stories by some of your favorite authors, beginning with Beverly Barton's THE OUTCAST, IM #614, featuring one very breathtaking bad boy!

Convict Reese Landry was running from the law—and the demons that tortured his soul. Psychic Elizabeth Mallory knew he was innocent...and in desperate need of the right woman's love.

ROMANTIC TRADITIONS continues in April 1995 with Patricia Coughlin's LOVE IN THE FIRST DEGREE, a must-read innovation on the "wrongly convicted" plot line. So start your new year off the romantic way with **ROMANTIC TRADITIONS**—only in

And now for something completely different....

**In January, look for
SAM'S WORLD (IM #615)
by Ann Williams**

Contemporary Woman: Marina Ross had
landed in the strangest of worlds: the future.
And her only ally was the man responsible for
bringing her there.

Future Man: Sam's world was one without
emotion or passion, one he was desperately
trying to save—even as he himself felt the first
stirrings of desire....

**Don't miss SAM'S WORLD,
by Ann Williams, available this January,
only from**

Maura Seger's
BELLE HAVEN

Four books. Four generations. Four indomitable females.

You met the Belle Haven women who started it all in Harlequin Historicals.
Now meet descendant Nora Delaney in the emotional contemporary conclusion to the Belle Haven saga:

THE SURRENDER OF NORA

When Nora's inheritance brings her home to Belle Haven, she finds more
than she bargained for. Deadly accidents prove someone wants her out of
town—fast. But the real problem is the prime suspect—handsome
Hamilton Fletcher. His quiet smile awakens the passion all Belle Haven
women are famous for. But does he want her heart...or her life?

Don't miss THE SURRENDER OF NORA
Silhouette Intimate Moments #617
Available in January!

If you missed the first three books in Maura Seger's BELLE HAVEN series,
The Taming of Amelia (Harlequin Historical #159), *The Seduction of Deanna*,
(Harlequin Historical #183) or *The Tempting of Julia* (Harlequin Historical #244),
order your copy now by sending your name, address, zip or postal code, along with a
check or money order (please do not send cash) for $3.99 for each book ordered
($4.50 in Canada for #244), plus 75¢ postage and handling ($1.00 in Canada), payable
to Harlequin Books, to:

In the U.S.:	In Canada:
Silhouette Books	Silhouette Books
3010 Walden Avenue	P.O. Box 613
P. O. Box 9047	Fort Erie, Ontario
Buffalo, NY 14269-9047	L2A 5X3

Please specify book title(s) with your order.
Canadian residents add applicable federal and provincial taxes.

BELLE95

EXTRA! EXTRA! READ ALL ABOUT...
MORE ROMANCE
MORE SUSPENSE
MORE INTIMATE MOMENTS

Join us in February 1995 when
Silhouette Intimate Moments introduces
the first title in a whole new program:
INTIMATE MOMENTS EXTRA. These break-
through, innovative novels by your favorite
category writers will come out every few
months, beginning with Karen Leabo's
Into Thin Air, IM #619.

Pregnant teenagers had been
disappearing without a trace, and
Detectives Caroline Triece and Austin Lomax
were called in for heavy-duty damage
control...because now the missing girls
were turning up dead.

In May, Merline Lovelace offers
Night of the Jaguar, and other
INTIMATE MOMENTS EXTRA novels will
follow throughout 1995, only in—